WHAT DO WOMEN WANT?
Is . . .

"HILARIOUS . . .
funky, outrageous . . . satirize(s) sexual politics, group therapy, the publishing industry,
celebrity namedropping in . . . Manhattan's
fashionable watering places, activist lawyers,
militant feminists, Jewish parents and airline
security . . . a picaresque saga"

—*Publishers Weekly*

"SOLID LAUGHS . . .
inspired raunchiness . . . tautly hilarious sex-
and-satire"

—*Kirkus Reviews*

"UPROARIOUS FUN . . .
wickedly absurdist comments on contempo-
rary society . . . a hilarious series of unlikely
liaisons and sexual experiments"

—*ALA Booklist*

"The *Portnoy's Complaint*
of the '80s. He has taken over where . . .
Philip Roth left off."

—*N.Y. Sunday News*

"READERS WILL FIND THEMSELVES
LAUGHING OUT LOUD . . . DAN
GREENBURG IS OUR FUNNIEST
NOVELIST."

—*John Barkham Reviews*

Books by Dan Greenburg

Love Kills
What Do Women Want?

Published by POCKET BOOKS

What Do Women Want?

Dan Greenburg

PUBLISHED BY POCKET BOOKS NEW YORK

For technical information on airline safety the author is indebted
to Laurence Gonzales—journalist, author and pilot.

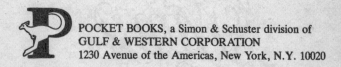

POCKET BOOKS, a Simon & Schuster division of
GULF & WESTERN CORPORATION
1230 Avenue of the Americas, New York, N.Y. 10020

Copyright © 1982 by Dan Greenburg

Published by arrangement with Simon & Schuster
Library of Congress Catalog Card Number: 81-23118

ISBN: 0-671-46735-2

First Pocket Books printing May, 1983

10 9 8 7 6 5 4 3 2 1

POCKET and colophon are registered trademarks
of Simon & Schuster.

Printed in the U.S.A.

To the memory of
Sam Greenburg,
my father and teacher

"What do women want?"

—Sigmund Freud

"There aren't any hard women, only soft men."

—Raquel Welch

1

On the last day of May, precisely three weeks before his fortieth birthday, Lance Lerner realized with suffocating clarity that his wife was having an affair with his best friend.

He had once too often walked into a room where the two of them, chatting together *sotto voce,* had abruptly and awkwardly fallen silent at his appearance. He didn't need a house to fall on him.

His first reaction was disbelief—it wasn't possible. His second reaction was belief—it was possible. His third reaction was rage, his fourth was a profound sense of having been betrayed, his fifth a horrid feeling of having been abandoned, his sixth a brief but overwhelming attack of nausea.

His seventh and most enduring reaction was something approaching calmness and acceptance. It was, he reasoned, after all not really so odd that his two favorite people in the world should be attracted to each other. He did not think that Cathy would want to leave him—he'd given her everything, what more could she want? He did not, he was sure, want her to leave him. And yet . . .

And yet this knowledge of his cuckolding—for, everything else aside, that is what it was—had made his marriage disconcertingly lopsided. For a man as compulsive, as *fanatical* about order and balance as was Lance Lerner, this lopsidedness could not be tolerated. It would have to be corrected. Balance would somehow have to be restored if the marriage was going to continue, but what was necessary to tip the scales back to flatness? Some kind of equal and opposite reaction was clearly called for, but what?

And then he knew. It was so simple, really. Even a child could appreciate its simplicity and its appropriateness: to redress the balance of their relationship (a term he hated), he would simply have a brief affair with his *wife's* best friend. The only problem, really, was in determining which of two quite different women that person might be.

Cathy Lerner was, at age thirty, what they called a beauty. Tall, long-boned, both big-breasted and delicately featured—an unlikely combination. Her straight shoulder-length hair was described as either light brown or dishwater blond, but in summer it was always streaked with sunshine. Her eyes varied between gray, blue, green and violet, depending on the weather and her mood—a sort of corneal litmus paper.

Like many beautiful women, she was ambivalent about her physical attributes—women as well as men focused on her looks and blurred her intellect and spirit. In self-defense she frequently hid behind high-necked blouses, baggy suits and trousers, even outsized horn-rimmed glasses.

The night that Lance met Cathy he thought she might be a little bookish for his taste. She was wearing the glasses and the baggy suit and she had told him she was an editor at the *New York Times Book Review*. To be honest about it, Lance, a prolific novelist, had at first considered her less a romantic partner than a good professional contact. The first time he saw her undressed he forgot about his professional life for sixteen consecutive hours—for him, a record.

Cathy was what Lance had always wanted—the male dream, the virgin whore. But she was more selves than two, she was a dozen at least, and she loved playing whichever one came up: smoldering temptress, petulant child, regal hostess, wide-eyed maiden, flaming bitch. Just which Cathy would come home to him at the end of the day he never could be sure. He almost never tired of the variety—it was like dating a dozen different women at once.

Sometimes Lance wondered what it was that Cathy saw in *him*. He guessed it was his ability to adapt to and take joy in whichever self she chose to be at the moment. Cathy could have been a fine photographer, an excellent model, a passable painter, a moderately good writer. Threatened equally by failure and success, she chose to do none of these. She became an editor, not out of any love she had for guiding or shaping a piece of writing but out of an ambivalence she had about being in the spotlight herself. Having come to it for the wrong reasons, she blamed editing for its limitations.

Lance found Cathy brilliant yet surprisingly naive—persistently new, like a child hearing something for the first time. That she had come to New York from Oklahoma didn't explain it. One of his terms of endearment for her was Cute Bunny. Once Lance had made reference to the old joke about Cecil B. De Mille—the one where De Mille laboriously stages the costliest shot in his biblical epic with thousands of extras and special effects, how he has the action covered by three different camera crews in various locations to ensure getting the coverage he needs, how as soon as the scene is over the first two camera crews shamefacedly radio in technical problems, and how he radios the third cameraman, who replies: "Ready when *you* are, C.B." Lance and Cathy were about to leave the apartment to go to dinner and Cathy had asked if Lance was ready. He'd replied, "Ready when *you* are, C.B.," then asked if she knew what the reference was. She said yes, but he sensed she was bluffing. "OK," he said, "what does C.B. stand for?" "Cute Bunny," she said, as if it were obvious.

At times Cathy told him extravagant stories about her adventures during the day, which trailed off into wistful resolutions. If Lance pressed her for details, she sometimes cocked her head and thought a moment, then replied, "I may have made that part up."

Lance wasn't sure Cathy always knew who she was. At times there seemed to be little connection between her intellectual and physical selves. It was as if she found her body a nice place to visit but didn't really live there. Once he found her brushing her hair in a distracted manner in front of the full-length mirror in the bathroom. Her robe accidentally fell open, revealing her amazing body, and she let out an audible gasp of surprised pleasure. "Sometimes I take my breath away," she explained, reddening, as if she'd been caught in an act of voyeurism.

When they had foolish spats about nothing at all and Lance was too stubborn to suggest making up, Cathy would hold out her arms to him and he would gratefully rush into them. At least at first.

Shortly after the first novel he'd written had become the best-selling book of 1973, Cathy had presented herself to Lance. Presented herself as a person with no needs, a person who lived only to serve him, his greatest fan. It was a promise she was later to retract—Cathy was to become the last woman in Manhattan to embrace the feminist movement—but Lance found no difficulty in accepting it. Spoiled all his life by an adoring Jewish mother, he was not in the least surprised that another woman wished to take over his mother's duties. That the woman was considerably younger than his mother and not remotely Jewish made it possible for sex to be part of the deal as well.

Cathy went to bed with Lance on their second date, stayed the night and never left. Her two roommates warned her not to sever ties with other men too quickly, but she paid them no attention. They had, she suspected, their own too personal reasons for being wary of the love that had sprung up so rapidly between her and Lance:

Cheryl, the blonde TWA stewardess, distrusted all men because of the ease with which she drew them to her side. Like Groucho Marx, she scorned membership in any club that would have her as a member.

Margaret, the junior CPA, was already spinsterly at twenty-three, distrusted all men because of the *difficulty* with which she drew them to her side, but used the guise of sexless frump to hide her true identity—a closet sensualist who secretly believed no man was good enough for her.

A year after Cathy moved in with Lance, she announced to Cheryl and Margaret that she was getting married. Both women shrieked with glee, danced around like dervishes, and were secretly appalled. The marriage, they knew, would never work. Although they were right, it was for the wrong reasons.

In any case, Cathy's marriage produced such profound depression in her former roommates that Cheryl moved in with a male flight attendant whom she outranked, and Margaret seduced a young securities analyst, was married three weeks after Cathy and Lance, and filed for divorce the day her processed marriage license arrived in the mail.

Lance and Cathy. Cathy and Lance. For seven years they had seemed the ideal couple. For seven years they had been the marriage against which their friends measured their own. Cathy was the perfect antidote for Lance's writerly neurosis, calming him during fits of depression, flattening out his lows and nimbly avoiding flattening his highs, planning and executing lavish dinner parties and casting them with influential people in both publishing and show business.

Lance took marvelous care of Cathy too, shoring her up when her self-confidence slipped, encouraging her short-lived projects in writing, painting or photography with hours of sober counseling, and being commendably patient about the half dozen or so men who always seemed to be hov-

4

ering around her like mosquitoes looking for a place to light.

Lance had always found the sight of a woman in garter belt and stockings very exciting, but Cathy refused to wear them. Garter belts, she said, were binding, cumbersome, old-fashioned and dumb. Once when Lance was out of town on business, though, Cathy went to her first porno film with a friend, saw women wearing garter belts, and decided they were sexy after all. The night Lance came back he and Cathy went to a formal dinner party. Shortly after they were seated Cathy took Lance's hand under the table, placed it on her knee and led him to discover she was wearing the much-longed-for lingerie. They went into the bathroom together between courses and managed a quickie standing up.

When they were first married Cathy took great delight in seducing Lance into making love out of doors. Once they had sex under a blanket at the beach and Lance got a severely chafed penis from a few grains of sand. Once they did it in the woods and Lance got a poison ivy rash on his butt. Thereafter, Lance balked at love in the great outdoors, but Cathy persuaded him to do it in the city on their terrace, certain they couldn't be seen. A crazed neighbor on an upper floor of an adjoining building lobbed rocks at them, however, and so, much to Cathy's disappointment, Lance moved his amatory activities permanently indoors.

Without realizing it, Lance was making Cathy into what he needed in a mate, although not what he wanted. He was nipping the peaks of her sexual passion because they made him uncomfortable. They made him feel he was losing control, and he was terrified of losing control.

Their sex together grew less passionate. Every single night became three nights a week, then twice a week, then mostly Sunday mornings—and not every Sunday, at that. Two- and three-hour sessions utilizing eight positions sifted down to twenty-minute sessions of your basic missionary position. They reassured each other and themselves that this didn't mean they were any less in love, only that their love was going into a different gear. A higher one, to be sure.

Several times Lance was tempted to play hide-the-salami with one or another of the women who meandered through his mostly happy marriage. Women who were turned on by his growing success and fame. Women who were turned on by his slim and well-tuned body, his dry wit, his droll and mildly self-mocking manner. Women who were turned on by his wife's considerable sexuality and didn't know how else to deal with it. Women who were turned on by the mere fact of Lance's being married and therefore inaccessible and safe.

Lance had always been willing to flirt with them, but never more. He was afraid of wounding Cathy, of being caught and damaging his marriage, although the prospect of exploring an unfamiliar female body was so exciting to him he sometimes found it hard to breathe, and although the prospect of conceiving and executing a secret plot to bring it off was possibly even more exciting to him than that of the adulterous act itself.

Lance was always able to sabotage his own best efforts at married flirting. If he and Cathy had gone to dinner at a friend's house and he had flirted with an attractive woman there, he tried to disguise his interest in her either by going on at some length about the woman's unattractive qualities, or else by doing the reverse—frankly stating how delicious he thought she was—on the theory that any pronouncement so blatant couldn't be anything but innocent. The only problem was that Lance often forgot which tack he had started out on, and consequently found himself saying wildly contradictory things about the woman in question.

Lance had never gone farther with these casual crushes than occasionally taking them to lunch, having a few too many vodka-tonics with them, and trading suggestive remarks. He consummated these crushes in fantasy while making love to Cathy, and he sublimated his growing horniness in his writing and in his vicarious joy in the sexual exploits of his best friend, Les.

Les French was dark, curly-headed, bearded, and full of the old piss-and-vinegar. Les was nearly fifteen years Lance's junior, yet Lance felt more comfortable sharing his daily frustrations and fantasies with Les than anyone he knew except for Cathy. Les was either quite a bit more mature than your average twenty-five-year-old, or else Lance was quite a bit less mature than your average forty-year-old. Recounting to Les in elaborate detail the circumstances of his latest unconsummated flirtation had always been enough for Lance. At least till now.

Lance resented the loss of Les as a confidante almost as much as he resented the fact that Les was slipping it to his wife. God, what kind of a man would slip it to his best friend's wife? After all he'd done for Les! Why, Les was not only his best friend, he was his goddamn protégé! What kind of a protégé slips it to his mentor's wife? The ungrateful little creep!

He wondered what Les and Cathy said about him when they discussed him. Did they make fun of him? Was Cathy telling Les the secret things about Lance that only Cathy knew? Like what they did in bed together? Like talking in bunny voices? He prayed that Cathy had more restraint than to tell Les about stuff like that. Perhaps Cathy had been the aggressor. Perhaps she had actively seduced him, and Les had mainly gone along with it so as not to seem impolite. If that were the case, perhaps it was not quite fair to blame Les for what had happened. It was something that, one day, they would have to work out if the friendship were to continue. For now, though, what he had to do was determine who was Cathy's closer friend, Margaret or Cheryl, and then steer that person into the sack at the earliest possible opportunity. That was the only course of action that seemed likely to bring peace to his fanatical, compulsive mind.

Lance was compulsive in all things. Compulsive in his work—about the way he had to have everything in his office lined up in neat stacks, parallel or perpendicular to everything else. Compulsive in his eating—about the way he always ate each thing on his plate separately, never mixing them together, always saving the best for last (early training in deferred gratification), always finishing everything on his plate, even if he hated it. Compulsive in his driving—he owned an old Porsche, and if he failed to respond to a passing Porsche owner's wave or toot or flash of headlights, he felt horrible about it, once even making a U-turn in the middle of the road and taking off after the startled motorist, madly waving and tooting and flashing his lights at him.

If Lance had been less of a compulsive, less of an extremist, less of a fanatic, the choice would have been easy: he would simply have begun plotting the seduction of the blond TWA stewardess. But because of his fanaticism—his conscientiousness, as he chose to view it—he suspected that Margaret was actually the closer friend and therefore the more appropriate target of his retaliatory mission.

To settle the issue, there was one way to find out whom he would pursue.

2

"Hey, Cathy?"

"Hmmm?"

"How's your old friend Cheryl these days?"

"Cheryl? I don't know. OK, I guess."

"She still living with that male stewardess of hers?"

"I think so. Why?"

"Oh, no reason, no reason. I was just thinking. Cheryl is a pretty good friend of yours, isn't she?"

"Sure. Why?"

"She's probably your *best* friend, wouldn't you say?"

"My *best* friend? Oh, I don't know. Certainly one of my *two* best. Her and Margaret, I mean."

"Mmmm. You know, I always thought you liked her just a tiny bit more than Margaret, somehow."

"Really? I don't know what would have given you *that* idea."

"I don't know. Maybe it's just that I sense that you *admire* her more than Margaret or something."

"Admire? Cheryl? No, I really admire Margaret a lot more than Cheryl. What's this about?"

"Wouldn't you say, though, that it's pretty much of a toss-up? That Cheryl and Margaret are about equally close to you?"

"Not really, no. I'm really closer to Margaret. What's this about, Lance?"

"Nothing, really. It just happened to cross my mind that you were pretty tight with both Cheryl and Margaret, and I started wondering who you liked more, that's all."

"I see."

"Funny how I always thought you liked Cheryl better."

"Yes, it is. I don't know why you would have thought that."

"Mmmm. Let me ask you this: Did you *ever* like Cheryl better than Margaret?"

Cathy burst out laughing.

"Lance, will you tell me what this is all about?"

"Nothing, honey. I was just wondering, that's all. Can't a person wonder about his wife's best friends and not have it be *about* something?"

"Sure, but it's sort of weird, that's all. Spending that much time thinking who I like better, Cheryl or Margaret. It just seems kind of weird, you know?"

"I don't see what's weird about it. Why do you think it's weird?"

Cathy looked at him strangely.

"If I didn't know better," she said, "I'd say you were deliberately trying to get me to say that I liked Cheryl better than Margaret."

He had gone too far.

"Why would I ever want you to say a thing like that?"

"I don't know, Lance. *You* tell *me*."

"Forget it," he said.

The choice, willy-nilly, had been made. In order to save his marriage, he was now *forced* to sleep with Margaret.

3

He had planned to call Margaret for a lunch date as soon as Cathy left the apartment, but Cathy was working at home while her office was being redecorated and seemed to be around whenever he managed to summon the courage to make the call.

Eventually, one particularly balmy day in early June, Lance decided to call from a pay phone in the street. At the first phone he tried an elderly man with a two-day growth of beard was permanently affixed to the receiver. The next two phones were out of order, and when he finally found one that worked it happened to be on one of the noisiest corners in midtown Manhattan.

He dialed the number and, as it started to ring, his pulse suddenly started pounding in his throat. He realized he was seven years removed from the practice of calling women for dates and he had forgotten what the rhythms sounded like. When he was in college he often wrote out entire scripts before phoning girls for dates, usually reading his lines right off the paper. Happily, he'd outgrown the practice when he graduated.

On the fifth ring somebody answered, but the voice didn't sound familiar.

"Is, uh, Margaret there?" said Lance.

"This is Margaret," said the unfamiliar voice. Was it really Margaret or was it somebody masquerading as Margaret?

"Margaret?" said Lance.

"Yes?" said the voice.

"Oh," said Lance. "Hi, Margaret, it didn't sound like you."

"Who is this?" said the voice.

Sweat suddenly prickled his forehead and the space between his shoulder blades.

"I'm sorry," said Lance. "This is—"

At that moment the driver of a passing cab gave in to the accumulated frustrations of having been able to move only three blocks in the past half hour and leaned on his horn for approximately sixty seconds.

"What did you say?" said Margaret.

"I *said* this is—"

The cabdriver, clearly an emissary from a God who did not approve of adulterous affairs, no matter now justifiable, gave the horn another thirty seconds.

"I can't *hear* you!" yelled Margaret.

"I'm sorry. This is . . ." Lance eyed the cabdriver warily, then screamed: "LANCE!"

"Jesus Christ," said Margaret, "I think you punctured my eardrum."

"I'm sorry," said Lance. "I thought he was going to honk again."

"Where are you calling from, Lance, the Holland Tunnel?"

"Ha ha. No, from the street, actually. I just happened to be walking along Madison Avenue and I thought I would call you up and say hello."

Now *there's* an assholic way to start a conversation, he thought. Maybe I should go back to writing out scripts.

"I see," said Margaret. "Well then, hello, Lance. How's Cathy?"

"Cathy?" he said. The sweat began flowing out of glands he didn't know he had, drenching his clothing.

"Your wife?" said Margaret helpfully. "Tall, good-looking woman with large breasts and dishwater blond hair?"

"Ha ha. Yes, I know the one you mean," said Lance, trying to get into the spirit of banter. "Cathy is fine. Saw her only this morning, as a matter of fact."

"Tell her I couldn't find the Ralph Lauren blouse she wanted," said Margaret. "Bloomingdale's had it in beige, but not in mauve. Ask her to call me if she wants it in beige."

"I, uh . . . don't know if I'll be able to do that," said Lance. What was he supposed to say: "Oh, Cathy, when I was phoning Margaret to see if I could get into her pants, she gave me a message about a blouse . . ."

"You what?" said Margaret.

"I mean I . . . might forget," said Lance. Then it occurred to him that Margaret would now phone Cathy and repeat their conversation, and Cathy would ask Lance why he was calling Margaret, and . . .

"On second thought," said Lance hurriedly, "I'm writing it down. Here . . ." He pretended to write on a piece of paper. "Bloomie's had . . . blouse in beige . . . not in mauve . . . call Margaret if . . . want in beige."

"Good boy," said Margaret.

"Listen, Margaret, the reason I'm calling—how's about lunch tomorrow?" Lance blurted.

"Tomorrow? Tomorrow's OK, I guess," said Margaret. "Just you and me and Cathy, you mean?"

"No no no," said Lance nervously, "not Cathy. You and me and . . . nobody."

There was a puzzled silence on the other end.

"Is this a surprise for Cathy?" said Margaret.

"In a way," said Lance.

"Well, sure," said Margaret. "Why not? Where do you want to eat?"

Lance was almost overcome with gratitude.

"How's about Maxwell's Plum? Sixty-fourth and First. About twelve-thirty?"

"Fine," said Margaret.

"Oh, and don't mention this to Cathy," he said. "I mean it would spoil the surprise."

When he hung up the phone, Lance was so drained of energy he could scarcely walk.

"Hi honey," said Cathy, as Lance let himself back into the apartment. "Where've you been?"

"Where've I been?" said Lance. "Out."

"I *know* you were *out,* silly," said Cathy. "I mean where?"

"Oh, I went to the store. To buy some yogurt."

"We have about twenty containers in the fridge," she said.

"I know," he said. "I mean, uh, I realized that once I got to the store."

"I see," she said, looking him over with interest. "Have you been running?"

"Running?" he said. "Why no. I mean why do you ask?"

"Well, you're all sweated up and you're out of breath."

"Oh, that," he said. "Well, I did do a little running, as a matter of fact. I was suddenly feeling kind of sleepy, so I ran around the block a couple of times to kind of get my heart going."

"You ran around the block a couple of times to get your *heart* going?" she said.

"Yeah."

What *is* this? he thought. *She's* the one who's sleeping around—why am *I* feeling so guilty?

Cathy shrugged and went into the bathroom to shower. Lance collapsed into a chair.

He thought he ought to prepare for the lunch better than he'd prepared for the phone call. It was a more difficult script, and he wouldn't have the luxury of reading it off a piece of paper either.

He wondered what Margaret's reaction would be. He wondered if she'd be shocked and disgusted at what he was going to propose to her. He wondered if she'd go straight to Cathy with the whole thing.

If he'd had any idea of what he was about to get into, he'd have thrown Margaret's phone number right into the toilet.

4

Maxwell's Plum was ornate and cheery. A million dollars' worth of Tiffany lamps, art deco figurines of naked ladies, and sculptures of animals hanging from the ceiling looked down on Lance Lerner as he waited in the darkest corner of the restaurant for the appearance of his wife's best friend, who was now twenty minutes late.

Had she misunderstood the arrangement? Hadn't he told her "Maxwell's Plum . . . Sixty-fourth and First . . . about twelve-thirty?" And hadn't she said "Fine"?

Maybe she'd got the day wrong. No, he'd definitely said "Tomorrow," meaning today. Maybe she knew what he had in mind and had called Cathy. Would she do that? No. If she were going to do that, she would have done it immediately, and he would have heard about it immediately too. The fact that she hadn't called Cathy suggested that she was planning to come. Regardless of whether she knew what he had on his mind.

A waiter appeared once more at his elbow.

"You wish to order another drink, sir? While you're waiting?" he said in an amused, patronizing voice. Clearly, the fucking waiter was enjoying the sight of a guy nervously waiting for somebody who appeared to be standing him up. Clearly the sonofabitch had never been stood up himself, the faggot bastard.

"Why, yes," said Lance, with a tone he hoped conveyed just the right mixture of disdain and boredom. "Another vodka-tonic will be fine."

"Very good, sir," said the waiter, and minced off to the bar to regale his colleagues with accounts of Lance's stoodupness.

Lance looked at his watch for the fortieth time. It was now one o'clock. She was a half hour late! How long could he be expected to wait for her, the miserable twat? He had half a mind to simply get up and leave.

He looked around for the waiter. He could just cancel the drink, pay the bill and leave. She clearly wasn't coming now, but how was he supposed to act toward her when he saw her again with Cathy? Would he be able to contain his anger?

Unless. Unless she had arrived punctually at twelve-thirty, maybe even a little before that, waited five or ten minutes, figured he'd changed his mind and left—he had, after all, been about five minutes late himself . . .

And then it hit him: she'd been struck by a cab on the way to the restaurant. She was so preoccupied with her own ambivalence, lust and guilt over the prospect of an illicit meeting with her best friend's husband that she didn't look where she was going, and a cab going much too fast ran a red light, swerved to avoid her at the last instant, but not quickly enough. Margaret's body was tossed into the air by the cab's fender like a hapless matador on the horns of a bull. She lay, even now, on a stretcher in a city ambulance, her life's blood drenching the pretty clothes she had worn especially to please him.

Poor Margaret! What a horrid way to die! He would have her death on his conscience for the rest of his life, and he'd never be able to tell Cathy about it either.

That must have been what happened. That *better* be what had happened, he thought—for *her* sake.

"Hi, Lance. Sorry I'm late."

He looked up. It was Margaret, alive and intact. She looked like she'd been running.

"Well, hi," he said coolly. "I didn't think you were coming."

"I'm sorry," she said, sliding down into the banquette, "I . . . got detained."

Was that it? Was that all he got after almost forty minutes of waiting and having to be humiliated in front of an entire corps of waiters—*I got detained?* He was fast becoming so furious he was not going to be able to speak at all.

"Monsieur?"

The waiter appeared with Lance's vodka-tonic and nodded to Margaret.

"I'll have a Tanqueray martini," she said. "Straight up."

"Very good, madam," said the waiter and withdrew.

Margaret smiled at Lance. He did not return the smile. She was wearing a tan blazer, tan skirt, and a beige silk blouse.

She had a dutchboy haircut with medium brown hair, flat brown eyes and horn-rimmed glasses. She wore practically no makeup, no lipstick or rouge, and no perceptible eyeliner. He did not find her the least bit attractive. For the first time he thought she might be a lesbian.

"I'm really sorry I was so late, Lance," she said in a quiet, feminine voice he had never heard her use before. "I'll tell you the reason, but first . . ." Her voice trailed off, and he thought she might be blushing.

"Yes . . . ?" he said.

"Well, first I want to hear why you wanted to see me."

"Why I wanted to see you?" he said stupidly.

He took his second drink and poured it down his throat.

"Yes," she said. She was looking at him very directly—almost sensuously, a slight smile on her face. And she was very definitely blushing. She *does* know why I wanted to see her, he thought. That makes it easier. And harder.

"Well," he said, beginning slowly, stalling for time, using the trick that all schoolboys learn when they don't know the answer to what the teacher has asked them, beginning the answer by restating the question, "why I wanted to see you was . . . I wanted to talk to you."

"About what?"

"About what? About a lot of things, actually. First of all, I wanted to talk to you about, uh, something that has been on my mind for quite a long . . . You see, Margaret, although you and I have known each other for several years, for almost eight years now, as a matter of fact, I don't think we have ever talked—really *talked*, you know?—about things like, uh, well, like the kinds of things that, perhaps, you and I would have talked about, assuming that we had had the opportunity to talk about them. To really *talk* about them, I mean, you know?"

He was awash in perspiration. She was looking at him closely. The slight smile was still on her face.

"Lance, do you want to fuck me? Is that it?"

He exhaled sharply. Blood surged into his cheeks and forehead.

"Well, yes," he said, finding his voice now slipping into an odd, quiet and slightly manic tone. "The fact is, Margaret, I've always found you incredibly attractive, incredibly sexual. I quite frankly didn't think it was appropriate to even *have* such thoughts, much less to voice them, and I swear I never intended to, but every time you've been in our house and

15

we've been physically close to each other, it's been all I could do to restrain myself from taking you in my arms."

"I know," she said quietly.

"What?" he said.

"I could tell how you felt about me," she said softly. "I'm afraid you weren't as discreet as you thought you were."

He fought the impulse to burst out laughing, deciding it would be a tactical error.

"You don't think that *Cathy* . . . ?" he began.

"Oh no. No no, I don't think Cathy noticed," she said. "I don't think Cathy would even *dream* that you—or *any* man of hers, for that matter—would so much as *look* at me, but I could certainly tell that you were interested."

"I see. And . . . how do you feel about that?" he asked cautiously.

She shrugged.

"You're not the *first* of Cathy's men who's wanted to sleep with me," she said.

"I'm not?"

She shook her head.

"Naturally, I feel some ambivalance about it," she said. "Cathy is, after all, one of my three closest friends. I wouldn't do anything to hurt her. And yet . ."

"Yes . . . ?"

"Well, I knew what you were going to say to me today. And I guess I *was* pretty ambivalent about it—that's why I was so late. I left the office three times. I almost didn't come at all. I was going to telephone you at the restaurant and tell you I wasn't coming, that I didn't think it was right. But then I thought, what if that wasn't what you wanted to talk to me about, you know? I would have looked like an ass. Tell me, why did you finally call me *now?* After all these years of lusting for me in silence?"

"Um, well, because of a couple of things, I guess. First of all, I've discovered that Cathy is . . . I've discovered that Cathy is having a little . . . fling herself."

Margaret's eyes widened.

"With whom?" she said.

"What does it matter?" he said.

"It doesn't," she said. "I'd just like to know."

"I'd rather not say," he said. "I mean, if she had wanted you to know, I guess she would have told you herself."

"I suppose you're right," she said. "You know, I *thought*

she was having an affair. Only I was afraid to ask. I'll bet I know who it is."

"Who?" he said.

"That cute guy at the health club. Sven. The one who teaches yoga. She's always kidding around with him. Is that it?"

Sven? The guy at the health club who teaches yoga? Was she having *two* affairs?

"It's not Sven," he said.

"It doesn't matter," she said. "If she'd wanted me to know, she'd have told me herself. So. What is this, an eye for an eye?"

"Pardon me?"

"What is this—evening the score? *She's* sleeping around, so you're going to do it too, to retaliate?"

"No no no, nothing like that. Of course not. No no. It's just that . . ."

"It wouldn't be so hard to understand if that were it," she said.

"It wouldn't?" he said. "Oh, well, I mean, I suppose there must be an *element* of that in this, you know, but it's certainly not the most important one."

"It isn't?"

"No. Of course not."

"Then what is?"

"The most important one is how I feel about *you*. This incredible attraction that I feel for you, that I've felt for some time now. That's the most important one. Of course, the fact that I've found out that Cathy herself is, uh, you know, having a fling sort of makes it easier. To tell you how I feel about you. How I've felt for some time. You know something? You haven't said yet how *you* feel about *me*."

She smiled again.

"I find you a . . . reasonably attractive man," she said.

He snorted with laughter.

"Jesus Christ," he said. "After all that, the most you can say is, 'I find you a reasonably attractive man'?"

Color came into her cheeks.

"All right," she said, "I fantasize about you a lot."

"You do? That's better. Tell me what you fantasize."

"Oh, I fantasize about a lot of things."

"C'mon," he said. "You can do better than that. What are you fantasizing right now? Right this second?"

Her face got redder. She started to say something so quietly that he could hardly hear her.

"What's that?" he said. "I can't hear you."

"I *said*," she said, "I am fantasizing that you are going to slide under the table right now as we're talking, pull down my panties, bury your face in my pussy, and lick me till I scream."

There was an immediate crash behind them. Lance looked around to see the waiter retrieving a tray that had once held several drinks. Lance was aware that the people at the tables on all sides of him had stopped talking and were pretending relentless interest in their silverware and ashtrays. He felt his penis begin to get hard.

"I'm sorry," she said, flustered. "I guess I shouldn't have been quite that honest."

"No no," he said, "I really admire an honest answer."

The waiter was still picking up pieces of glass and ice cubes, hoping that there would be more.

"You haven't said how you feel about what I just told you," she said.

He checked the people at the adjacent tables and waited till his gaze forced them to resume their conversations. Then he turned back to the waiter, who was mopping up liquid as slowly as possible.

"How's about I just mail you a transcript of our conversation?" Lance said pleasantly. The waiter got very huffy and stood up.

"I'm sure I have better things to do than to eavesdrop on your asinine sexual conversations," he said and flounced away.

Lance leaned across the table toward Margaret. He was aware of her perfume. She had never before, to his knowledge, used perfume.

"Can we go back to your apartment right now so I can do what you were fantasizing?" he said hoarsely.

Margaret looked away. Her breathing was beginning to be labored. She hadn't needed rouge after all.

"I don't know what I want to do," she whispered.

"You don't?" He was incredulous.

"I mean I *do* know what I want to do. I just don't know if I *can*."

"Because of Cathy?"

"Because of Cathy. I don't know if I can do this to her. I *love* Cathy."

"*You* love Cathy? How about *me*? I don't love Cathy? I *worship* Cathy, for God's sake. Cathy's a goddam *saint*, that's what she is."

"You're telling me? Cathy was my *roommate*, Lance."

"Your *roommate*? She's my *wife*, for Christ's sake!"

"Well, I know that. And that's why I don't know if I can do such a thing to her."

"You don't know? What do you need to make up your mind?" he hissed, sliding his hand underneath the table and grabbing her knee.

"Don't," she said softly.

"Don't what?" he said, leaning farther forward, sliding his hand under the hem of her skirt, up the inside of her thigh.

"Please don't," she said even more softly.

"Why not?" he said, sliding his hand up to the flesh of her upper thigh adjoining her pudendum.

"Because," she whispered.

"Because what?" he whispered, leaning even farther forward and slipping his hand over the silky crotch of her panties. The position he was forced to take to reach his hand that far under the table was giving him a pronounced pain in his right shoulder.

"Because it isn't fair," she whispered.

"Why isn't it?" he whispered, and just then a muscle in his shoulder began to spasm and he emitted a sharp cry.

"What's wrong?" she said, alarmed.

"Nothing," he said, withdrawing his arm from under the table and wincing in pain. "Just a little muscle spasm, that's all. Margaret, I think we should leave here. I think we should go back to your apartment."

"I don't know if I can do that, Lance. I need time to think."

"O.K., we'll walk there—you can think on the way."

"I need more time than that."

"How much more?"

"I don't know. A few days. Maybe a week or so."

"Can't you think any faster than that?"

"Please, Lance. You have to let me get accustomed to the idea. It's going to take time. I'll let you know as soon as I've thought it through."

She got up.

"Where are you going?" he said.

"I'm very conflicted. I have to leave."

"But we haven't even ordered yet."

"I couldn't eat anything now anyway. I'm too upset."

19

He got up and followed her to the door of the restaurant. Every head in the place charted their progress from table to door.

"Will you call me when you decide?" he said.

"How can I call you?" she said. "How do I know Cathy won't answer the phone?"

"I'll answer all calls for the next few days," he said.

"What if you have to go to the bathroom?" she said.

"It's a long cord," he said, "I'll take the phone in with me."

"You'd better call *me*," she said, opening the door to the restaurant.

"When shall I call you? Is tonight too soon?"

"Yes. Don't call for several days. Don't call me for a week."

"A week? I can't wait a whole week."

"Please, Lance. Wait a week. Promise me you'll wait a week."

The waiter, suddenly afraid that Lance was attempting to leave without paying, raced up to the door, waving the check.

"Just a moment!" he yelled. "Just a moment there, fellow!"

"A week, then," said Lance. "June 14th. But no later."

"Aren't you forgetting something?" said the waiter unpleasantly, reaching the door and barring Lance's passage with his outstretched arm. Lance turned to face him, incredulous.

"If you don't drop your arm this instant," said Lance, "I'm going to stick my fingers up your nose and rip it off your face."

5

By the time Lance reached home he had almost recovered from the drinks at Maxwell's Plum. He let himself into the apartment and went to the bathroom to change.

"Honey, that you?" called Cathy from another room.

"No, it's the cat burglar," he said, swiftly removing his tie and jacket to avoid answering questions about where he'd been. Cathy came into the bathroom just as he was slipping into a denim work shirt. She grabbed him from behind and kissed the back of his neck.

"You're pretty cute for a cat burglar," she said, hugging him hard. "You want to fool around a little before my husband gets home?"

Lance winced, was about to make a bitter retort, and stopped in the nick of time. Cathy turned him around and kissed him on the mouth.

"Hey," she said. "Where've *you* been?"

"Out shopping," he said. "I had to get a couple things from the hardware store."

"Then why is there vodka on your breath?" she said.

"Vodka? On my breath?" he said. "What do you mean?"

"I mean I smell vodka on your breath," she said.

He realized that Wolfschmidt had sold him out.

"Vodka," he said inanely, "has no taste. You can't smell it on somebody's breath."

There may have been one or two acceptable replies to the question she'd posed. This had not been one of them. The smile and the playfulness slowly dissolved.

"Where have you been?" she said.

"To the hardware store," he said. "I told you."

"They serve vodka now at the hardware store?"

"As a matter of fact, smart-ass, today they did. It just so happens that today was Midtown Hardware Store's twenty-

21

fifth anniversary in business, and they were serving vodka and white wine and little canapes with red caviar and sour cream. I thought you'd be pissed at me for drinking on a day when I had work to do, but I may as well confess, since you've got the nose of a bloodhound. I admit it, Officer Lerner—I've been drinking."

He chuckled and tried to hug her, but she couldn't be jollied back into her playful mood. He knew he had made a big mistake.

Soon he would make one about eighty times worse.

6

Cathy and Margaret walked into the locker room of the New York Health and Racquet Club. The buxom Puerto Rican attendant opened two lockers for them and gave them two towels. Both women began undressing. Both seemed preoccupied.

"You know what I think, Margaret?" said Cathy, pulling her sweater over her head, "I think Lance might be having an affair."

Margaret counted slowly to ten before she trusted her voice to reply.

"What do you mean?" she said.

"I don't know," said Cathy, stepping out of her skirt. "He's acting very weird. He came home a few days ago with vodka on his breath and tried to sell me some cockamamy story about the hardware store having an anniversary and serving liquor."

"Oh, I've heard of things like that," said Margaret. "The hardware store around my house did that about a month ago, in fact. They served liquor and champagne. That's quite a common practice for hardware stores these days."

Cathy hung her skirt and sweater inside the locker and

turned to her friend. The familiar sight of Cathy's briefly attired body always made Margaret vaguely uncomfortable.

"You don't think Lance is having an affair then?" said Cathy hopefully.

"Oh no," said Margaret, shaking her head vigorously, "absolutely not. I mean I'd know if he was, and he isn't." She couldn't believe the words which had just walked out of her mouth.

Cathy frowned.

"What do you mean you'd know if he was?"

Margaret's mind raced for an explanation.

"I mean," she said, "that if Lance was having an affair, there wouldn't be any doubt in *your* mind. And if there wouldn't be any doubt in *your* mind, then there wouldn't be any doubt in *mine*. After looking at you, I mean. I mean you couldn't hide it. From your friend, I mean."

Cathy sighed and regarded her reflection in the mirror on the wall.

"I guess you're right," she said. She unhooked her bra, paused, flashed first one breast and then the other at the mirror, stripper style, then hung her bra in the locker. "I guess I *would* know if Lance was having an affair. I guess he probably isn't," she said.

"I'm sure *he* isn't," said Margaret. "Are *you?*"

"Me?" Cathy burst into laughter. "Hell no. Why did you ask me that?"

"I don't know."

"Well, I'm not," said Cathy.

7

True to his word, Lance waited an entire week, till June 14th, before seeking out another pay phone and calling Margaret. In the intervening seven days his apathy toward Margaret had reversed itself and hardened into a fine obsession. He replayed the fantasy she had described in the restaurant with endless variations. It was all he could think about.

He made love to Cathy and imagined it was her plain-looking friend. He had endless visions of Margaret—of her pulling down her panties under the table in the restaurant and his going down on her, of her slipping under the table to go down on *him,* and so on. The concept of making love to someone as beautiful as Cathy and having fantasies about someone as plain-looking as Margaret was ludicrous, though not, he suspected, at all unusual. Wasn't it George Burns who said even if you were married to Marilyn Monroe you would still be out trying to pick up pigs?

By the seventh day following Lance's lunch with Margaret he could stand it no more. He went out into the street and, after losing six dimes in the first two pay phones, finally reached her.

"Have you decided?" he said.

"Who is this?" said Margaret.

"Oh, I'm sorry. It's Lance."

"Oh, Lance. I didn't recognize your voice. You're back in the Holland Tunnel, I see."

"Ha ha. Look, you've had a week now. What did you decide?"

"Well, I don't know yet. I need a little more time."

"More time? How much more time?"

"Another week."

"Another *week!* I can't wait another week. Why can't you decide now? Why don't you know what you want?"

24

"Lance, Cathy thinks you're having an affair."

"*What?*"

"She said you came home with vodka on your breath. She said you told her you got it at an anniversary celebration for a *hardware* store."

"It was all I could think of on the spur of the moment," he said sheepishly.

"I told her hardware stores in my neighborhood had anniversary celebrations with liquor all the time."

"Oh God. Look, when can I see you?"

"I need more time."

"When can I see you?"

"I don't know, I don't know. O.K., a week from today. Next Thursday."

"Thursday? The twenty-first? That's my birthday."

"So? How are you planning to celebrate it?" she said. "Is Cathy taking you to dinner or what?"

"I guess so. I don't know. It's my fortieth birthday. Cathy hasn't mentioned it, though. Frankly, I think she's forgotten. I'm not exactly uppermost in her mind these days."

"I'm sure you're wrong."

"No I'm not. Well, what the hell. If she doesn't remember, I'll tell her myself. But I guess I can meet you before dinner for a drink. A drink and . . . whatever else you decide to do. O.K. then, Thursday it is. What time Thursday?"

"Five-thirty. At my place."

He chuckled.

"At *your* place, eh? Then I won't *ask* what you're planning to give me for my birthday."

8

Thursday. June 21st. The first day of summer. Lance's fortieth birthday. He studies his barely noticeable bald spot in two strategically placed mirrors in the bathroom and makes a mental note to consult a dermatologist about it—right after he consults a nutritionist about a more healthful diet and a program of vitamins, and right after he renews his lapsed membership in the health club where he used to swim laps.

On the morning of his fortieth birthday he actually breaks down and reminds Cathy it's his birthday. Actually has to *remind* her. He inquires what she would like to do for dinner. She says it's up to him. Up to *him. On his fortieth birthday.*

He is now doubly justified in fucking her best friend. It is only fitting that he will be doing it today. It is now four-thirty. Feeling sorry for himself, he pours two quickie drinks and downs them before he leaves the house. He tells Cathy he is going to Bloomingdale's and Hammacher-Schlemmer to buy himself some birthday presents and will be back at eight to take her to dinner.

He leaves the apartment and walks slowly uptown to Margaret's. He stops in a bar and has another drink. He tries to picture what he will be doing with Margaret only an hour from now. He tries to picture Margaret naked. The nononsense Margaret without her clothes. Without her horn-rimmed glasses. Without her dry accountant's manner. What will she feel like naked? What will she smell like? What will her dry accountant's body taste like when he begins to devour it with tongue and teeth? What noises will she make, if any, in the throes of orgasm?

He arrives at her apartment building. He looks at his watch: 5:25. He is five minutes early. He goes on in anyway. Heart hammering in his chest. Pulse pounding in his pants. This will be the first woman other than Cathy in more than seven years. Will it be heaven? Will he even be able to get it up?

He rings the doorbell. She buzzes him in. He takes the elevator up. He pauses briefly before her closed door. Is this really what he wants to do? Fuck his wife's best friend on his fortieth birthday? It is. His wife has given him no choice. He knocks.

It takes at least three minutes for her to come to the door.

"Who is it?" she says.

"Who do you think?" he says.

The door is unlocked. It swings inward. It is dark inside. She had drawn the blinds and drapes. He slips into her apartment. He reaches out for her, touches her shoulder. She pulls away, giggling. He thinks he smells bourbon on her breath—so she has had to sneak a couple of drinks for courage too!

"Come here," he whispers.

"Not yet," she says, her voice retreating.

"Where are you going?" he says.

"To get something. Make yourself comfortable."

A door at the other end of the room opens, then clicks shut.

He sighs, sits down. He imagines her in her bedroom, pulling her dress over her head, stripping down to bra and panties or a flimsy negligee. The image is too much for him. He feels his penis begin to stiffen. The room is warm. He slips out of his jacket. Takes off his tie. He carefully removes his boots and socks and tiptoes across the living room to her bedroom door. He starts to knock, stops, has a better idea. He slips out of his shirt, slacks and undershorts. Stark naked, his now-hard-as-a-rock penis preceding him, he raps at her bedroom door.

"Here I come, ready or not!" he calls.

"Come on in," says Margaret in a strange, high, possibly ambivalent voice.

He turns the knob and walks into the darkened bedroom.

Blinding lights. And forty people yell: "SURPRISE!"

9

In a perfect world it would never have happened. In a perfect world Margaret would not have perversely neglected to warn Lance in case he might at the last moment decide to do something spontaneous like this. In a perfect world he would have entered the bedroom *before* taking off all his clothing.

In a perfect world he might have realized somewhat before the lights were switched on that what he had mistaken for the evidence of an affair between Cathy and Les had been merely the clandestine arrangements for a mammoth surprise party.

Now time has stopped dead and he stands staring into the faces of his wife and his best friend, who are holding a long rectangular mocha cake with forty lit candles on it, flanked by Margaret and Cheryl and thirty-six other utterly paralyzed people who are all desperately wishing to be somewhere else.

There is total silence. No one so much as draws a breath. Forty mouths are open, frozen in position. Eighty eyes bulge forward, staring at his nakedness, at his rapidly deflating erection. Eighty lungs are holding in their already used-up oxygen, pending potential deliverance by means of the next words from Lance's lips.

"I can explain this," he begins, wildly ransacking his mind for anything—anything at all in the memory core—that will get him out of this. "This isn't what it seems," he babbles, but by now those in the room have already sensed disaster—like fans whose team is losing the championship game by a single point and who watch the basketball leave the hands of the team's star center and hear the final gun go off and know even though it has not even reached the zenith of its trajectory through the air that the ball will never in a million billion trillion years go through that hoop but will bounce impotently off the rim and the game and the championship if not their very lives are lost lost lost and their prayers have once more gone unanswered by an indifferent God.

The next five minutes would be among the worst ever experienced by any person in the room who had not been in a major war. If a passing vendor had suddenly appeared with a tray of cyanide pellets and single-edged razor blades he would have sold out his entire stock in twenty seconds.

"As you may or may not be aware," Lance continued, "Margaret's apartment happens to have a fairly heavy infestation of cockroaches. The instant I entered the living room, a roach dropped off the ceiling and fell into the space between my shirt collar and the back of my neck . . ."

Both Cathy and Margaret had burst into tears. Everybody else, faces averted and mumbling unintelligible phrases, was pleading pressing engagements upstate and making for the door.

". . . As I happen to have an almost pathological aversion to cockroaches," Lance continued, his tone now approaching hysteria, "I immediately began pulling off articles of my clothing in a vain attempt to . . ."

It was hopeless. Nobody was even listening to him anymore.

10

At home Cathy was surprisingly adult about the whole thing. All right, so she broke a few dishes and screamed a little. But then she stopped. She dried her tears. She composed herself. She packed a small canvas bag and went to stay with Cheryl and her male stewardess.

Lance wondered whether the neighbors had been able to hear her screaming, and then berated himself for caring about such insignificant things in the midst of something as serious as having your wife leave you.

Lance was miserable, but he knew she'd be back in the morning.

She was not back in the morning. He called Cheryl and asked to speak to Cathy.

"I don't think she wants to speak to you," said Cheryl.

"What makes you think that?" he asked.

"Because every time the phone rings she says, 'If that's Lance I don't want to speak to him.'"

"Ask her."

"It won't help, Lance."

"Ask her anyway."

A sigh.

"OK, but it won't help."

He heard her put the phone down. He heard voices in the background. He heard the phone being picked up.

"Cath?" he said gently.

"No," said Cheryl, "it's Cheryl. She won't speak to you, Lance. I told you."

"How about if I come over there and try to speak to her in person?"

"I wouldn't advise it."

"Why not?"

"I don't think it would help."

"Why not?"

"I think it would just make her angrier. I don't think you want to make her any angrier now than you have already. I'd just give her a while to cool off."

"How long?"

"I don't know. Couple of months, maybe."

"Ha ha. How long, Cheryl?"

"I don't know, Lance. But I don't think she plans on coming back to you for a while."

"What do you mean? How do you know that?"

"Because. Since she's been here she's been going through the real estate section of the *Times*, circling ads for apartment rentals."

"Oh my God. Are you serious?"

"Absolutely."

"What should I do, Cheryl?"

"Like I said. Just give her some time to cool off."

"OK. Will you let me know if there's anything I can do?"

"Of course."

"Thanks, Cheryl."

11

There being no longer any need to use a pay phone on the street, Lance telephoned Margaret from the apartment. She hung up the moment she heard his voice. He called back and began shouting before she could disconnect:

"You hang up on *me?* After cockteasing me into dropping my pants in front of my wife and forty of my closest friends, *you* hang up on *me?"*

"Did you wish to speak to Margaret Pusser?" said a fey male secretary.

"Uh, oh, excuse me," said Lance pitching his voice several octaves lower, "yes, may I please?"

"I'll see if she's in."

"Don't see if she's in," said Lance, getting heated up again, "I just *talked* to her. Tell her she has a choice—either come to the phone to hear what I have to say now, or else read it tomorrow in a full-page ad in the *New York Post.*"

"I'll see if Miss Pusser can come to the phone," said the voice.

The line was put on hold. Easy Listening Muzak was piped into Lance's ear, getting him hotter. If he'd wanted to hear Easy Listening Muzak he'd have taken an elevator ride. Somebody came back on the line.

"Margaret?" said Lance tentatively.

"Yes?"

"You hang up on *me?"* he shouted. "After cockteasing me into dropping my pants in front of my wife and forty of my closest friends, *you* hang up on *me?"*

"What do you mean *cockteasing?"* she said. *"I* didn't tell you to take off your pants in front of all those people."

"What do I mean by cockteasing? Were you or were you not the person who invited me up to her apartment to have sex?"

31

"I didn't invite you up to my apartment to have sex, I invited you up to my apartment to have a surprise birthday party. Cathy and Les and I had been planning that party for weeks."

"Is that so? And what did you tell Cathy you were going to say to get me up there?"

"I told her I was going to be very mysterious and even a little flirtatious and say I had something very important to discuss with you."

"'A little flirtatious,' is that it? Did you tell her being 'a little flirtatious' included an invitation to bury my face in your pussy and lick it till you scream?"

"I don't recall saying anything that specific to you."

"No? What *do* you recall saying, *specifically?*"

"I recall saying that I had had some . . . romantic notions about you and that I—"

"'Romantic notions'? Those are the words you recall? Nothing about burying faces in pussies or licking anybody till they screamed?"

"I'm afraid not. I *did* want to be enticing enough to lure you to my apartment in time for the party, but I certainly wouldn't have said anything that vulgar to the husband of one of my best friends."

"I see. Did being 'enticing enough' include allowing me to slide my hand up your thigh and stroke your pudenda, or don't you recall that either?"

"I recall your grabbing my knee and my pulling away from you, and that is all I recall," said Margaret. "And now, if you don't mind, I really do have to get back to work."

"Listen to me, Margaret—please," said Lance, softening his tone. "Do you at least admit that you had sexual feelings for me at Maxwell's Plum and that you were seriously considering going to bed with me? Will you at least admit to that? It's important that you be completely honest with me."

"Lance, I'll be completely honest with you. I think you're a very interesting man, and I'm very fond of both you and Cathy, and I'm sorry you two are having this trouble now, but I'd be less than fair unless I told you the absolute honest-to-God truth. And the absolute honest-to-God truth, Lance, is that I do *not* find you physically attractive. I know you've always had the hots for me and it must be painful to hear that the feeling is not reciprocated. As I told you in the restaurant, you're not the first of Cathy's men who's wanted to sleep with me. You *did* ask me to be completely honest with you."

"Yes," said Lance, "I guess I did. Well, that's about it, then, Margaret. Thanks for being honest."

Margaret put down the receiver and stared into the middle distance for several minutes. Most of what she'd told Lance was the truth. She really *had* invited him up to her apartment for a surprise birthday party rather than sex. She really *had* told Cathy and Les she was going to be mysterious and a little flirtatious and say she had something important to discuss with Lance in her apartment. It was ironic that Lance had invited her to lunch at Maxwell's Plum the very week that she and Les and Cathy were trying to figure out where to have the party and how to get him there. When he called, she realized she could use the vague promise of sex to accomplish their goal, and she immediately told Cathy and Les her plan.

All right, maybe not immediately. There *had* been a short period of time in which she considered slipping into bed with Lance. So she'd told him a tiny fib. Not that Cathy would ever have suspected. Not that Cathy would ever think for one single second that any husband of hers would find Margaret even the slightest bit attractive. Cathy, as much as Margaret loved her, had a somewhat inflated opinion of her fatal attractiveness to men. Cathy would have been amazed at how many of her old boyfriends had made flagrant passes at Margaret. Not just Lance. There was also Randy.

Randy had pursued Margaret and pursued her, the whole time he was dating Cathy. Finally Margaret gave in and slept with him. Randy was amazed at how hot Margaret was in bed—that was exactly how he put it—but he never wanted to sleep with her a second time. Which was just as well, because Margaret didn't really like Randy all that much, for one thing, and for another thing she felt a little guilty about Cathy. Which was probably one of the main reasons she finally decided not to sleep with Lance and to turn his sexual invitation into merely a means to get him to the party. If there hadn't been a Randy, Margaret might have slept with Lance. But there *had* been a Randy, and Margaret didn't think she could handle another one.

Too bad she had to tell Lance she found him unattractive. However, she suspected the main reason he wanted to sleep with her was to get even with Cathy for allegedly sleeping with Les, so it probably served the bastard right after all.

* * *

Lance thought of calling Les for advice, but then he decided not to. He had been so upset by the notion that Les was slipping it to Cathy that, even now that he knew it wasn't true, he could only forgive him about eighty-five percent. There was still resentment. It made no sense, but there it was.

He impulsively called Cathy at the *Times Book Review* to tell her that he loved her. It rang about forty times and then a secretary answered and put him on hold before he could ask for Cathy, and then they were disconnected. He dialed again and the line was busy, but he finally got through and asked for Cathy. She said that Cathy was in a meeting and was there any message.

"Yes," he said, "just tell her that Lance called to say he loves her."

"Will she know what this is in reference to?" said the secretary.

He finally called up his old psychotherapist and made an appointment to talk it over with her. His therapist was a marvelous middle-aged woman named Helen Olden. Helen was a former Freudian and a high-cheekboned former beauty who was now silver-haired and distinguished-looking instead of a beauty, and who no longer felt limited in her replies to patients' questions by the two official Freudian responses of "Well, what do *you* think?" and "What comes to mind about that?" It was partly that Helen had discovered that the Freudian approach wasn't doing much for patients like Lance who tended to overintellectualize everything at the expense of their feelings, and it was perhaps even more that she had been repressing her natural chattiness over the years and it had finally welled up and spilled over the top.

Lance had gone to Helen for a couple of years before he married Cathy. He'd seen psychotherapy as being a bit like surgery—like taking apart a living being to remove an organ which had once been necessary for survival but now interfered with it. He and Helen thought they'd removed all the unnecessary organs and decided to sew him up shortly after he was married. Now he had returned to her, badly shaken, mystified at the sudden turn of events in his life, and ready for more exploratory surgery.

They began the session with Lance allowing Helen to tell him all about the new book she was writing and, even though it was technically on his time, he gave her what advice he could about book promotion and distribution, trying hard not to feel envious at hearing that the advance she was getting for her first book was more than his last three advances combined.

Then Lance told her about his false perception of an affair between Cathy and Les, and of his attempts to balance the scales, of the lights coming on and forty people yelling "Surprise!"

Helen—she encouraged her patients to call her Helen instead of Dr. Olden, now that she was no longer a Freudian —took a long drag on her Gauloise, let out the smoke and said:

"What made you think that fucking your wife's best friend was going to solve your problem?"

Helen used words like "fucking" a lot since she had quit being a Freudian. She was the only person Lance knew who could use vulgar language and still sound classy.

"I don't know," he said. "I guess I was trying to even the score."

Helen made no reply but looked at him in the infuriating way he remembered from when he had been in therapy years before, a vague I-know-something-but-I'm-not-telling half-smile on her face.

"You don't think I was trying to even the score?" said Lance.

She shook her head.

"OK," he said, "what *was* I trying to do?"

"I'd rather have you tell me what *you* think," she said.

"C'mon, Helen. Don't give me that neo-Freudian bit of answering a question with another question. I asked you what you think I was trying to do."

"If I told you now it wouldn't mean very much to you."

"Try me. What was I attempting to do?"

"You were attempting to get out of the marriage."

"You're crazy," he said. "Get out of the marriage? Why would I want to do *that?* I *love* Cathy. Why would I want to get out of the marriage?"

"I *told* you it wouldn't have much meaning for you now."

"C'mon, Helen, for Christ's sake—why would I be attempting to get out of the marriage?"

"Because it threatened you."

"How did it threaten me? What threatened me?"

"The closeness. The intimacy. Separation, like underarm deodorant, takes the worry out of being close."

"Why would closeness worry or threaten me?"

"Why do *you* think?"

"Oh Christ, we're not back to that old Oedipal crap, are we?"

"I don't know, are we?"

He sighed.

"Great," he said, then declaimed in a singsong voice: "I'm threatened because I think my wife is my Mommy, and if I'm fucking my Mommy, then Daddy will kill me. Is that it?"

"Let's put it another way. Let's put it in terms of the incest taboo. We grow up being taught it's not nice to have lustful feelings about anybody we live with—Mommy, Daddy, sister, brother, and so on. Then we grow up and move in with a wife or husband, and suddenly it's supposed to be OK for us to have lustful feelings about them. But deep down inside, our early training is telling us that it's still wrong, that the old rules still apply. That it's wrong to be sexual toward anybody we live with."

"So?"

"So we lose interest in having sex with the person we live with. We feel anxious, depressed, suffocated, guilty. We find ways of putting distance between our mates and ourselves. We convince ourselves we're not feeling well enough to make love. We pick fights over nothing at all. We get sexually interested in people with whom we could have only distant relationships and we have affairs. Or we imagine that our *mates* are having affairs with others and are cuckolding *us*. The means hardly matters. The end is the point: to create distance. To push away the threat of having taboo sex with somebody you live with."

Lance thought it over.

"Look," he said, "maybe there's something in what you say. But that's not my problem right now. My problem is that I acted like an asshole and my wife has left me and she's now circling rental ads in the *Times*. My problem is how do I get her to come back to me?"

"As long as you think that's what your problem is, you're not going to be able to solve it," said Helen flatly. She looked at her watch and stood up. "I'm afraid our hour is up, Lance."

"Hey, look," he said, "I need help. Are you saying you won't help me?"

"I'm saying that if all you want me to do for you is help you get Cathy back, then it's going to be a waste of my time and your money. You may get her back for a while, but you'll just drive her away again. Or you'll fall in love with someone else and just repeat the same pattern. I'm not interested in helping you continue self-destructive patterns, Lance. If you want to work on the larger problems, I'll be glad to help you."

"I've had so much therapy already," said Lance. "Do you really think there's any point in starting the whole thing over again?"

"I think it would be very helpful for you to get into a group," she said.

"A group?"

He made a face.

"I think it would be very helpful to you," she said, walking to the door. "But right now we really do have to stop."

She opened the door and smiled a professional smile.

"I'll think about it," he said.

He noted with some satisfaction that he had managed to squeeze an additional five minutes out of her that he wasn't paying for.

12

Cathy came back to the apartment the following day. He was overjoyed to see her and went to hug her, but she eluded his arms.

"I've been doing a lot of thinking," she said.

"I know," said Lance, "so have I. I realize how upset you are with me and I just want you to know that if you—"

"I'm not upset anymore," she said.

"Good," he said.

"I was very upset the other night, I admit it," she said, "but I'm not upset now."

"Wonderful," he said.

"I've thought everything out very carefully," she said. "I found a nice little place in the West Eighties. One small bedroom, a tiny living room, a kitchenette. It's not gorgeous, but it's clean, and it's only $875 a month. You can have this place. All I want is the furniture."

He chuckled tentatively, suspecting that she was kidding. She left, knowing that she was not. She had said she wasn't upset anymore, but he could tell from how she had eluded his arms and slammed the door on her way out that this was not quite accurate. He knew it was useless to try to talk to her until she calmed down. He spent a horrid, sleepless night, managing finally to drop off to sleep at six in the morning.

Promptly at seven the doorbell rang.

He lurched out of bed, his lips and eyelids glued together, his hair pasted to his forehead. He pulled on jeans and a T-shirt and staggered to the door. He pressed the intercom.

"Who's there?" he said.

"The Motherloaders," said the voice of an android.

"The *what?*" he said.

There was no further response from the intercom. Instead, the door was unlocked and opened. In walked Cathy, followed by four females in work shoes and coveralls on which was stenciled the word "Motherloaders." They were built like stevedores, uniformly short and stocky and very broad in the chest and shoulders. Their necks looked about a size 18. The four women trooped into the living room, followed by their leader.

"What's going on?" said Lance.

"I told you yesterday," said Cathy. "You're keeping the apartment, I'm taking the furniture."

"But this is so abrupt," said Lance. "Can't we talk about it?"

"We talked yesterday," she said, turning toward the four androids. "Start with the living room and work your way to the door. Everything goes."

As Lance watched helplessly, the four mannish movers, smirking faintly, carted out all their furniture—their expensive chrome and leather chairs and modular seating sections, their glass and stainless-steel coffee tables, cartons hastily piled with pots and pans and dishes and glassware and stainless-steel flatware they had got for their wedding, boxes packed haphazardly with books, including some he had bought long before he'd even met her.

He said nothing, partly because he felt so guilty over what had precipitated this action that he thought he had no right to object to anything she did to him, partly because he figured she was simply overdramatizing and would be back with all their stuff in a week or so—the moment she calmed down and came to her senses—and partly because he sensed that, were he to hurl himself in the path of the quartet of muscular Motherloaders they would simply trample him into the parquet floor.

He looked at the four Motherloaders and was unable to differentiate between them; they were all short, squat, muscular and unattractive. He recalled Cathy recently saying he viewed women as sexist stereotypes, that he never bothered to differentiate between them, that he couldn't bring himself to make one-to-one contact with women and therefore dehumanized them. Here he was, doing the very thing she had accused him of.

The toughest of the four Motherloaders galumphed by him, carrying a heavy armchair over her head. He sprang in front of her and opened the door for her. He heard her grunt something. He decided to behave as though she'd said thank you.

"You're welcome," he said.

She grunted something else and moved through the doorway with the chair. He followed after her, suddenly determined to make one-to-one contact with her.

"That must be pretty heavy," he said, trailing her down the stairs.

"Yep."

There seemed to be nothing else to say to her. He raced ahead of her to open the downstairs door and nearly tripped her in the process.

"Sorry," he said. "I was just trying to help."

She grunted something.

"My name's Lance," he said. "What's yours?"

"June," she said, and left him standing stupidly on the curb.

Well, he thought, so much for one-to-one contact.

In less than two hours they were gone.

He was alone in an empty apartment. She had left him only their bed, his clothes, the liquor in the liquor cabinet, his manuscripts and electric typewriter. He sat down in the middle of the dusty floor and cried like an infant.

For the next several days Lance was immobilized. He had no desire to receive visitors, shower, shave, dress, look at the mound of unopened mail that was beginning to collect under the mail slot in the front door, answer his constantly ringing telephone, or call up his answering service to find out why they waited till the thirty-seventh ring to answer, or to have them dictate a long list of cryptically encoded callers' names and numbers and then have to try to decipher them. A message from "Canoes Arts" had once proved to be from the Cuisinart company, one from "Pastor Galley" turned out to be from the Poster Gallery, and one from a "Miss Terry Gardes" was revealed to be from his old friend in Hollywood, Harry Gittes.

Les came to the door twice and asked if he could do anything, but Lance, fresh from his noncuckolding trauma with Les, sent his friend away.

Lance drank unknown quantities of vodka, and ate canned ravioli at erratic intervals during the day and night, after removing the tops of the cans with a hacksaw because, along with everything else, Cathy had taken all the can openers.

Lance awoke most mornings at four a.m. with a throbbing, skull-pounding, eyeball-squeezing, forehead-shattering headache, stumbled into the bathroom and then struggled for ten minutes, trying to get the child-proof cap off the Bufferin bottle. There were no children in his household, and yet he seemed incapable of buying any kind of medicine that had a cover on it he could remove without getting contusions of the fingertips. If these bottlecaps gave *him*, a comparatively grown man, that much trouble, then what the hell did they expect a *child* with a roaring hangover to do at four a.m.?

Lance alternately watched TV and slept, fully clothed, lying face down across the bed. There was no program, however mindless, that he did not watch—game shows, kiddie cartoon shows, inspirational religious programs—he devoured them all hungrily and without judgment because they permitted him to not think about what had happened.

Lance felt pain, sorrow, fear, anger, depression, and wondered whether he was losing his mind. All the assumptions he had ever made about living with a woman no longer seemed to be valid. He was dimly aware that it was July 4th, Independence Day. He did not feel at all independent. He found himself unable to do any of the things he used to be able to do before Cathy had left him. Although he had been a passable cook, he could no longer quite recall how to turn on the stove. In some preconscious section of his mind he felt that, were he to starve, Cathy would somehow hear about it and come back and feed him.

What little food remained in the apartment went moldy in the refrigerator or furry on the shelves, but he was reluctant to throw it out, seeing it as the last nostalgic remnants of a happier life with Cathy. Indeed, foodstuffs were only the first of a series of things that lurked in cupboards, waiting to be discovered by him and—like emotional land mines—inflict tremendous damage, recalling memories of happier times with his loving wife.

There was another reason he was reluctant to throw out the spoiled food. When he was very small he was a skinny, sickly child. His parents tried to fatten him up, having been told that he wouldn't survive if he remained so thin. They force-fed him like a Strasbourg goose, cajoled and shamed him into eating every last bit of food on his plate, alluding to starving children in Poland who lusted after his soggy mashed potatoes and cold spinach, even anthropomorphizing the food in their desperation to prevent him from rejecting it: "If you don't eat your nice spinach, you'll hurt its *feelings*," they'd whimper when he disdained the proffered spoonful.

Oh-oh. Now that was something he could get into, the notion that spinach had feelings and could be offended. He had a very weird imagination—all little kids do, particularly those who grow up to be fiction writers—and the idea that he would be hurting tender spinach sensibilities if he didn't eat it was unbearable. He was already carrying around a fairly heavy load of nonspecific guilt as it was, and he didn't need wounded spinach feelings on top of it. So that was what they used on him the most: "You don't want that lovely cauliflower? The little cauliflower is *crying*." Oh God, crying cauliflower—he couldn't stand it! "You don't want that lovely glass of warm milk? The poor little milk is *crying*."

No, *stop*, he thought, I'll eat *anything, anything*, only don't tell me it's crying. If he had been a little sharper he might have noticed that it was only certain foods that cried when you didn't eat them. Ice cream he never remembered crying, for example. Not one piece of chocolate cake shed a single tear during his entire childhood. It was only the unpopular foods that always seemed on the edge of despair.

His parents were delighted they'd found a way to make little Lance eat. He eventually gained enough weight to make it into adulthood, but he had paid a terrible price: compulsiveness in all things and a continuing tendency to anthropomorphize everything. Not only was he unable to throw away cauliflower, warm milk, mashed potatoes and spinach, he got teary when he had to part with chicken bones, squeezed oranges, old coffee grounds, and used Kleenexes. His parents literally had to sneak the garbage out of the house while he slept.

The important thing, of course, was that it had got him to eat. He grew up healthy. Only the other day his internist had told him he was the ideal weight for his height. And whenever he went to a restaurant, the waiter always remarked what a good eater he was. The only irony was that the woman he married had never even *heard* of the Clean Plate Club. And whenever Lance had chided her by saying that the poor little breadcrusts were crying, she only laughed. Lance would get so upset he'd end up eating them himself.

Till now, that is. Now the only breadcrusts he had to worry about were his own. And the idea of throwing out any of the rotting food they'd owned together was unthinkable.

He began making late-night forays to an all-night supermarket, looking unshaven and seedy, and realized that there was very little in the way of foodstuffs that he could buy whose preparation did not now totally befuddle him. He loaded up on frozen TV dinners, canned ravioli, tortilla chips, beer and Mallomars.

He made a few abortive attempts at cooking, with awful results—his unwatched pot bubbled over, charred and burnt out, with thick gooey stuff forever doomed to be encrusted in the innermost recesses of stove and sink and countertop.

He ran out of socks and underwear. He tried washing the dirty ones in the sink, but managed to get them neither clean nor totally dry. Wearing a bathing suit instead of undershorts, and no socks inside his boots, he took a pile of his dirty laundry in a pillowcase to the laundromat.

He did not know how to operate the washers and driers. When he attempted to ask the women there the most rudimentary questions about how the machines worked, they shied away from his wild-eyed unkemptness as if he were a leper, a child molester or worse. He managed at last to do his laundry without their help, although his whites were permanently stained from running colors, and several of his garments shrank down to toddler size.

On July 14th, Bastille Day, he showered and shaved and went to the housewares section at Bloomingdale's to buy pots and pans and a guide to basic cooking information. Once more he was at a loss about how to proceed, but a matronly

42

saleswoman took pity on him and showed him what to buy to stock a basic kitchen. He was childishly grateful and repressed a powerful urge to hug her to him and rest his head on her bosom and sob.

One day he was having a dream that Cathy had come back to him and was giving him a bath in the bathtub and he was happily showing her his rubber ducky when the rubber ducky rang like a telephone and he knew it was Cathy calling to say she was coming back. He reached out for the phone by the bed, knocked the receiver off the hook and finally managed to pick it up and croak: "Cathy, is that you?"

There was a puzzled pause on the other end of the line.

"Mr. Lerner, please," said a shy teenaged voice.

"Who is this?" he said warily.

"Is this Mr. Lerner?" she said.

"It depends," he said. "Who's *this?*"

His caller giggled.

"This is Dorothy Chu," she said, as if he would instantly recognize the name.

"I'm sorry," he said, "am I supposed to know you?"

"I . . . thought you would," she said. "I guess I was presumptuous. It sounds like I caught you at a bad time. I'll let you go back to whatever you were doing."

"OK," he said.

"It's just that I did something I'm ashamed of and I wanted to apologize."

"Apologize?" he said. "For what?"

"You really don't know?" she said.

"I really don't know," he said.

There was a short pause.

"Mr. Lerner, I'm a senior at the High School of Music and Art and, well, I'm a writer myself, you know? I sent you a fan letter a few months ago. I asked you for advice on writing, and you were kind enough to tell me a lot of stuff—formulas for fiction and nonfiction and stuff. Do you remember now?"

"I'm . . . afraid not," he said. "I get a lot of mail like that, frankly, and I try to answer all of it. It's hard to remember what I say or whom I say it to, though. What was it you wanted to apologize for?"

"Well," she said, "my friend Janie and I—she's a writer too, sort of—we were going over your letter about a week ago with all the stuff you told me about how to write fiction and nonfiction and everything? And we were both pretty stoned, and I said I thought you were very sexy for an older man, and, well, that's why we took those Polaroids and sent them to you. We're both author groupies, you might say."

"You say you sent me Polaroids?" he said.

"You mean you didn't get any letter with Polaroids? Of a seminude Chinese girl? I mailed it about a week ago."

"Oh, *those* Polaroids," he said, thinking fast. "Just a minute. I'll see if I still have them."

He scrambled out of bed and out into the hall and began feverishly digging into the several pounds of mail by the mail slot. He found and tore open three letters addressed to him in fairly childish handwriting before he found the right one. Out tumbled five Polaroid pictures. Three of them featured a girl of about seventeen or eighteen with long black hair to her waist, Oriental features, and a very pretty face. She was wearing white panties and no bra. Her breasts were small but they stirred something in him immediately. The other two pictures featured the same girl with another slightly older-looking Oriental girl behind her, also seminude, with her arms around the first girl's waist. Both girls were grinning idiotically.

Lance raced back to the phone, tripped on the cord and sent the phone crashing into the wall. When he picked up the receiver, the line was dead.

13

He couldn't believe it. The line was absolutely dead.

"Dorothy!" he shouted into the dial tone. "Dorothy, come back!"

He could hear nothing but the dial tone. He slammed down the receiver, cursing. He went to get the letter with the Polaroids again, desperately hoping there would be a phone number, and found a note written on lined yellow notepaper:

Dear Mr. Lerner,

Or may I call you Lance? I thought it was really sweet of you to write to me and answer all my questions at such length. If you can drag your fingers off the typewriter long enough to dial a phone number, please give me a call. I am hoping the enclosed pictures will be an inducement to call.

Love,
Dorothy

There was no telephone number anywhere on the letter, front or back. He picked up the envelope. On the back of it she had scrawled: "Chu/16 Mott St./NYC."

He picked up the phone and dialed Information, but the operator could find no listing at that address. He hung up and was just considering taking a subway to Chinatown to hunt her down when the phone rang again. He snatched the receiver out of its cradle on the first ring.

"Dorothy?" he said.

There was silence at the other end. Then:

"Lance?"

The voice sent shivers through him.

"Cathy?"

"That's right," she said coolly. "Perhaps I should hang up so that you can talk to Dorothy."

"No! Cathy, my God—how are you, darling?"

"All right, I suppose. I was just calling to see how *you* were, but I suppose you've already told me. I must say, you certainly don't let the grass grow under your feet. Where did you meet Dorothy?"

"Dorothy is nobody," he said. "When can I see you?"

"Well, I don't know," she said. "How about lunch this afternoon? Or is that too short notice?"

"Come on, Cathy, give me a break. This afternoon is fine. Where and when?"

"How about Maxwell's Plum at one o'clock?"

"I'd . . . prefer another place, if it's all the same to you."

"OK. How about the Russian Tea Room? At one?"

"The Russian Tea Room at one. You got it."

He arrived at the Russian Tea Room twenty minutes early, got a booth near the front door and ordered a double White Russian from the Puerto Rican waiter in the high-necked Slavic peasant costume. Lance was clean-shaven and showered and shampooed and as nervous as a high-school kid on

45

his first date. He had totally forgotten Dorothy Chu and whatever it was she needed to apologize for and was rehearsing his own set of apologies when Cathy walked into the restaurant.

She looked sensational. She was wearing a pair of tight chocolate-brown slacks, a brown tweed jacket and a café-au-lait cotton shirt with the buttons open almost to her navel. Was it a good sign or a bad one that she looked so terrific? Had she dressed this spiffily to entice him into a reconciliation, or did she do it because she was now free of him and on the prowl for men?

She offered him her cheek for a perfunctory kiss, and sat down in the booth. She looked at once happier and sadder than he'd ever seen her before. It was impossible to tell what she was feeling.

"What are you drinking?" she said. "It matches my outfit."

"Oh, this? It's called a White Russian. It's Kahlua and cream and vodka, I think. You want one?"

"Sure."

He tried to signal the waiter but couldn't manage to make himself sufficiently visible. He and Cathy looked at each other and smiled. It was going to all be OK, he thought. Thank God, it was all going to be OK. He wanted to take her in his arms and tell her how happy he was. He got a flash of the depth of love he felt for her and his eyes filled up.

"I love you," he said.

"I love you too," she said, and took a breath. "But I want a legal separation."

He couldn't believe he'd heard what he'd just heard. She couldn't have said what he thought she'd said.

"What are you saying?" he said.

Tears sprang to her eyes and spilled down her cheeks.

"I've thought about it a lot, Lance. I've talked to about a thousand women I know over the past month—I even had two sessions with a shrink—and I've decided that that is what I want."

He felt sick to his stomach. His vision was strangely blurred, like looking through a movie camera lens that had been covered with Vaseline. He thought he might vomit up White Russians all over the perky little red leatherette and brass booth.

"I don't understand," he said. "You want a legal separation just because I made a fool of myself in front of all our friends? Just because I wanted to have sex with Margaret to punish you for the affair I thought you were having with Les? I admit what I did was moronic and thoughtless and demeaning, but is it a reason to end a happy seven-year marriage?"

"No, of course not. What you did *was* moronic and thoughtless and demeaning, but that's not the reason I want to end our marriage."

"What then?"

"You said we had a *happy* seven-year marriage. Is that what you really think we had, Lance?"

"Sure. Don't you?"

"No, not really. Oh, I admit I was pretty happy at first. I didn't know any better."

"What do you mean you didn't know any better?"

"I mean that I didn't know what I needed. I thought it was enough to be your servant. Your slave. I thought it was enough merely to live in your shadow, merely to be the wife of Lance Lerner, best-selling author and charming talk-show guest. I thought I had no needs of my own. I was wrong, Lance. I'm sorry. I misled you."

"Cathy, listen to me. I *know* you have needs. Honest to *God* I do."

"You do?"

"Yes. Do you really think you were my slave, though? I mean is that what you really think or is that just feminist rhetoric?"

Her eyes narrowed.

"You weren't thinking of attacking feminists now, by any chance, were you?"

"No, of course not. I have nothing but admiration for the movement."

"Good."

"And I'm sure that splinter groups like MATE don't, as they say, necessarily reflect the views of the management."

"*Mate?*" she said.

"You don't know about MATE? M-A-T-E? Men Are The Enemy? Don't tell me you haven't heard of them."

She shook her head.

"It was on *Eyewitness News* only last night. Men Are The Enemy. They abduct a man, they tear his clothes off, abuse him sexually, then write slogans all over his body in spray enamel, like 'Rape is a political crime.' I can't believe you haven't heard about MATE."

Her manner turned chilly.

"I'm sure that's a very amusing concept you made up. You

ought to use it in your next novel. I'm glad you have such a sense of humor about the movement."

"Cathy, I'm not making it it up—it was on the goddamn *news* last night—goddamn *Eyewitness News*."

"I'm sure you're right," she said. "And I'm sure you've never made cruel and satiric remarks about the women's movement before, either."

"I think the women's movement has accomplished some marvelous things, I really do. I'm behind them one hundred percent. But nobody has ever accused the movement of having a sense of humor about itself, either."

"I did not," she said icily, "come here to talk about the women's movement. I *did* come here to talk about us."

"Good," he said. "So did I. Let's talk about us."

"Fine," she said. "Now then. As I said before, I have done a lot of thinking, and what I have decided would be best for both of us would be to have a legal separation. I'm not saying a divorce—not at this point, at least—and even if it came to that, I wouldn't want any alimony. I don't even think we need to have a lawyer, if you're willing to—"

"Cathy. Stop. Listen to me. How can you do this? Doesn't our relationship mean *anything* to you?"

"It means a great deal to me. But so does my relationship with myself. So far I've been giving that one the short end of the stick."

"But we're so good together, Cathy. We take care of each other. We have good times. Don't we have good times?"

She shrugged.

"Sometimes they're good," she said. "Sometimes they're not. Do you know how much I hate the process you go through every time you write a novel?"

"God, no," he said. "What part of the process is it that you hate?"

"Every goddamned part," she said. "When you're writing it and it isn't going well, you're depressed and cranky and a pain in the ass to be with. When you're writing it and it *is* going well, you're at your desk sixteen or seventeen hours a day, and it's like you don't even know I exist. When you've finished a draft and you ask me to read it, you *watch* me, for God's sake—you watch me while I read it. And then if I say anything that's the least bit critical about it, you jump on me and practically tear my *throat* out."

"I do not," he said in a wounded voice. "I happen to take criticism very well for a novelist."

"The hell you do," she said. "The slightest thing I point out that I think needs changing and you go and sulk for about three days. So then you turn it in to your editor, and you're so nervous till you get a reaction from him that you're practically jumping right out of your skin."

"But then I get better, right?" he said hopefully.

"The hell you do," she said. "When you've finished all your revisions and your editor thinks it's perfect, *then* is the time you start worrying about how the publisher is going to screw you by not advertising it or promoting it properly, and you become absolutely obsessed with various stratagems to get the book into the media and to get the publisher to send you out on a promotional tour."

"Cathy, you *have* to do that. If you don't—"

"I *know* you think you have to do that. So then you finally persuade them to send you out on tour, and I get to see you about twice in the next six weeks. And when it's over you come home exhausted, you have laryngitis from doing eight talk shows a day, you're usually running a fever of about a hundred and three, and I not only get to be your Mommy and take care of you, I also have to hear all the usual atrocity stories of how the books weren't in any of the stores, and how some of the shows you were supposed to be on didn't even know you were coming, and how others were so ineptly run that you—"

"But it's all *true*—"

"I'm sure it is—and that doesn't make it any more fun to listen to, either. So then, after a couple of weeks you've recuperated, but you've managed to think of an idea for a new novel, and the whole goddamned process begins all over again."

"Jesus," he said. "That's what you've been feeling all these years?"

"That's what I've been feeling," she said.

"I don't know what to say," he said. "I mean, you've just described my life. That's what I do for a living. I write and sell novels. I had no idea it was so painful for you. How come you never told me this before?"

"I did," she said quietly. "You just never listened to me."

"Is it really so terrible for you during the writing phase?" he said gently.

"No," she said. "The other phases are the terrible ones. The writing phase is like living alone. And that's what I'm doing now."

"God," he said, "I had no idea. I mean I feel I ought to apologize to you and promise to change, but I don't really think I could do my work any other way, you know? If I didn't throw myself into my writing when it was going well and work sixteen hours a day, I'd never be able to finish anything. And if I didn't agonize about each book's promotion and then go out on tour with it, the public would never hear about it."

She shook her head sadly.

"You're just a workaholic, Lance—why don't you admit it?"

"Maybe I am," he said. "Workaholics are people who have to overcompensate for their own laziness and their urge to procrastinate, for their inner voices telling them that however much they're doing it's not enough, it's *never* enough, they're still not a good boy. But I also happen to love my work. I hate it when I'm not working. It's more than hate—I'm terrified when I'm not working. I'm like a shark—if I stopped moving I'm sure I'd die."

"I know that's what you think," she said.

"It happens to be true," he said. "But look, forget the work for a moment, because I don't even know what to suggest in that area. At least there are other areas that are good in our marriage, right? I mean, we still have a good sex life, for example, don't we?"

"Is that what you think?" she said.

Lance was badly shaken. He looked around quickly to see if any waiters or other diners had heard this.

"You don't think we have a good sex life?"

"How often do we make love now, Lance? Will you tell me that?"

"I don't know. I mean, I don't keep score on the headboard, I—"

"When we first started living together we made love every day. More than once a day at times. How often do we do it now—once every Sunday? Once every other Sunday?"

"Ssssshhhhhh," he said. He glanced around again. The people at the other tables weren't looking at them, but they weren't talking, either. He leaned across the table to her and continued the conversation in whispers.

"The last week we were together," he whispered, "we did it twice."

"Sunday and when else?" she said.

"Sunday and Wednesday," he whispered.

"And the previous two weeks not once," she said.

"There was a reason for that," he said. "First I was sick, and then we had all those late evenings and we were both too tired—you said so yourself."

"*You* were too tired," she said. "*I* wasn't too tired. I am *never* too tired."

"You are *so*," he said.

"Are not," she said.

"Are so."

"Are not."

"Well, maybe you're right," he said. "After all, why should you be tired? What's tiring about lying there like a lox while I do all the work?"

Her eyes widened and her nostrils got very big.

"Is that what you think I do?" she said. "Lie there like a lox?"

"Do you deny that you don't respond right away when I stroke you? Do you deny that you don't let me do anything but massage your legs for about forty minutes before you even *begin* to let me touch your—"

"Do *you* deny that you would go straight for the old crotch every single time if I didn't stop you?" she said. "Whatever happened to foreplay? Whatever happened to afterplay? Whatever happened to experimentation?"

"What are you *talking* about?" he said. "I ask you all the *time* about all *kinds* of experimentation."

"What you ask me about all the time is not experimentation, it's perversion! You honestly think that having me dress up in a nurse's uniform or wanting to do it with me and another woman or wanting to tie me to the bed is *healthy*?"

"Why isn't it healthy?" he said, but just then the Puerto Rican waiter in the peasant's costume returned to their table with luncheon menus and Lance ordered White Russians for both of them.

"You're so damned predictable," she said even before the waiter was entirely out of earshot. "Whatever happened to spontaneity? You used to be so spontaneous. We used to make love in the bathtub, on the living-room floor, in the car, under a blanket on the beach, in swimming pools . . . Nowadays it's only in bed and we never do anything but the straight missionary position."

"Who the hell's fault is that?" he hissed. "You told me that's the only one you can have an orgasm in."

"Sssssshhhh!" she said.

"Did you or did you not tell me that the missionary position was the only one you could come in?" he whispered.

"I might have told you that," she admitted, "but who says I have to come every time we make love?"

"Who says?" he said. "*You* say, that's who says."

"I told you I have to come every time we make love?" she said.

"Maybe not in so many words," he said. "But if you *don't* come, you keep guiding me back there till I get a chafed penis or a spasm in my finger or lockjaw."

She glared at him.

"*God,* you're horrible," she said. "I never realized how horrible you really are. I'm seeing you now for the first time."

It was not, he decided, going as well as he had hoped.

14

"Women waste their whole *lives* on men," said Cathy heatedly, sitting, not lying, on the therapist's couch. "You meet a man, you fall in love with him, and then you do whatever it takes to land him and keep him happy—no matter how humiliating—because you've been taught that that is woman's *role.* To wait on a man and to compromise yourself for him."

"Mrs. Lerner . . . ?"

"The man, of course, just accepts it as his *due,* because most men have gotten away with such spoiled treatment all their *lives*—first from their mothers, and then from their mates. Women are—"

"Mrs. Lerner, I wonder if we might—"

"Women are in endless pursuit of the man they love," Cathy continued. "Men are in endless pursuit of *all* women. The only time a man will pursue a woman is when she stops waiting on him. Then he'll do anything—*anything*—to get her back again and restore the status quo."

"Mrs. Lerner, can we—?"

"If he can just get her back, then he can pretend that things are still the way he imagined them to be—that he's still the prince, that he will still be waited on, that she will always be devoted to him no matter what he does, and that he wasn't wrong about how he perceived the world before she left him. That's why it's so important to get her back, to—"

"Mrs. Lerner, I—"

"*Please,* Dr. Freundlich," said Cathy, "it's important that you understand this. Now then, the woman's level of rage gets to a certain point—she realizes the dream isn't going to work, and suddenly it's over for her. She's through with him. Finished. The man is *astounded.* From his point of view, nothing's changed—he's done nothing different, she's done nothing different, nothing's changed—so what could be wrong? Then, if the woman continues to ignore the man's *earnest* entreaties to return, he says, 'Well, that's women for you—you can't live *with* 'em, and you can't live *without* 'em.' He forgets the whole thing. He pretends it never happened. And then he meets a new woman and he does the same thing all over again, having learned absolutely nothing from the entire experience. And that's why men are assholes."

The doctor smiled at her.

"Am *I* an asshole?" he said.

"You're a man," said Cathy, "so you're an asshole."

"And yet you chose to come to me—a man—for counseling, instead of a woman."

"I'm an asshole too," said Cathy.

The doctor gave her a bland, professional smile.

"You say that women are in endless pursuit of the man they love," said the doctor. "But most of them *want* endless pursuit, because victory is too threatening to them."

"Are you saying that I waited on Lance and compromised myself for him for almost eight years because I *wanted* him to act as though I wasn't there?" said Cathy. "Because I would've been threatened if he'd acted like I *was* there?"

"Since I still don't know you very well," said the doctor, "I'd be foolish to say such a thing. What I can tell you, though, is this: Very often in intimate relationships, one of the partners will be very generous and very giving and very self-sacrificing, hoping that the message that's being conveyed is, 'This is how I want *you* to take care of *me*—with the same unselfish, unstinting, nothing-held-back attitude,' but—"

"But the other partner is a Jewish Prince and he just accepts it as his due because he's spoiled rotten," Cathy snapped. "He's so spoiled he'll always ask his mate where something is, rather than look for it himself. He's so spoiled he'll—"

"What I was going to *say*," said the doctor carefully, "was that this sort of behavior is very seductive. It seduces the partner into thinking you don't need anything at all from him in return, that you're just one great big giver—a walking human cornucopia. So then you become resentful that you're giving too much, that you're not getting anything in return, and then you feel justified in leaving him. But if you had merely communicated your true feelings to him in the first place, and not given him this seductive and untrue picture of yourself as a human cornucopia, then he might have reciprocated, and you wouldn't have had any justification for getting mad and leaving."

"Are you saying I set it up?" said Cathy.

The doctor shook his head and sighed.

"I'm saying," he said, "that the situation you describe is not something that was *done* to you, it's a situation that you helped create. You are not its victim."

"You think I'm portraying myself as a victim?"

"Don't *you?*"

"I asked you first."

"I think that many people try to show how impotent and victimized they are in order to preserve their sense of innocence. There's a word that always comes with 'victim' and that's 'innocent.' Innocent victim. The victim is innocent by definition. Unfortunately, what you do when you become a victim is forfeit any possibility of helping yourself—as if to be able to help yourself is to admit not only your strength but your guilt."

Cathy pondered this for several moments before she spoke again.

"Do you think I have any strength?" she asked.

"I think it took *enormous* strength to leave Lance," he said. "And I think it took enormous strength to come here."

Cathy nodded her head slowly, apparently satisfied with both answers.

15

"I can't believe the things she said to me," said Lance.

"What did she say to you?" said Helen, taking a drag on her Gauloise.

"That we don't make love long enough, that I don't give her enough foreplay, that I'm not spontaneous enough, that I'm not imaginative enough, that I'm kinky—things like that."

"Are they true?"

"Some are, some aren't."

"Which are?"

A long sigh.

"When Freud said 'What do women want?,' I could have told him. You know what they want? Three hours of goddamn foreplay, that's what."

"How long do you generally spend on foreplay with Cathy?"

"I don't know, Helen, I never timed it with a cake timer."

"Less than three hours?"

"Yeah, less than three hours."

"Less than half an hour?"

"I don't know. Maybe less than half an hour."

"Less than three minutes?"

"Hey, Helen, give me a break, will you? I said it was maybe less than half an *hour,* I didn't say it was less than three *minutes,* for God's sake."

"I'm sorry. So after you've spent less than half an hour on foreplay, then what?"

"Then we make love."

"For how long?"

"I don't know. More than half an hour. Sometimes an hour, sometimes an hour and a half. Sometimes two hours. Sometimes longer than that."

"It sounds to me like you have a fairly active sex life."

"It's active all right. It's so active I can hardly *move* afterwards. I work as hard at sex with my wife as I do working twelve hours at the typewriter."

"Does it take you that long to achieve an orgasm?"

"Hell no. I can do that in about three minutes. But if I do, she doesn't have time to have one herself. So I hold it back, and I hold it back, and when I hold it back long enough I lose my erection. I feel like I have to stay hard long enough to make her come."

"You resent that, don't you?"

"You're damn right."

"And that's why you lose your erection—out of resentment?"

"I guess. I feel I have to be ready for her anytime she wants it. Sometimes I'll come to bed after working very late in my study, when I think she's asleep, and just as I'm dozing off she'll reach over to my groin and start caressing me. I feel guilty if I can't get hard immediately. Even if I'm half asleep, or if I'm just not in the mood."

"And how does that make you feel—angry?"

"Sort of. And less than manly, too."

"Why do you feel that to be a man you have to be able to produce hard-ons on demand?"

"I don't know, Helen. Men have been getting really bad press for the last few years, you know? They say we're selfish lovers, they say we're insensitive to women's needs. Some say a *woman* can satisfy a woman better than a man. Well, probably all of that is true. I've become a selfish and insensitive and unimaginative lover, and I didn't use to be. I used to be fucking dynamite in bed, Helen, and now I'm a lousy lay."

"Why do you say that?"

"It's true. I used to be spontaneous and imaginative. We made love everywhere—on the beach, in the car, in swimming pools, in the ocean, in revolving doors—everywhere. And then I was married awhile and I became a lousy lay. I've lost interest in sex, unless I've had a lot to drink or unless I'm looking at another woman and fantasizing, and I think part of the reason is that it's just not that much fun anymore. It's a job. It's mostly give and very little get. I don't get that much out of it anymore."

"Then why do you do it at all?"

"I want to do what's right. I think my wife is entitled to be

56

satisfied sexually, so I do it. I know that sounds horrible, but that's what I feel."

"It sounds horrible all right."

"It's so horrible I try to forget about it most of the time. I pretend it isn't happening. I pretend that things are still really great between us, that we're still the perfect couple, you know? And sometimes I try to do something to improve our sex life, but I always find some way to sabotage it. Like sometimes I ask her what I can do that particularly turns her on, but then when she tells me, I feel controlled and resentful, even though I asked her to tell me—isn't that crazy?"

"Yep."

"Sometimes when I get into bed at night after I've been working late I'm thankful it's a king-size bed because I can get into it without touching her and risking waking her up and starting something, and I think, 'Jesus Christ, what kind of a man are you to be feeling like that?' I mean, I'm still horny, I still have constant fantasies about sex, but I don't have much desire to have sex with her, you know?"

"Do you masturbate?"

"Yeah. I go into the john and do it and hope she won't find out, feeling like I'm about fifteen years old. And then when I come out, usually she wants to make love and I have to think of an excuse. What the hell is wrong with me, Helen—am I turning into a fag or what?"

"I don't think you're turning into a fag. I do think you're very resentful and very angry about the sexual demands you feel are being made of you, whether they are or not. I also think it's as hostile and controlling for a man to become impotent with a woman as it is for a woman to be unable to have an orgasm with a man. We're going through a difficult transitional period now, from a culture that looked reproachfully on sex to one that suddenly places a lot of emphasis on frequent and varied sexual activity and on performance . . ."

"Yeah . . ."

"But part of it is that women have *always* known they had the right to refuse to have sex. Men haven't had as much practice as women in saying no, so they aren't too sure how to handle a woman's advances without feeling guilty. You have to remember that nobody is *always* in the mood for love, no matter what the songs say. And you have to be able to say *no* if you're ever going to want to say *yes*."

16

It was not a call he looked forward to making, but it was a month since he and Cathy had separated and the longer he delayed making it the worse it was going to be. They would have to be told eventually. He dreaded their reaction. He heard the line ring about five times and then it was picked up.

"Hello?" said the voice of his mother, certain that whoever it was couldn't possibly be calling with news of anything good.

"Hi, Mom," said Lance, then added needlessly for an only child, "it's Lance."

"Lance!" shrieked his mother. "It's Lance!" she called to his father. It was as if he didn't talk to them once a week. Why was a call from him such a big deal? And if it was, why didn't he dole out more of them?

"How are you doing?" said Lance, trying to offset his mother's relentless premonitions of disaster. Lawyers and mothers, he mused, always know the worst that could happen in any given situation.

"Lance, what's wrong, dear?" said his mother, then yelled again to his father: "It's Lance!"

"Lance is in town?" he heard his father call out from somewhere in the background.

"No, Harry, on the *phone*—Lance is on the *phone!*"

"Oh," said his father, "on the *phone*. Why didn't you *say* so!"

"Lance," said his mother, "what's the trouble, darling?"

"Trouble?" said Lance. "Why do you always assume when I call you that there's trouble?" It irritated him that she did that, the more so because she was usually right.

"Hello, Lance?" said his father, getting on the extension. "How are you, son? What's new in the Big Apple?"

"Hi, Dad. Nothing much. How are you?" said Lance. His technique of breaking bad news to them was to start off slowly and then sort of quickly pop it in there like a surprise lay-up.

"Can't complain," said his Dad. "How's the writing?"

"The writing?" said Lance.

"What?" said his father. Neither of his folks was hard of hearing, but both were absentminded and tended not to listen very closely.

"How's the *writing?*" said Lance.

"*You're* the writer," said his father, "what're you asking *me* about the writing?"

"No, no," said Lance, wondering if his family might have blood ties to Abbott and Costello, "you asked me about the writing, you see, and I . . . The writing is fine, Dad. Although I've been doing less writing of late than reading."

"Than what?" said his mother. "*Bleeding?*"

"*Bleeding? Who's* bleeding?" shouted his father.

"*Nobody's* bleeding," said Lance. "I didn't say 'bleeding,' I said 'reading.' I said I've been doing less writing than *reading.*"

"Oh, *reading,*" said his father. "Reading is perfectly fine. I thought he said *bleeding.*"

"So did I," said his mother. "I almost had a coronary."

Lance winced. Any talk of coronaries from his parents triggered ancient fears of their dying, of him being left to fend unsuccessfully for himself.

"So," said his father, "then nobody is hemorrhaging there in New York after all. I'm relieved to hear that. And things are going well?"

"Yeah," said Lance. "Pretty well."

"So how is Cathy?" said his mother.

"Cathy?" said Lance. "Cathy is . . . fine. I mean we just got separated, but she's fine."

"Oh, God!" cried his mother, "I *knew* it was bad news. Didn't I tell you it was bad news, Harry?"

"You got what, *separated?*" said his father.

"Yeah," said Lance, "but it's no big deal. She'll probably come waltzing back in here tomorrow or the next day just like nothing happened."

It was a lie so blatant that nobody could possibly mistake it for the truth, even people who heard "bleeding" for "reading." Why, then, did he say it—to convince the operator?

"What happened?" said his mother. "You both seemed so happy when we saw you last."

"I know it," said Lance. "It was just one of those things, you know?"

"Is it another fella?" said his father, quietly, so the neighbors shouldn't hear. It was no mystery to Lance where he'd learned his anxiety about eavesdropping strangers.

"No, no, it's not another man, nothing like that," said Lance.

"Then what is it?" said his mother.

"A misunderstanding," said Lance. "Nothing more than that. We'll get it patched up again, don't worry."

"Worry?" said his mother. "Why should I worry? You're a grown man, forty years of age. You think I'm worried you can't take care of yourself?"

"No, Mom, I don't think that . . ."

"Don't you think I know you can cook and wash your own clothes and clean up a little around the house whenever the dust gets so thick you can't see the furniture?"

"Yes, Mom, I know you know that."

There was a pause.

"Honey, do you want your Mom to come to New York to take care of you for a little while?" said his mother softly, as if she wanted to speak quietly enough so that he himself wouldn't have to hear the question and be embarrassed by it. Her query and the enormous love which had obviously prompted it momentarily connected with the terrible feelings of abandonment and helplessness he thought he had successfully repressed, and he had to bite back a sob. Tears filled his eyes, but he managed to make his voice absolutely calm again in seconds.

"I'm fine, Mom," he said, "honest to God. I appreciate the offer, and I may even take you up on it sometime, but for now I'm OK, and I think it would be better if I worked this all out by myself."

"All right, dear," she said.

"Do you need some money, son?" said his father softly. Lance had at least ten times as much money as his Dad, but whenever he was in trouble his father always offered him money.

"No thanks, Dad," said Lance. "I have enough money."

"Do you want to tell us what the fight was about?" said his mother. "After all, your father and I have been married fifty years—about fighting we happen to know a little something."

"I don't think I really want to talk about it just now," said

Lance, shuddering at the prospect of describing the moment when the lights came on and forty people stood staring at a naked Lance with a hard-on and the word 'Surprise' came halfway out of their throats and froze there.

"Well," said his father, "whatever it is, I'm sure you'll be able to work it out. We both have a lot of faith in you, kid."

"Thanks, Dad," said Lance. "That means a lot to me."

17

"My *God*, Lance," said Howard Leventhal, ushering him into his neatly cluttered office, "you look absolutely *awful!*"

"It's good to see you, too, Howard," said Lance, pushing a pile of perfectly squared-off manuscripts aside and sitting down on the brown velvet couch opposite his editor's desk, a study in controlled chaos.

Howard, a prissy, paunchy man with thinning sandy hair, an unexpectedly handsome face and Ben Franklin glasses, was actually eight years younger than Lance and leapt upon any apparent flaw in Lance's generally superior appearance with thinly disguised relish. Since Lance knew where it came from, he found it more flattering than insulting.

"Really," said Howard, "you look *ghastly*—is anything *wrong?*"

"Well no, not really," said Lance with elaborate casualness. "I have a mild headache and a slight upset stomach, and Cathy has left me, but other than that, everything is perfect."

"Cathy's *left* you?" Howard slapped his forehead. "Oh, my *God*. When did this *happen?* Where did she *go?* How are you *surviving?*"

Howard tended to speak in the italicized cadences generally employed by homosexual men, though Lance doubted Howard was a fag. Howard, in fact, appeared to have quite a crush on Cathy.

"Get a grip on yourself, Howard," said Lance. *"I'm* handling it nicely, there's no reason why *you* shouldn't."

People like Howard were always trying to co-opt your troubles and get more pain out of them than you did yourself. Lance resented such behavior. He had worked hard to get himself into the mess with Cathy, and he was damned if he was going to share his pain with anybody.

"Do you want to *talk* about it?" Howard asked, adopting a confidential and solicitous tone.

"Sure," said Lance, "but not now. Now I'd rather talk about the promotion of *Gallivanting.*"

"I understand, I understand," said Howard, grabbing Lance's hand and squeezing it. "Is there another *man* or what?"

"Not exactly," said Lance. "But we can discuss it at greater length some other time."

"Good," said Howard. "I don't *blame* you for not wanting to talk about it. We'll just go on into Mike Fieldston's office—Mike is our head of promotion and advertising, I don't believe you've met him yet—and we can talk about personal matters later. It's *not* another man, you say?"

His father, Lance decided, was allowed to ask about other men. His editor was not.

"No, Howard," said Lance, "it's not another man."

"Good," said Howard. "Say, it's not another *woman,* is it?"

"No, Howard," said Lance, beginning to get annoyed, "it's not another woman, either. Five down, and over to you, Arlene Francis."

Howard flashed Lance a forced smile and took him on into Mike Fieldston's office. Mike Fieldston was tall, Waspy, blond, and, like Howard, had a paunch, thinning hair and somewhat Benfranklinesque glasses. Maybe those were prerequisites for working at Firestone.

Mike stood up and shook hands with Lance as he and Howard entered. Then he introduced Lance to three other people who were already there for the meeting: a mousy woman of twenty-five named Charlene who worked in publicity, an acne-scarred but otherwise attractive brunette named Judy or Julie who was also about twenty-five and also worked in publicity and who was either slightly below or slightly above Charlene in rank, and a pipe-smoking blond chap of about thirty by the name of Brad who worked in advertising and was merely teetering on the *brink* of paunchiness and thin-hairedness.

Everybody found seats. Mike cleared his throat. Lance wondered idly how Judy-or-Julie's acne scars had affected her love life. He wondered what he'd do if someone offered to return Cathy to him with the provision that serious acne scars came with the deal. He'd take the deal even if it were leprosy.

"Lance," said Mike, "Judy, Charlene, Brad and I have been kicking around some ideas for the promotion of your book, and, well, frankly, I think we've come up with a helluva campaign."

"Great," said Lance. "What's our budget, by the way?"

"What's our what, Lance?" said Mike, frowning as though the word might be new to him.

"Our budget. How much is Firestone allocating for the promotion and advertising campaigns of my book?"

Mike looked quickly at Howard and then back to Lance and cleared his throat. Lance began to get uncomfortable. It made him uncomfortable any time others in a room knew something he didn't.

"The budget," said Mike, "has not as yet been finalized."

"I see," said Lance, waiting for the rest of it.

"We do not, quite frankly, have a whole carload of money to play around with," said Mike, flashing Lance a smile to let him know he knew that "a whole carload of money" was a helluva charming metaphor. "I think I'd better say that right off the bat."

Lance's discomfort began edging smoothly into anxiety. From experiences with his previous six novels he knew that the act of publishing a book was largely a self-fulfilling prophecy. Three of his previous books had been dubbed bestsellers by their respective publishers before they had even been set in type. They were advertised and promoted like bestsellers, and bestsellers is what they became. His other three novels had been dubbed dogs by their publishers at about the same point. They were scarcely advertised or promoted, and dogs they surely became. This of course caused Lance to take a loss on the years invested in the books, but it also made it hard to find a publisher for his next novel after each failure, since it is authors who get blamed for lack of sales and not their negligent publishers.

When Lance had made his deal with Firestone on *Gallivanting,* his latest, they seemed to feel it would be a blockbuster. They promised him a promotion and advertising budget in excess of a hundred thousand dollars, just for starters, and a twenty-four city promotional tour.

"Is the budget less than a hundred thousand dollars?" said Lance.

"Oh yes," said Mike. "Quite a bit less than that, I'm afraid."

"I see," said Lance. "Is it less than fifty thousand?"

"Oh yes," said Mike. "Quite a bit less than that."

"Is it less than twenty-five?" said Lance.

Mike looked at Howard again. Howard shrugged.

"I'm going to be honest with you, Lance," said Mike. "The budget is five thousand dollars."

Lance turned to Howard. He was stunned. He felt slightly dizzy.

"Is this true, Howard?" said Lance.

"Lance," said Howard, "there's a *hell* of a lot you can do with even *that* amount of—"

"I want my book back," said Lance, feeling like a five-year-old. "If you're spending that little, you're throwing it right into the toilet. I'd rather publish it *myself* than—"

"Now hold *on* there, Lance," said Mike, "let's not be childish."

"No, let's not be childish," said Lance, getting more and more excited and childish. "Let's be really grown up and professional and pretend that five thousand dollars is going to be able to do anything at all to let the reading public know my book even *exists.*"

"Lance," said Howard, "it's not *our* decision to limit the budget to five thousand—"

"Whose decision is it?" said Lance.

"The head of *sales*. And old man Firestone *himself*," said Howard.

"I thought you were going to give me a big send-off," said Lance, hating the five-year-old tone that clung to his voice, but unable to mature it. "That's the only reason I signed with Firestone in the first place. You promised me a twenty-four city promotional tour and a hundred-thousand-dollar budget, do you remember that?"

"I remember . . . that we were *hoping* it would be a bigger book than the men now feel it's going to *be*," said Howard carefully.

"The *men?*" said Lance. "You're telling me that the sales

force has already decided—before the book has even been *printed*—that it's a dog?"

"That's their feeling, Lance," said Howard. "The men are usually *right* about these things, too."

"On what are they basing their feelings?" said Lance. "Have they all read the manuscript?"

"Lance," said Howard patronizingly, "we publish three hundred and sixty-five books a *year*. That's a book a *day*. Do you honestly expect the men to read every *one* of them?"

"No," said Lance, "just mine."

Mike, Brad, Judy and Charlene chuckled, anxious for the opportunity to lighten up the mood.

"If they haven't read my book," said Lance, "then on what did they base their feeling it's not going to sell?"

"On what I told them about it at *Sales* Conference," said Howard.

"How long did you talk to them about it at Sales Conference?" said Lance.

"Well, they only gave me a couple minutes for each book on my *list*," said Howard, "but don't worry, I gave yours quite a build-up."

"I'll just *bet* you did," said Lance. "What did you say about it?"

"I read them the paragraph I wrote about it for the spring *catalogue*," said Howard.

Lance took a deep breath. He felt he was in quicksand, and someone had thrown him a breath mint.

"Howard, how can they tell anything about whether my book is going to sell from merely hearing a paragraph that you wrote about it?"

Howard looked at Mike. Brad looked at Judy and Charlene. They wondered why every single author they handled had to be certifiable.

"Lance, they didn't think your book was very well *written*," said Howard in a vaguely accusatory tone.

"They didn't *read* my book," said Lance. "They listened to you read them a paragraph *you* wrote. Was the paragraph *you* wrote well written?"

"It . . . frankly needed work, Lance," said Howard, "I'm not going to deny that. Look, *you're* the writer, not *me*."

"Yeah, I'm the writer. And my writing is being judged by what a self-confessed *non*writer wrote about it."

Lance looked from face to face. They showed him tight,

fakey little smiles. It wasn't fair. Their logic made no sense at all, yet they were acting as though *he* were the crazy one.

"Lance," said Howard patiently. "The initial orders from the *stores* have borne out the men's pessimism—the orders aren't, frankly, very *good*, Lance."

"How *could* they be good?" said Lance. "The men didn't like what you told them at Sales Conference. How do you think that made them sell my book?"

It was futile to continue this, but he couldn't seem to stop.

"Look, Lance," said Howard, "if the word-of-mouth on the book is *good* among the public and it really takes *off*, then I'm sure the house will really get behind it."

"If the word-of-mouth on the book is good and the book takes off," said Lance, "who the hell *needs* the house to get behind it?"

"Look, Lance," said Mike, "there's still a helluva lot of mileage we can get out of that five thousand dollars."

"Like what?" said Lance.

"Well," he said, "first of all, we'll get you a lot of interviews in the New York area, then we'll take a couple small space ads and, uh . . ."

Lance turned to Judy and Charlene.

"What kind of interviews are you working on for me in the New York area so far?" he said.

"Well," said Judy, "we've got a few interviews tentatively lined up . . ."

"Anything on network TV?" said Lance. Network TV could make a book a bestseller.

"Not really," said Judy, "but . . ."

"Anything on *local* TV?" said Lance. Local TV could be very effective in certain cities.

"Not really," said Judy. "Pub date isn't till September 15th, but we do have tentative interviews set up on a couple of FM radio shows in New Jersey, and I'm working on a press interview in the Moonie newspaper . . ."

"The Moonie newspaper?" said Lance incredulously. He thought she might be joking, then realized she had no sense of humor.

"The Moonie newspaper has quite a circulation," said Charlene defensively, "you'd be surprised."

"So that's it, eh?" said Lance, vaguely nauseated, turning to Howard. "That is what you're giving me to bring my book before the public—FM radio in New Jersey and Moonie newspapers?"

"It's not a bad start," said Mike.

"It's better than *nothing,*" said Howard.

"No, it isn't," said Lance. "It is *not* better than nothing, Howard. That's where you're wrong."

Howard sighed.

"You know, Lance," said Mike, "half the problem is that it's just a bitch to promote fiction."

"It's also hard as hell to sell anything with sex in it," said Judy.

"The one thing they absolutely won't *touch* on most of your TV talk shows today," said Charlene, "is sex."

"Sex," said Judy, "or humor."

"Sex, humor, or politics," said Mike. "And I'm afraid you've got a helluva lot of all three in this book."

"What the hell's the difference?" said Lance. "If I took all the sex, humor and politics out of my book and turned it into a piece of straight reportage, you still don't have any budget to promote it with."

"Lance, why don't you contact old man Firestone and see if *he'd* be willing to increase our budget?" said Howard wearily.

"I may just do that," said Lance.

To the absolute surprise of nobody, Firestone never responded to Lance's phone call nor to the three messages he left on subsequent calls. He was assured every time that Firestone had received his messages and was trying to find time to return his calls.

It was clear how much Firestone valued his authors. Someone ought to teach the sonofabitch a lesson. If only authors weren't such independent bastards. If only they'd band together and force some basic issues. Like guaranteeing, when you were on a tour to promote a book, that there would be copies of it available for sale in bookstores. It didn't seem a lot to ask, and yet finding your book in stores when you were on tour was the exception rather than the rule.

In all fairness, Lance knew, it was not possible for any author to be satisfied with the way his book is published. To use a metaphor common among authors, it was like carrying a baby through nine months of pregnancy and then surrendering it to someone else to bring up while you hung around and watched. Even if the person were doing the best job she could, you still wouldn't be satisfied with the way she was raising your kid. But what usually happens is that the person decides that she can't afford to buy your baby clothes, so the child runs naked; the person often forgets to feed it, and so the child grows sickly. Eventually the person forgets the child exists altogether and one day sits down on it by mistake and crushes it to death. And then this person has the gall to tell you that your child was never really healthy to begin with and that what happened simply put it out of its misery.

Even if publishers did the best jobs they could, most authors would still find something to be bitter about, Lance knew. But why did publishers give authors so *much* to be bitter about? Why, for example, was it the exception rather than the rule when a book appeared without major typographical or production errors, or when it was actually to be found in the bookstores on publication day? Why, he wondered, was it the exception rather than the rule when a book was advertised or promoted enough to even come to the attention of potential readers, or when it was actually available to be bought when people came to buy it? If they sold bread the way they sold books, Lance mused, the bakers wouldn't stand for it. Why did the authors?

The first time Lance had ever gone into Brooks Brothers and had seen the suit coats turned inside out and stacked on tables instead of hanging on a rack, he was greatly intrigued. He approached a salesman and asked him why they stacked their jackets this way. "We've *always* done it this way," said the salesman haughtily.

"Because you found out that a jacket keeps its shape better this way or what?" said Lance.

"No," said the salesman, bored with Lance's obtuseness, "because we've always *done* it this way."

Although conglomerates had bought most of the publishing houses and forced them to update their sales and distribution methods, publishing was still a lot like Brooks Brothers, Lance felt.

Charlene in publicity called him on the phone.

"Well, I finally heard from the *Tonight Show*," she said. "It's a no."

"What talent coordinator did you talk to?" said Lance.

"Sheldon Aronson," she said.

"Well, I don't know that name," said Lance, "but I've been on the *Tonight Show* a couple of times before, and my talent coordinators were Jamie Severeid and Bob Shirley. Why don't you try one of them?"

"I'm sorry," she said, "I only deal with Sheldon Aronson."

"How come?" said Lance. "Do you have such a good

batting average with him you're afraid to jeopardize it or what?"

There was a short silence at the other end of the line.

"I have never managed to get anyone on the *Tonight Show*," she said.

"I can see why you wouldn't want to jeopardize that record," said Lance.

18

Cathy was exhilarated. Exhilarated and frightened. She had rented the first apartment she'd looked at, a tiny three-room job in an old building on the far West Side. It wasn't anything to look at, but it was available, it was $875 a month, which was relatively cheap, and mainly it was *hers*.

Hers. Hers to do with whatever she wished. Hers to fix up beautifully and keep looking immaculate or hers to throw soiled laundry around and pick it up only when or if she pleased and not when one's obsessive, anal-compulsive husband thought one ought to. Hers to listen to loud rock music in, even though one's husband hated it and only liked classical—she had never listened to rock music when she lived with Lance, even when he wasn't home! OK, so it wasn't as fancy as the place she'd lived in with Lance. That was all right—she'd always felt something of a fraud living in a swell apartment that was strictly a reflection of *his* income, not hers.

She had a phone installed immediately and fell in love with its whiteness and its newness and its absolute *hersness*. She had never owned her very own phone before, never had a number at which only *she* could be reached. In her apartment with Lance, people who called were calling for either of them, but mostly for Lance. In the apartment she had shared with Margaret and Cheryl, people were calling for any of them, but mostly for Cheryl. Before that she had lived in a college dorm and before that with her parents, and neither of those phones were hers by a long shot. But with this phone, anybody who called would be calling only for *her*. Except for wrong numbers, of course.

Cathy spent the first Saturday in her new apartment painting it white—virginal white. She chose a glossy enamel so that the walls and ceilings would look exceptionally clean. She didn't have to buy any furniture but a bed—the stuff she had brought from Lance's apartment filled the tiny rooms so tightly she could scarcely squeeze between the pieces. Perhaps she should have left a few pieces for Lance. Perhaps not. If he needed furniture, let him *buy* it. Fuck him.

Her rage at Lance, she realized, was a little stronger than it needed to be. His moronic attempt at seducing Margaret at his fortieth birthday party was too pathetic to inspire the kind of fury she was now feeling. Perhaps it went deeper than Lance. Perhaps it didn't. The incident at the surprise party elicited less anger from her than the mere image of Lance sitting at his desk, typing away at his novels, totally oblivious to her existence.

Her father, whom she loved very much—too much to even talk to more than twice a year—had had a similar ability to lose himself in his work and disappear totally from his family in every sense but the physical. Cathy's father wrote insurance policies instead of novels, but the effect was the same. Cathy didn't believe in the existence of such mystical phenomena as out-of-body travel, but she supposed that if such a thing were possible, the bodies which out-of-body travelers left behind would appear to their families the way that Lance's had to Cathy during their marriage and the way that Cathy's father's had to her and her mother while her mother was still alive.

It had been Lance's idea that Cathy's mother's cancer was psychogenically induced, which Cathy felt was as disrespectful as it was absurd. Cancer was cancer, as far as Cathy was concerned, and she worried constantly that it was hereditary and that sooner or later it would show up in her own breasts or her cervix or her ovaries or something. She was always discovering lumps in her breasts, which lasted long enough to produce fantasies of mastectomies and of being abandoned by Lance before she made appointments to have the lumps inspected by a doctor, following which they generally went away.

Lance maintained that Cathy's mother was never able to

get her father's attention except when she was ill, which was simply not fair, although probably true to some extent. Every time her mother got sick, Cathy's father had dropped his work and waited on her hand and foot. And every time she got well he withdrew his attention and returned to his insurance policies. That much was certainly true.

And what was also true was that every time Cathy's mother got sick her father was just a little less attentive to her with each successive illness. Until Cathy's mother got lumps in her breasts and it looked as though she might have cancer. Then her father was as attentive to her as he had ever been since they'd gotten married. And when it turned out that the lumps were benign, Cathy's father was immensely relieved, but after a while he returned to his work and it seemed to Cathy and her mother that he had never left it.

Cathy's mother had two more cancer scares before they finally discovered a malignancy. Lance said—unfairly and cruelly—that Cathy's mother had finally, through trial and error, figured out how to do it right. Why would Lance *say* such a thing? Why would anybody deliberately give themselves cancer, assuming that such a thing were physiologically possible? Never mind what Lance thought. One of Lance's favorite things to argue about at dinner parties was that all illness was psychogenically induced, even his own.

Well, if Cathy—God forbid—ever got cancer, it wouldn't be because she'd wished it on herself, and that was for sure, and the fact that she occasionally got sick when she was living with Lance and enjoyed the fabulously attentive care he gave her did not at all prove he was right. She did not need his care, she rejected absolutely his support: "So long, succor!" she yelled out suddenly and giggled.

She wondered who would take care of her now if she did get sick. She supposed that whichever man she was dating at the time would do as much for her as Lance had. Well, almost as much. The thing was to hold off getting sick until she was involved with another man seriously enough to have him take care of her if she were ill.

Another man. The prospect of becoming involved with another man was wildly exciting and delicious. Who would she become involved with? Which of the dozen or more men who had constantly buzzed around her while she was with Lance would now become her lover? The thought of taking other lovers made her feel guilty. Well, there was ample time for that. Right now she was more interested in getting her

71

new life together than in having lovers. She was on her own now for the first time in her life and she liked it. "I *like* myself, I *like* myself!" she chanted, prancing through her new apartment. She went into the tiny white bathroom and took a long, luxurious bubblebath. She got out and sat on the bed, rubbing scented creamy lotion lovingly on her body. She absentmindedly kissed her right knee and giggled at what she'd done.

She didn't need Lance. She didn't need other men. She didn't need anyone at all—she had *herself* now. She would take more bubblebaths. She would masturbate. She had surprisingly little guilt about masturbation, probably because of the matter-of-fact way her mother had dealt with the subject. Cathy thought that female masturbation was normal and healthy and even beautiful, unlike male masturbation, which was gross and tacky and perverted.

She might even start using the Ben Wa balls that Lance had given her a couple of years ago. She hadn't at first known what the two little gold balls in their purple velvet jewelry box were when Lance gave them to her. She thought he was kidding when he said that women wore them inside their vaginas, especially in the Orient, for the pleasant sexual sensations they produced. But she had dutifully tried them, and if they hadn't exactly driven her mad with pleasure, they were, as Lance put it, better than a poke in the eye with a sharp stick.

She went over to the top dresser drawer where she kept the Ben Wa balls and was surprised not to find them there. She looked through her other drawers as well. She searched every drawer in every piece of furniture she'd brought with her, but she couldn't find them. Where the hell could they have gone? She was positive she had taken everything with her when she'd moved. She was positive they weren't still in Lance's apartment. So where could they be? It wasn't even that important to find them, but the idea that they were lost and she couldn't have them when she wanted them was causing her to get unduly upset.

19

Lance was finally able to speak to Les, and to forgive Les for seeming to have been humping his wife. Les urged Lance to begin dating other women.

Lance told Les he didn't think he was ready yet. It had been years since Lance had had to think about the business of picking up and seducing women, and he didn't know if he was up to it. Not that it was so hard to do. Not that he hadn't flirted with lots of women in the eight years he had lived with Cathy, because he had—Margaret was the latest example of that, of course. But married flirting was different, somehow, from singles pickups. Married flirting was sneakier, naughtier, less serious. There seemed little likelihood that it would ever lead to anything hardcore.

He wondered what sex would be like with someone other than Cathy. He wondered if he'd even be able to get it up.

A publishing party in a cavernous nine-room West Side apartment. Three people who could afford separate but smaller apartments on the more fashionable East Side of Manhattan shared the apartment—a handsome and well-connected city editor of a large metropolitan newspaper, a bespectacled, relentlessly polite chap who wrote caustic reviews of Off-Broadway plays, and a sexy, redheaded police reporter who wasn't sleeping with either of them as far as anybody could tell.

Lance downed two vodka-tonics in a plastic glass without ice, because they'd run out, and chatted with an author he knew named Arthur Arthur. Arthur Arthur was one of the dozen successful authors that Lance knew well enough to bullshit with at parties. Arthur Arthur, who earned $100,000 to $200,000 per book on hardcover advances, had once confessed to Lance that he despised writing, and that the whole process was utter, unrelieved agony to him. Arthur Arthur was a more commercial writer than Lance, and took pride in the fact that he had never spent more than three months writing any of his fifty-seven books.

"You know," said Arthur Arthur reflectively, "I guess I must be the only member of our crowd who's made it really big."

Lance didn't know which part of the remark was the more surprising—that the fellow felt he had made it really big, or that the two of them were in anything approaching the same crowd.

A woman he knew named Marlene Orman caught sight of Lance and scurried over. She and her husband, Fred, had been friends of Lance and Cathy's up till a couple of years ago, when Marlene left Fred for a much younger man.

"Lance," said Marlene, "I almost didn't recognize you!"

"How are you, Marlene?"

"Well, I'm *fine*," she said grabbing his upper arm and squeezing it, while frowning into his face, "but how are *you?*"

"Fine," said Lance.

"I *heard*," said Marlene, still frowning into his face. Why was it some people stood too close to you, he wondered, and why was it always those with halitosis?

"What did you hear?" said Lance.

"About you and Cathy. I'm so sorry. You look pretty broken up—you must be taking it hard."

"You think I look broken up?" said Lance. "I thought I looked terrific."

Marlene shook her head sadly.

"Don't worry," she said. "This too shall pass. The pain gets lighter and lighter, and then, in two or three years, it will hardly hurt at all, and you can start looking around for someone else."

"Well," he said, "thanks for buoying up my spirits, Marlene."

"Look around you, Lance," she said, looking around her. "Look at the friends we used to know. What do you see?"

Lance looked around. He didn't know what he was supposed to be looking at.

"There's Ralph Aron. Do you remember what a cute couple Ralph and Rona Aron used to be? Look at what he's married to *now*."

Lance looked at Ralph. Ralph had aged somewhat—lost

crown and forehead hair, gained eye and neck wrinkles and waist flesh. Ralph was standing next to a very sexy-looking, very intense, very *young* woman who was wearing a suit and tie.

"She looks all right to *me,*" said Lance.

"Ralph is forty," said Marlene. "This girl is barely *twenty-one.*"

"What's the difference how old he is if they're happy?" said Lance.

"*Happy?*" said Marlene. "That's what I mean—we thought Ralph and *Rona* were happy. We thought you and *Cathy* were happy. You probably thought Fred and *I* were happy. We all put on such a happy facade—we all invested such effort to try to convince our friends how goddamned *happy* we were—and now here we all are with different mates. Fred is here tonight too, you know."

"He is? Where?"

Marlene pointed. Lance could make out Fred standing next to a young blonde girl who had her arm familiarly around his waist. Fred, he saw, had aged as much as Ralph. Lance was secretly pleased that he looked better than they did. Fred was a fairly funny writer. He wondered how a writer as funny as Fred had managed to put up with such halitosis for all those years.

"Can you imagine him bringing that girl to a party he knew I'd be at?" said Marlene. "I could hardly believe my *eyes* when I saw him walk in that door."

"Marlene," said Lance, "didn't you leave *him?*"

"What's the *difference* who left whom?" she said. "I think it displays a certain lack of sensitivity for him to be standing there with his arms around that . . . girl. How would you feel if *Cathy* had brought somebody tonight and was standing there in plain sight of you, pawing him?"

"Speaking of Cathy," said Lance, "I guess there's a possibility she just might show up here tonight."

"You mean you haven't *seen* her?" said Marlene.

"You mean she's *here?*" said Lance, feeling his lower gastrointestinal tract suddenly drop into his boots.

"Right around the corner," said Marlene, "in the dining room. By the hors d'oeuvres. Oh, you poor *thing,* I thought you'd already *seen* her."

"Uh, no," said Lance, moving toward the bar. "Hey, listen, Marlene, it was nice running into you. I'm going to go and freshen my drink."

"I don't blame you," she said. "Liquor will ease the pain, for a little while at least."

Lance refilled his drink, knocked it down, had another, and drifted around the corner. Sure enough, there was Cathy, talking animatedly to a guy he didn't know and to Howard Leventhal. He was debating whether or not to go over to her when Howard said something to her. Cathy glanced in Lance's direction, her face got fairly flushed, and then she turned around and headed in the opposite direction.

Lance, nursing his fifth vodka-tonic, was forcing endless drinks on a plumpish but otherwise presentable-looking young woman named Joyce who wore a see-through black blouse in which nipples were clearly visible. After about seven of the Lance-forced drinks, Joyce appeared to be having a modicum of difficulty standing upright. Lance suggested that they go back to his place for a nightcap. Joyce said why not?

Lance steered Joyce into the bedroom and burrowed into the yard-high mound of coats, finally extracting both hers and his, and was weaving tipsily toward the door when a tough-looking brunette in black leather jeans and boots tapped him on the shoulder.

"You going to the East Side, chief?"

Lance had not, to the best of his recollection, ever been called "chief" before, and he was intrigued.

"I'm going as far as 48th and Second," he said.

"Terrif," said the brunette. "Mind if I share your cab?"

Lance shrugged.

"Why not?"

Lance guided Joyce into the elevator, through the lobby, and out onto the street, as the brunette gave a running critique of everybody at the party. The brunette's name was Stevie, she was a policewoman and although she had had as many drinks as Joyce, she carried it better.

The three of them got into a cab, with Lance in the middle, and Stevie began a surprisingly knowledgeable interrogation of Joyce on literary subjects as far-ranging as the influence of Gertrude Stein on the style of Ernest Hemingway and the religious symbolism in *Ulysses*. Stevie, it developed, aside from being a plainclothes police detective, also taught English to cops at John Jay College.

As Stevie interrogated Joyce and Joyce replied as best she could under the influence of seven Manhattans-in-a-plastic-cup-without-ice, Stevie surreptitiously ran her hand slowly up the inside of Lance's inner thigh, pausing millimeters short of paydirt.

Lance was wildly ambivalent. What did Stevie want—a threesome? Would Joyce want that too? The possibility of having to sexually satisfy *one* total stranger after years of nobody but Cathy had produced a certain amount of anxiety in him as it was, but now it seemed possible he was going to have to perform for *two*—a lifelong fantasy of his, but one that multiplied his anxieties geometrically.

The cab sped down Fifth Avenue. Lance suggested to Stevie that she accompany him and Joyce back to his apartment for a nightcap. To his immense disappointment and relief, Stevie declined and got out of the cab at 57th Street.

Lance was perplexed. He cursed himself for not getting Stevie's phone number. When they reached his apartment, Lance paid the cabbie and guided Joyce up the stairs to his door. The moment he closed the door behind them and triple-locked it in anticipation of not having to unlock it again till morning, Joyce announced that she was going to be sick.

Lance led her swiftly into the bathroom, and just barely managed to raise the toilet seat and point her towards the bowl before Joyce brought up all seven drinks and remnants of her last few meals. Lance, his romantic ardor considerably dampened, held her forehead and comforted her till the last drop of bile had been retched out of her guts.

"How the hell did I manage to put away that much liquor?" Joyce moaned.

"I have a confession to make," said Lance. "I kept refilling your glass every time you weren't looking."

"But why?" she said.

"Well," he replied, embarrassed, "I wanted to get you drunk. I thought it would be easier to seduce you that way."

"*Seduce* me?" she said. "You didn't need to seduce me. I wanted to go to bed with you the minute I *saw* you."

Lance was amazed. Intellectually, he knew that women wanted sex as much as men, but years of brainwashing were hard to overcome. Emotionally, he still believed you had to trick them into it.

Joyce began having dry heaves, and Lance was persuaded to take her home. On the way out she noticed the lack of furniture for the first time. Lance dismissed her questions with the vague explanation that he was in the process of redecorating. When he put her in the cab he said he'd call her, but he knew he wouldn't. The memory of all that puking had squelched his lust for her.

The next morning he called his hosts and inquired how to get in touch with Stevie. The relentlessly polite drama critic gave Lance her number and a warning:

"Don't get too aggressive with her physically," he said. "She's a brown belt in *tae kwon do.*"

Lance called Stevie and made a dinner date for the following night. They went to a charming restaurant called Café Europa that featured chicken curry baked in thick brioches, and they talked about the literary life.

"The trouble with Norman," she said, "is that he has never really lived up to the promise of *The Naked and the Dead*, you know?"

"You're familiar with all of the work that Mailer has done since *The Naked and the Dead?*" he asked.

"Familiar? I'm familiar all right, don't worry. Sometimes I wish it was only his *work* I was familiar with."

"Oh, you know Mailer *personally*, then," said Lance.

"I met him in the Village," she said. "At the Lion's Head. He was there with Jimmy and Pete."

"Jimmy and Pete . . . Breslin and Hamill, you mean?"

"Yeah. They were trying to teach Joe Torres how to throw a left hook. My *grandmother* throws a better left hook than any of those guys, Torres included."

It went like that for three hours. Stevie succeeded in dropping upwards of eighty names from the New York literary-showbiz community. Then Lance invited her back to his place for a drink. She accepted. Despite the enormous quantity of liquor he had consumed at dinner, he was not perceptibly high. His extreme nervousness at the prospect of sex with his first unfamiliar woman in eight years had neutralized the alcohol in his brain.

"What's the matter," she said, surveying his barren apartment, "you don't believe in furniture?"

"My furniture," said Lance, "was stolen by a gang of lesbians."

Lest he appear too aggressive and set himself up for painful *tae kwon do* body-blocks, Lance waited until almost three a.m. before finally making a pass at her. He was a little off his timing, but she responded hungrily to his kisses. They necked for about twenty minutes and then she looked up at him and said in a voice softer than he had heard her use all night:

"You're very tender."

"Thank you," he said, but he had missed the point.

"Sometimes," she said, even more softly, "I like a man to hurt me a little."

He wasn't sure how to react. He was initially surprised, but then figured it made sense—any woman who had that much invested in tough talk, police techniques and *tae kwon do* was probably overcompensating for a red-hot streak of masochism. She clearly wanted to be dominated.

"I'll see what I can do," he said, but he knew it wasn't going to work until he'd had time to research a few techniques in sophisticated hurting. He grabbed her by the hair and pulled her violently toward him to kiss her and almost broke his left front tooth. While unbuttoning her blouse he gave her several swift pinches along the arm, which caused her to push him away and hold him at arm's length for a closer look.

"You're new at this, aren't you?" she said.

"I've done my share of it," he said as casually as possible, "it's just that I'm a little out of practice."

Stevie stifled a yawn, noted the hour was late, and made her way to the door. Lance asked if she wanted him to put her in a cab. She smiled, bent over slightly, and patted the inside of the top of her left boot. Lance obviously didn't get it, so she pulled up her pant leg and showed him the small, stainless-steel, snub-nosed .38 caliber revolver in her boot.

20

Ernest H. Roosevelt was beginning to see how it could all work. Never mind that nothing ever had in his whole life practically. Never mind that his life so far was one bad black joke. Never mind that he was six feet five, had hands big enough to comfortably hold a basketball in each, but was so uncoordinated that he couldn't even dribble ten feet without falling down. Never mind that blacks were supposed to have natural rhythm and be dynamite dancers and that he'd never so much as learned to boogie. Never mind that blacks were supposed to be terrific in bed and he could hardly get it up at all, much less keep it up long enough to put it anywhere that mattered.

There were, for Ernest H. Roosevelt, more important things in life. Like writing.

Ernest H. Roosevelt's middle name was Hemingway. He had been named for the great novelist by his Mamma, whose only contact with Hemingway was a book in which, when the Spanish lady was screwing, it said that the earth moved. The earth had never moved for Ernest's Mamma when she screwed, but she loved the idea that it could for somebody, even a Spanish lady in a book.

Ernest's name and obvious lack of physical coordination had caused all of his teachers in school to encourage him to write. The two things often went together. Ernest had got most of Hemingway's books out of the library and read them several times each. He was disappointed by *The Green Hills of Africa,* having thought it might be about The Black Experience, but he liked the ones about bullfighting and war and fishing and hunting, and in his early attempts at writing he tried to bring together many of these elements.

The teachers had always been very encouraging. They hoped he'd be able to go to college and study writing in a university. They suggested that his writing would improve considerably if he would pay more attention to grammar and spelling, but he happened to know that professional writers had editors who corrected their grammar and spelling, so he wasn't too worried.

Other kids he knew read magazines like *Penthouse* and *Hustler.* Ernest read *Writer's Digest* and *Publishers Weekly.* He was mesmerized by reports of the kind of money authors earned on their hardcover advances. A hundred thousand dollars was not uncommon for a first novelist to make for a hardcover advance against royalties, he had read, and soft-cover rights frequently went for over a million dollars. Every time he read about another record advance, he took note of the publishing house and editor who had paid it, and of the agent who had made the deal. When his own book was ready, he had to know where to take it. At the moment it looked like it might be a toss-up between two agents: Lynn Nesbit at International Creative Management, and Mort Janklow of Morton L. Janklow Associates. There was only one problem.

The problem was the book itself. He didn't know what he wanted to write it about. The teachers in school had always told him to write about what he knew. All he knew about was being a lousy basketball player and an even worse dancer and a nonlover in a society where those were the three things everybody expected you to be able to do for *sure*. All he knew about was fighting roaches and rats for your food and getting stoned or drunk or hooked on bad drugs and having to rip off liquor stores and gas stations and deal drugs to earn enough to live on. Who the hell wanted to read about *that*?

There were other writers besides Hemingway that he admired. He had read several stories in *Playboy* by a dude named Lance Lerner, and Ernest had written the dude a letter addressed to the *Playboy* office in Chicago, asking for advice on how to write. The dude had even written him back, telling him a lot of stuff about plot construction, character building, and so on, but not mentioning anything at all about the things he really needed to know, like whether to publish in hardcover first or whether to go to a combined hard-and-soft deal immediately or whether to forget about hardcover altogether and just do a straight paperback original. The one thing the dude kept emphasizing, though, was that Ernest should write about what he knew.

Well, there it was again, the same old shit—write about what you know. Maybe he'd write about ripping off a store—how you cased the joint, how you planned the ripoff, how you made your getaway, how you fenced the merchandise, and so on. He'd been doing that kind of thing ever since he was twelve. Maybe he would write about that.

While browsing one hot July evening in the B. Dalton bookstore on Fifth Avenue and 52nd Street, he came across a copy of the *Random House Dictionary* which he knew he had to have if he was going to become a professional writer. The only problem was that the mother cost a fortune and he didn't have the first nickel. What if he ripped off, not a liquor store or a gas station or a pawnshop, but a *book*store—where he could get not only the bread out of the register but the *Random House Dictionary* as *well!*

That was what he would do. And the B. Dalton on Fifth Avenue and 52nd was right in the heart of the Man's biggest high-rent area too—which meant if he got caught the media would probably give him a lot of play. All the p.r. would only help his book, which he could then finish in Riker's Island. The hardcover advance would pay his bail and his court costs, and the paperback advance would put him in fat city. If they sold it to the movies, he would arrange to play a featured role just for the exposure.

Smiling for the first time in weeks, Ernest began to make quick sketches of the floor plan and the locations of exits and registers on the back of a copy of the *Writer's Yearbook* he had just ripped off in the next aisle.

21

A publishing party in an elegant suite at the St. Regis Hotel. Butlers in tuxedos circulated with drinks and trays neatly stacked with miniature quiches, stuffed mushrooms, miniature eggrolls and rumaki.

Lance, who couldn't bear the sight of another TV dinner or frozen lasagna, was loading up on hors d'oeuvres. The butlers wore disdainful expressions as he snagged half a dozen miniature quiches and eggrolls at a crack, but he didn't care.

It was, he noted, an "A" list of invited guests. He recognized three fellow editors of Cathy's from *The New York Times Book Review,* two from *The New Yorker,* one from *The New York Review of Books,* half a dozen freelance literary critics, a dozen name authors, and a couple dozen of the top echelon of staff from the publishing house that was giving the party.

He deftly scooped seven more miniature quiches off the tray of a passing butler, then noted he was being observed with no little amusement by a stunning woman with platinum hair, absurdly high cheekbones, and a plain black gown which revealed the elegantly slim body of a high-fashion model. The woman was six feet tall.

Lance felt himself blushing furiously.

"Tapeworm?" she said with a smirk.

"Mmmmm," said Lance, nodding, chewing and swallowing three of the quiches and washing them down with a glass of champagne. "Nasty business. Have to consume at least forty pounds of food a day or I starve to death."

The woman giggled. Lance, realizing he had given a reasonably amusing retort despite his discomfort, allowed himself to approach closer. The woman met his gaze coolly with gray eyes so light in color they were almost unattractive. The little lines around the eyes and the slight slack below the chin told him she was probably no longer a high-fashion model. He figured her to be close to forty. She'd probably not look much the worse for wear at fifty-five.

"All forty pounds of it have to be in the form of hors d'oeuvres too, I imagine," she said. Her voice, he noted, was deeper than usual, and it had a slight British flavor, which was probably an affectation. Perhaps she was an actress.

"Absolutely," he replied. "The tapeworm can't handle anything but miniatures. Anything bigger, he sends it back. My name is Lance. Lance Lerner. What's yours?"

"Claire."

"Claire," he said. "Glad to meet you, Claire. You an actress?"

The woman found this a comical notion.

"No," she said, "not an actress. At least not in the sense *you* mean."

"Ah. A high-fashion model, then," he said.

She shook her head.

"An international courier," he said.

She closed her eyes and shook her head.

"Nothing that glamorous, I'm afraid," she said. "I'm just a businessman's wife."

Well, so much for that, he thought. The slight suspicion he'd had that she might be single and available was clearly not a possibility.

"What business is your husband in?" he asked, envisioning an automobile dealership that leased Rolls Royces.

"Publishing," she said and emptied the glass of champagne she was holding.

"Really?" he said. "What's his name?"

"Austin Firestone," she said. "Do you know him?"

Lance, chewing an eggroll, missed a beat and bit a hole in his inner lip.

"I . . . don't know him *personally*," he said, touching his lip experimentally with a forefinger and noting that he was bleeding slightly. "I have, however, been trying to reach him by phone for several days. Unsuccessfully, I might add."

"Really?" she said. "Why are you trying to reach him?"

"Well," said Lance, trying to decide how much he ought to tell her, then realizing he'd drunk too much champagne to apply whatever decision he might make in that area, "I wrote a novel which your husband is publishing in a few weeks, and I wanted to tell him I thought he was about to make an unsound business decision."

"Unsound? In what way?" she said.

"Well," he said, "he has allocated only five thousand dollars for the advertising and promotion of my book. Five thousand dollars is not enough to do anything. I wanted to suggest to him that either he increase the budget substantially so we'd have a chance to sell a few copies of the book, or else save the five thousand altogether, and spend it on something more apt to give him a return on his investment. Like municipal bonds."

She held his gaze for several moments.

"I think Austin would be interested in hearing your views on this subject in person," she said. "Would you like to meet him?"

"Are you kidding me? I'd *kill* to meet him," he replied.

She nodded.

"I'll arrange a dinner," she said. "Nothing fancy. Just a few couples at our apartment. I won't tell him anything about this. You'll have an opportunity to meet him in a relaxed atmosphere. Then, when you think you've got his attention, you can raise the topic yourself. I think he might be intrigued."

"God," said Lance, "would you really do that for me? I'd really appreciate it, no kidding."

She smiled at his boyish eagerness.

"I'd be glad to do that for you, Lance," she said. "Perhaps some day you'll be able to do something for *me.*"

"Anything," said Lance. "You name it, you got it."

"Anything?" she said. "That's quite an offer."

"I mean it," he said, "I swear to God."

"We'll see," she said, "we'll see."

22

If there was one thing Stevie Petrocelli couldn't stand it was coming home after a night tour in the goddamn 9th precinct, with the stench of human garbage on her body, and not being able to take a long hot shower. For the past two months, every time she turned on the shower and got the temperature of the water adjusted so it wasn't either freezing or scalding and climbed into the stall, the fucking pressure dropped off to almost nothing, and then it built back up again and spurted out either thirty degrees colder or thirty degrees hotter, with the result that Stevie had on several occasions been badly burned.

She had spoken of the problem numerous times with Gladys Oliphant—Gladys the *Elephant* she called her because the woman was so big and fat—but the bitch kept saying that she was only the super and not a goddamn plumber. Stevie called the landlord and threatened to get the building cited for numerous building code violations, but the landlord advised her that she could also find herself another apartment. The tiny one-bedroom rental was nothing to look at, she knew, but the location on West 57th almost made it worth the $800 a month she had to pay for it.

She had recently changed her tactics with Gladys, figuring you could catch more flies with honey than vinegar, which was a stupid expression because as far as she knew you couldn't catch flies with vinegar at *all*. The threats hadn't gotten her any closer to having her shower fixed, so she'd started trying to be nice instead. Complimenting the Elephant on her hair (it was frizzy and red), complimenting her on her clothes (they were mostly tentlike, pastel-colored, nylon dressing gowns). Maybe the new tactics were beginning to pay off. Gladys had actually for the first time come up and taken a look at the shower, removed the head with a huge crescent wrench, and announced that what it needed was a new gizmo that controlled the mixture of hot and cold water or something. Gladys said she would go down to a plumbing supply place on Canal Street in the next day or two, get the gizmo, and come back and put it in. She thought it would be fixed by Wednesday or Thursday.

Very interesting, if true, thought Stevie. Wednesday she was working the late tour at the precinct, but Thursday she was off all day. In fact, Thursday she was planning to have dinner with crazy Lance Lerner.

There was something terribly sweet about Lance, she mused. She had picked up a copy of his last book in paperback and not liked it very much—the character delineations had been pretty shallow and the imagery not really up to snuff—but he was a good kisser, and he'd tried so earnestly to hurt her when she'd foolishly said that was what she wanted.

She had obviously given him the wrong impression by saying that. He was probably off shopping for whips and shackles, when all she'd meant was that she didn't like a man to be too soft, that she hated to feel she was tougher than the guys she went to bed with, although she almost always was. Contrary to the impression she'd given Lance, she'd never really done any S&M before, although she'd certainly fantasized about it. Still, if that's what he thought she liked, then maybe she would give it a try. He certainly didn't appear to be shocked by the idea. Which was nice. It showed he had imagination in bed. There was nothing worse than a boring bed partner.

Well, whether he brought over chains or not, she would throw him a fuck on Thursday anyway. Just to see what he was like.

23

Goose Washington was an idiot, but he was the only one of the brothers that Ernest H. Roosevelt had talked to that was willing to help him rip off the bookstore. Goose got his name from the way he was always grabbing folks between the legs, no matter who they were or what the situation. Goose didn't care if he was in church, for God's sake, if he felt like grabbing somebody.

The one thing Goose had going for him, outside of he would go along with anything you asked him, no matter how stupid, was that he always knew where to locate a piece. Goose had gotten them two pieces for the bookstore job that were as fine as any Ernest had ever seen. One of them was a .357 Smith & Wesson Highway Patrolman model, a cop gun that was so big most dudes couldn't even fire it without using both hands. The other was a little .380 Walther PPK Automatic, the gun that James Bond dude used in all the "007" movies. You were supposed to get rid of whatever piece you used after the job you got it for was finished, but Ernest was tempted to hang onto whichever one of these he could.

He and Goose had kind of moseyed through the B. Dalton bookstore a couple of times, just generally getting the feel of the floor plan. Goose thought he was crazy to want to rip off a bookstore, but Ernest said that the publishing business was going through a boom and that there would probably be a lot of bread in the register. Ernest figured that Thursday night around eight o'clock was a good time to hit the store. Goose said it was all the same to him.

Ernest gave Goose his choice of pieces, but, just as Ernest had figured, Goose could barely lift the .357 Smith & Wesson, much less fire it with one hand, so Goose chose the Walther instead. Ernest hoped he wouldn't have to shoot anybody, but if he had to he would. It wouldn't be the first time, and it kind of came with the territory.

Thursday was only three days away. He went home to take notes on what he had done so far.

24

Gladys Oliphant had never been svelte. Since grammar school she had had to endure names like Tubby, Tiny, Porky, Fats, and of course, Oliphant the Elephant, her least favorite name of all.

In point of fact, Gladys was five feet ten and weighed two hundred and forty pounds. If she lost only ninety pounds she'd be just about perfect, she felt. Not that a hundred and fifty was svelte either, but it was a weight that Gladys aspired to, a weight that Gladys had passed briefly at the age of twelve and never again seen. The truth was that Gladys *preferred* being fat to being thin. Being fat kept most men, especially the disconcertingly sexual ones, at a distance. Her father and mother and all her sisters and brothers had been fat. Fat people were thought to be jollier than skinny people. She didn't think that was true, but she knew that skinny people usually looked undernourished and depressed.

She had only gone out with fat boys in high school and college, of course. Not that she had gone out that much with boys at all. After the incident in New Mexico, she had sworn off men of all ages for several years. Particularly Indians. Not that there were that many Indians in New York who were asking her out on dates, but she really did have a thing about Indians after the incident in New Mexico, and she didn't think that anybody in his right mind could blame her.

The way it had happened was that she and Thelma, a friend of hers who lived down the street, had gone one August on a camping trip to New Mexico. They had camped three nights on the edge of a huge Indian reservation near Taos without even so much as *seeing* an Indian. And then one day, when Thelma had gone off to look at kachina dolls, Gladys went wandering in the desert, looking for cactus flowers, and who should she meet up with but four Indian braves on dirt bikes, in jeans and T-shirts, who were out of their minds on firewater.

Because it was such a hot day Gladys was wearing just short shorts and a halter top. Large folds of fat peeked through the openings of her clothing. This must have aroused the Indians, because they surrounded her and began making suggestive remarks. She was a little frightened, but tried to cover her fear with wisecracks. She even chuckled when they spoke of staking her to the ground and initiating her into the tribe. She assumed they were kidding. They were not.

Two of them wrestled her to the ground and the other two spread-eagled her on the desert floor, drove four stakes into the hot clay and tied her wrists and ankles to them. She stopped chuckling. She tried to reason with them. They tore off her shorts, her halter top, her brassiere and her panties and, after dancing around her in a modified war dance with wild war whoops for a while, they pulled down their jeans and gang-banged her.

She screamed and cried, but that only seemed to excite them, so she finally shut up and endured the indignities in silence. When they had finished raping her, they simply left her there, baking in the hot sun, and rode their dirt bikes back to the reservation.

She didn't know how many hours she lay there, staked to the ground, frying on the clay, before a kindly old Indian woman found her, cut her loose with a machete, and took her back to the reservation in a rusted-out Dodge stationwagon to treat her for shock and sunstroke.

When Thelma came back and found Gladys missing she called out the state police, and when they finally found her on the reservation they took her directly to the hospital, where she remained for several days.

The four Indians who had raped Gladys were never caught. Gladys peeled for six weeks after returning to New York.

In many ways the rape by the Indians had killed off most of Gladys's once high spirit. She'd had hopes of becoming a dancer and was not ungraceful for her size, but she gave up ballet shortly after the rape, knowing it was hopeless. She'd

had some feeling she might one day do a little acting—
everybody said she had a beautiful face—but there weren't a
whole lot of parts for obese ingenues, and after the rape she
simply stopped kidding herself. She figured some day she'd
try her hand at writing. In the meantime she'd lucked into a
rent-free job as superintendent of an old apartment building
on West 57th Street. Her father had been a building contrac-
tor and she had gone along with him on so many jobs as a
youngster that she knew the rudiments of plumbing, wiring
and carpentry and was able to make most repairs on tenants'
apartments without outside help, assuming she was in the
mood, a fact which the landlord particularly appreciated.

Gladys's tenants were something else again. There were a
number of elderly people, several foreign persons, a handful
of young men living alone, and a policewoman. Most of the
young men were either dancers or actors—obvious
homosexuals—but one of them looked like he could go either
way. He was the only man she had ever flirted with since the
rape, mostly because he seemed gentle and shy and she felt he
posed no threat to her. She had numerous fantasies about
him, including one of making a baby with him, either in or out
of wedlock—it hardly mattered to her since she wanted a
baby even more than she wanted a man and, at age thirty-
seven, she didn't have too many mongoloid-free years left.
But all the flirting she did with the young man produced no
results. She decided he was a fag after all.

The policewoman was at first the most unpleasant tenant in
the building. Just because she had some problem with her
shower—who *didn't* in a building this old!—she expected you
to drop everything you were doing and go down to Canal
Street and ransack plumbing supply houses for parts. As if
she didn't have her hands full with all the other tenants'
complaints, to say nothing of the assignments she had to
complete each and every week for her correspondence course
from the Famous Writers School.

The Famous Writers School just *happened* to consider
Gladys Oliphant one of their most promising students. Or so
they said. Under their tutelage she had begun a romantic
novel which, they absolutely swore, was as brilliant as anything ever written by Barbara Cartland! It was only a matter
of time before she would be selling her novel for a huge
advance and moving to the East Side and hanging out at
Elaine's with all the other famous writers.

It was very likely the prospect of her imminent success as a romantic novelist that was causing Gladys to appear less ill-humored to her tenants, and that may have been why the policewoman was acting more polite towards her. Now that she was acting so polite, perhaps Gladys would even see about fixing up that shower of hers. Besides, she'd heard that the policewoman had a few connections in the literary world, and Gladys was planning to use her as a stepping-stone in her career.

While she was in there fixing the shower, Gladys might just casually feel the policewoman out about the possibility of the two of them maybe sauntering up to Elaine's one night and getting a head start on meeting some of her future colleagues.

25

Fifty dollars a pair was a preposterous price to pay for shackles, Lance decided. If the owners of slave ships had had to buy their shackles at the Pleasure Chest there never would have been any trade to the New World.

He'd settled instead on handcuffs—four sets of them. They weren't cheap either, but they were a better bargain than the shackles. He practiced unlocking them and snapping them closed again so as not to appear a total neophyte to Stevie when he put them on her tonight. He wasn't entirely sure why he was doing all this in the first place, but he thought she expected it, and besides he figured the experience would broaden him as a writer.

He had wanted to take her to an early dinner at the Russian Tea Room since it was so close to her apartment, but she insisted on dragging him all the way down to Soho to eat in some tiny little Italian place that had just opened and was already a hangout for artists and writers. The pasta was average, but he had several White Russians, his new favorite drink, and he somehow managed to down enough of them to endure her relentless name-dropping and have a moderately good time.

About seven-thirty they left the restaurant and headed back to her apartment. He was beginning to get turned on by the prospect of putting the cuffs on her, and his anticipatory excitement was in no way diminished by the realization that he would be locking up a cop.

"I have a little surprise for you," he said as they walked into her apartment and triple-locked the door behind them.

"I know," she said. "You've got about sixteen pairs of cuffs in your pocket."

He was amazed.

"How the hell did you know that?" he said.

She shrugged.

"Lance, give me a break. You don't think a cop knows the sound that handcuffs make in someone's pocket? You don't think several pairs of cuffs would make even *more* of that sound? Let's see 'em."

He took out the four pairs of cuffs and handed them to her. She looked them over with professional detachment.

"Jay-Pees," she said. "Not a bad make. Although any perp in *my* precinct could probably get out of them in about three minutes flat."

"Show me," he said. He unlocked one pair of cuffs with the tiny key it had come with. "Hold out your wrists."

"Hey hey," she said. "Slow down there, chief."

"What do you mean?" he said.

She looked at him and cocked her head.

"You brought these over here to have a little B&D fun, am I right?"

"B&D? Oh, Bondage and Domination. Right."

"Well, take it easy. I hardly know you. What makes you think I'd let you lock me up on our second date?"

"How many dates do you usually have to have with a man before you let him lock you up?"

"Whoa, there, buster," she said. "Slow down. What makes you think I've ever done this before?"

"You mean you haven't? I thought you were an old hand at this. In fact I was looking forward to learning some pointers from you."

She chuckled and went to the kitchen and poured herself a beer.

"You want a Lowenbrau?" she called. "Hunter Thompson bought me a case."

"No thanks," he said. "I've had enough drinks for a while."

She came back into the room, sipping her beer.

"So," she said, "you want to do a little experimenting in B&D, do you?"

"Sure," he said, "why not?"

"And you actually think that I—a policewoman—would let you lock me up, do you?"

"What's the matter," he said, "don't you trust me?"

"Of course not," she said. "Why in the name of Christ would I trust you?"

"I trust *you*," he said.

"You do?"

"Sure."

"O.K.," she said, "then let *me* put the cuffs on *you*."

It was a possibility he frankly hadn't considered. But it did seem reasonable that he couldn't expect her to submit to something he was unwilling to undergo himself.

"If I let you lock *me* up, then will you let me lock *you* up?" he said.

She nodded her head. He tried to picture himself totally immobilized, totally at her mercy. He found it titillating.

"How long will you keep me locked up?" he said, beginning to get aroused.

"Not long. Ten minutes or so. The minute you get uptight I'll unlock you. I assume you'll do the same for me."

"Of course," he said, "of course. Tell me, what, uh, do you plan to do to me once you have me all locked up?"

She cackled evilly.

"We'll see," she said. "Don't worry, it won't hurt. Much."

"Are you going to, uh, have your way with me?" he said, suddenly coy.

"Why else do you think we're *doing* this?" she said.

He nodded.

"O.K.," he said. "I'll trust you, Stevie. Tell me what to do."

"First take off your clothes," she said. "If I lock you up with them on, I'm going to have to tear them apart to get them off you."

Lance smiled and began undressing. He took off his sportcoat and tie and handed them to her. She opened the closet and hung them on a hanger. He took off his boots and socks. She put the socks in the boots and the boots in the bottom of the closet.

He paused and smiled at her uncertainly. He didn't know how aroused it was permissible to be while doing this. He didn't want to find he was enjoying it too much and then have to face the fact that he might be a closet pervert.

"C'mon," she said, "we don't have all night here."

He unbuttoned his shirt, took it off and handed it to her. He unbuckled his jeans, stepped out of them and gave them to her as well. She could clearly see the shape of his erection through his jockey shorts. She raised an eyebrow at it, and hung up the shirt and pants in the closet. Then she ushered him into the tiny bedroom and pulled back the spread on the queen-size bed. The head and foot of the bed had beautiful polished brass fittings. The sheets were black satin. Stevie was evidently somebody who entertained a bit in bed.

"OK," she said, "lie down. On your back, and spread those arms and legs. Spread 'em!"

He did as he was told. She unlocked two pairs of cuffs and chained each of his wrists to the brass pipes at the head of the bed. Then, chuckling softly, she pulled off his jockey shorts, cupped his stiff member briefly in her hand and kissed the tip. Then she secured each of his ankles to the brass rails at the foot of the bed. It was a weird feeling. He was a little ashamed at being aroused. He started to giggle.

"Undt now," she said, adopting a passable German accent, "Herr Lerner, I haff you completely in mein power!"

She burst into a long, maniacal laugh.

"W-what are you g-going to do to me?" he stammered, going along with the gag.

"Vat am I goink to *do* to you?" She cackled. "Chust vait undt *see,* Herr Lerner, chust vait undt *see!*"

She went and got a feather and began tickling him all over his body. He found he was extremely ticklish and began whooping with laughter. She kept it up slightly longer than he hoped she would. Then she took some baby oil and began to give him a massage. It was exceedingly pleasant and he began to relax.

"I think I'd like a drink now, if you don't mind," he said.

"Oh, you do, do you?" she said. "And what would you like to drink, may I ask?"

"A White Russian."

"Is that so?" she said. "What makes you think I even know how to make one?"

"You can do anything," he said.

Unexpectedly pleased by this response, she went into the kitchen, mixed his drink, and came back to the bed.

"Here," she said, "tilt your head this way and I'll dribble it into your mouth."

She began dribbling, but more of it got on the black satin sheets than in his mouth. They both found the process fairly amusing.

"You know," he said, "you really used a bit too much Kahlua. Would you please make me a new one?"

She exploded with laughter.

"You certainly are a pushy prisoner," she said. But she loved his audacity and she went back into the kitchen to mix a fresh one. When she returned to the bedroom, however, her hands were empty. She grabbed her coat and headed for the door.

"Hey," he said, "where are you going?"

"To get more Kahlua," she said. "I used up practically all I had."

"Hey, listen, don't leave," he said. "Forget about the Kahlua."

"Don't worry," she said, "the liquor store is right down-stairs. I won't be more than a minute."

She opened the door.

"Stevie, come back!" he yelled, but it was no use. He heard the door close behind her and he heard her key in the lock.

Well, he thought, what could possibly go wrong in the couple of minutes it would take her to return with the Kahlua?

26

Goose Washington and Ernest Hemingway Roosevelt made their way down Fifth Avenue along the edge of Central Park in a leisurely fashion. The night was warm and they were a little stoned.

Ernest fondled the .357 Smith & Wesson in his jacket pocket and tried to make mental notes of what his thoughts were as they approached the B. Dalton bookstore so that he'd be able to write about them afterwards.

"How ya feeling, bro'?" said Ernest to his friend.

"O.K., bro'," said Goose, and goosed the taller Ernest.

Ernest was the slightest bit nervous about trusting Goose with the loaded Walther, but he didn't figure he had much choice. Besides, this was hardly the first time either of them had used a piece in a holdup, and, even though none of the jobs had been bookstores, and even though none of them had been pulled outside of Harlem, it couldn't be that much different than what they were used to.

They crossed 59th Street and headed South on Fifth. Just six blocks more. Ernest ran over the layout of the store once more in his head. He had rehearsed it over and over until Goose had gotten irritated. Well, shit, what if he *was* irritated! This was important. This was going to be one of the key scenes in his novel. They couldn't fuck it up.

They crossed 53rd Street. There it was, half a block ahead.

"You ready, bro'?" said Ernest.

"Ready, bro'," said Goose.

They walked into the store.

27

Gladys Oliphant was happy. She'd managed to find the part for the policewoman's shower head without much searching at all. She'd spent some extra time wandering through the shops on Canal Street, browsing among the grimy tools and fittings that had been so much a part of the pleasant years with her father. Although she didn't really see an immediate use for them, she picked up a container of epoxy putty, two cans of WD-40 and a complete forty-piece fine thread tap and die set. She loved fooling around with tools, and you never knew when you might need them.

She came home and ate a leisurely dinner watching television, and had four or five cans of beer. She took a little nap with the TV on, and when she woke up she remembered the policewoman and her shower. While she'd been napping she thought she heard the policewoman's voice in the hallway. If she hopped up there now and fixed that shower head, perhaps the policewoman would invite her to stay for a beer.

Gladys went to her toolbox, took out an adjustable crescent wrench, picked up the shower head part and walked out of the apartment. The policewoman lived three flights up. By the time Gladys reached the right door she was slightly out of breath and puffing. She knocked on the door and waited, but there was no reply. Strange. She was fairly certain it was the policewoman's voice she had heard in the hallway. It was quite a distinctive voice.

She knocked again. Still there was no reply. Gladys's heart sank. The policewoman had probably only come back for a short time and then left again. Should she try her again tomorrow, or should she fix it now? If she came back tomorrow, she could fix the shower, then stay for a beer and discuss the literary life. On the other hand, she could fix it now, and then when she came back tomorrow the policewoman would be even happier to see her and would be even more likely to ask her to stay and chat.

All right, it was decided. Gladys put her hand into her pocket, took out her ring of keys, found the ones to the policewoman's apartment, and opened the door.

That's strange, she thought. The lights were on. The policewoman was a frugal tenant and never left more than a single light on when she wasn't home. Perhaps she was home and hadn't heard her knock?

"Hello," said Gladys. "Anybody here?"

"Stevie?" said a tentative male voice from the bedroom.

What was this? A male voice? Maybe a prowler? Gladys became very nervous. Should she leave while there was still time to call the police? She did have her heavy crescent wrench with her. Perhaps that was protection enough.

"Hello?" called Gladys once more, and crept, with wrench upraised, to the bedroom door. She peeked inside, and gasped.

She didn't know what she expected to see in the policewoman's bedroom, but if she had been asked to guess, a naked skinny man handcuffed to the bed would not have been one of the first hundred and fifty guesses she would have come up with.

28

Goose and Ernest walked into the store. Ernest nodded to Goose. Goose stationed himself at the door and Ernest ambled casually over to the main cashier's desk.

"S'cuse me, mah man," said Ernest softly to the man behind the cashier's desk, who was reading from a book entitled *Books in Print*.

The man, a white dude about fifty, bald, wearing wire-rimmed glasses and a white shirt and silk tie, looked up to see a very tall black man with a pleasant expression on his face.

"Yes, can I help you?" said the man.

"Ah'd like a copy of the *Random House Dictionary*, mah man," said Ernest amiably. "And then Ah'd like all the bread you got in that register."

The bald man didn't quite hear what Ernest had said, and then he saw the enormous pistol that Ernest had taken out of his pocket and his heart stopped beating.

Ernest looked back at Goose and Goose nodded. Goose took out the Walther and held it over his head. Ernest turned back to the dozen or so clerks and customers in the store.

"S'cuse me, folks," said Ernest in a fairly loud voice. "Ah hate to bother you, but this here is a holdup. Mah brothuh over theah has a gun, as do Ah, and we would not like to have to use them, but we will if we has to."

Everybody had looked up and stopped what they were doing. Nobody moved a muscle. Somebody whimpered. Somebody else prayed in a monotone.

"Please don't shoot anybody," said the bald man behind the cashier's desk in a polite voice. "We'll give you whatever you want, just please don't shoot anybody, all right?"

"Tha's fine with me," said Ernest cheerfully.

"What is it you want now," said the man, "the money in the register?"

"Tha's right, mah man," said Ernest. "The money in the register and the *Random House Dictionary*."

"The what?" said the man. "The *Random House Dictionary?*"

"Tha's right, mah man," said Ernest.

"Stephanie, bring this man the *Random House Dictionary*," said the clerk. "And step on it."

A young woman of about twenty, wearing horn-rimmed glasses and an exceedingly nervous expression, went to the reference book section, picked out a copy of the *Random House Dictionary* and brought it to the cashier's desk. She stared at the gun in Ernest's hand as though it had hypnotic powers.

"Thankya, sweet child," said Ernest, his heart suddenly welling up with love for the nervous white fox with the glasses, who was actually scared of *him*, of dumb old Ernest who couldn't dance or ball or dribble.

"Yo' name Stephanie, sweet child?" said Ernest to the nervous girl.

She nodded her head, unable to take her eyes off the Smith & Wesson.

"Don' be scared, Stephanie," he said. "Ah ain't gonna hurt ya."

Ernest turned back to the bald man.

"O.K., mah man, now Ah need the bread in that register and all the other registers in the store."

Ernest handed the bald man an empty El Al flight bag. The bald man nodded several times, turned around, opened the cash drawer and began putting money into the bag.

"Ah need the bread from the other registers too, mah man," said Ernest gently.

The man looked out at the rest of the store, got on the p.a. system and addressed everyone in a loud, quavery voice:

"Will cashiers at all the registers please empty their cash drawers and bring the contents here immediately?"

There was a small flurry of activity as all the cashiers emptied their cash drawers and brought the money up to the main cashier's desk and emptied it into the El Al flight bag. Ernest coolly surveyed the room, pointing his revolver this way and that, directing activity like a symphony conductor. Ernest checked Goose at the door and saw, to his irritation, that a short elderly woman was just coming through the door that Goose was blocking.

"*Excuse* me, young man," said the elderly woman, trying to push past him.

"Ma'am," said Ernest loudly, "please stop right theah, if you will. We havin' a holdup just now at the present moment, but we be through shortly."

Goose smiled sweetly at the elderly woman and then goosed her. She gave an outraged cry but didn't move.

Ernest made sure all the cash was in the flight bag, then jammed the *Random House Dictionary* in on top of it. It was a very tight fit.

"Pardon me for asking," said the bald man behind the desk, "but what do you want with the *Random House Dictionary*, if you don't mind my asking?"

"No problem, mah man," said Ernest. "Ah needs it for mah work. Ah'm a author."

"I see," said the bald man.

Ernest smiled broadly and backed away from the main cashier's desk and began edging toward the door.

"Ah thank all of you for bein' so cooperative," he said. "It was a pleasure doin' business with y'all. Ah would suggest for your own comfort and safety that you don' call the po–lice for about fahv minutes or so, or else we gonna have to shoot somebody."

He nodded to Goose, who opened the door.

"Take care now," Ernest called to the people inside the store. "Nice meetin' ya, Stephanie. And y'all have a nice day now, heah?"

Ernest and Goose moved swiftly through the door and began walking very rapidly north on Fifth Avenue. It had gone beautifully.

"Way to *go,* bro'!" said Ernest and slapped Goose's open hand.

And then they heard it:

"Stop them! Help! Police! Robbers! Stop them! Help! Police! Help!"

It was the little old lady, out on the street and screaming her lungs out.

Ernest fired one shot straight up in the air, cursed, and then both he and Goose broke into a dead run. A man on the north side of 53rd Street yelled something at them that they couldn't make out, then fired a shot in their direction.

Ernest and Goose raced uptown four blocks, then made a sharp left at the corner of 57th and Fifth, heading west on 57th Street. Pedestrians sprang out of their way like antelope, but they were now running so fast that they collided with at least five people between Fifth and Sixth Avenues.

At Sixth Avenue Goose didn't know which way to turn, so Ernest yanked him by the arm and they tore across 57th Street against the light, causing several cars to swerve to avoid them. If they could just make it two more blocks north to 59th Street, they could disappear into Central Park and they'd be home free.

29

Still chuckling to herself, Stevie walked out of her apartment building and down two doors to the liquor store. She nodded hello to the owner and pointed to the liqueurs.

"One bottle of Kahlua, please, Sol," she said.

"The large or the small?" he said.

She thought a moment. If she wasn't going to be seeing Lance much after tonight, then maybe the small would be enough. But he *was* sort of sweet—after all, he'd bought her the cuffs.

"Oh, what the hell," she said. "Gimme the large."

The man smiled, took the quart bottle of Kahlua down off the shelf and put it in a brown paper bag. Stevie gave him the exact change. Just then she heard the sounds of yelling and running outside. She went quickly to the door, just as two black men raced past her.

In scarcely more than a second her snub-nosed .38 was out of her boot and she was racing up 57th Street, shouting:

"Freeze, turkeys—*police!"*

30

The naked skinny man on the bed looked a lot more worried than Gladys felt. And he *was* chained to the bedstead. She didn't really seem to be in any immediate danger.

"Hi there," said the naked skinny man on the bed.

She wasn't too sure what you were supposed to say to naked skinny men handcuffed to bedsteads, so for the time being she said nothing. It was just possible that he was a sex criminal that the policewoman had apprehended, and that she had cuffed him to the bed and gone to get help. If that was the case, Gladys didn't think she ought to get too chummy with him. She continued to stand at the foot of the bed, her wrench upraised.

"Who, uh, are you?" said the naked skinny man on the bed.

He managed a forced smile. She thought it an inappropriate facial expression under the circumstances. He was behaving just like some guy trying to be polite at a bar or a party, except that they weren't *at* a bar or a party, they were in a policewoman's bedroom, and the man who had addressed her was naked and skinny and handcuffed to the bed.

Gladys appraised him thoughtfully. Aside from skinny, his body wasn't really all that disgusting to look at. And his sexual organs did seem to be in at least a mild state of arousal, which Gladys considered interesting. The penis wasn't badly shaped, she found herself thinking. Not that she was any expert in penises. She hadn't seen all that many of them, and the ones that she had seen were either the rather small and pathetic ones of the fat men she'd been to bed with, or else the rather menacing ones of the four Indians who had raped her.

No, as penises went, the one that this fellow owned was certainly not that displeasing to look at. She wondered why it seemed to be in a state of mild arousal—a "semi," she believed men called it. Perhaps the thing was in a mild state of arousal due to *her* presence in the room. The notion that she might be causing this strange man to be sexually excited made her blush.

It was ironic, she thought. The last sexual contact she had had with any man, it had been *she* who was spread-eagled and tied down and unable to move. And now the roles were reversed. Here was a naked man before her, totally helpless, totally at her mercy, and she could do anything she wanted to him, avenge herself for the Indian rapes or anything at all, and nobody would be there to stop her. She started getting excited and angry.

"Shut up!" she screamed suddenly.

The man, who had not uttered a word in the last two minutes or so, seemed startled.

"Shut up and let me think!" she said not quite as loudly. Her mind was racing, as various possible courses of action flitted through it.

She could hit him on the head with the wrench. She could scratch his eyes out. She could go and get a sharp kitchen knife and cut off that penis of his, that symbol of male aggression which had caused her so much pain and humiliation and suffering, and it would serve him right! She could always justify it afterwards as a political act.

She could also just walk over there and examine his sexual organs quite closely and in great detail in a way that she had never dared to do with any man before and would probably never have such an opportunity to do again, and when the paddy wagon or whatever the policewoman had gone to get finally arrived, she would merely say that she'd been helping to guard the prisoner, and if he told them anything she'd done before they arrived they wouldn't believe him, because it would be his word against hers and he was a criminal and she was not.

"Uh, may I be permitted to say something?" said the naked skinny man.

"No!" she shouted, suddenly enraged. "You'll speak when I ask you to speak, and not before!"

Now where the hell had *that* line come from, she wondered, shocked at the vehemence of her response. Probably from a movie she'd seen late at night on TV.

"I'm sorry," said the man.

"I didn't mean to yell," she replied. "I'm just a little . . . upset."

"So am I," he said. "Are you a friend of Stevie's?"

She turned her attention from the penis to the face.

"What?" she said.

"I said are you a friend of Stevie's?" he said pleasantly.

"In a way," she said. "I'm the super of this building."

"Ah," he said. "So *that's* why you had a key to her apartment."

"Yeah," she said. "I came up here to fix the shower head. She's been after me to do it for months."

"I see," he said. "I suppose you're wondering what I'm doing here like this."

She watched him carefully, waiting for the first hint of a trick.

"It did cross my mind to wonder that," she said.

"It's rather simple, really," he said. "Stevie and I went out to dinner together and, knowing her, uh, interest in . . . unusual sexual practices, I, uh, brought over four pairs of handcuffs as a sort of surprise . . ."

"She's interested in unusual sexual practices, you say?"

"Why, yes."

"I had no idea," said Gladys.

"Well, there's no reason why you would have," he said.

"Look, maybe you shouldn't ought to be telling me this," said Gladys.

"Why not?" said the naked skinny man. "These are very intimate circumstances we find ourselves in."

Gladys noted that the mild state of arousal which the man's penis had been in when she entered the room had considerably diminished since he'd started talking. In a way she preferred him more aroused. Perhaps that was simply the way she affected men: at first they were turned on by her, and then the more they got to know her the less turned on they were.

"What are you," she said, "a sex criminal?"

"No," said the naked skinny man, "a writer."

Gladys's ears perked up.

"A *writer?*" she said. "*I'm* a writer."

"No kidding?" he said. "Who do you write for?"

"For the Famous Writers School," she said, not without pride. "I'm writing a romantic novel under their direct supervision."

"Well," said the man, "isn't that something."

"Yeah," she said. "The one thing that always bothers me, though, is . . ." She changed her mind and shook the thought away.

"Yes?" he said. "What bothers you?"

"Never mind," she said. "You probably wouldn't be interested."

"Sure I would," he said. "In fact, I used to teach a course in writing at the New School."

"Honest?"

"Honest. What is it that bothers you?"

"Well," she said, "I'm not real sure what makes a novel, you know? I mean I'm not sure what's supposed to be *in* it."

He nodded.

"Well," he said, "there's a little catch-phrase that I learned from a writer at the *Saturday Evening Post* many years ago which might help you: 'An appealing character strives against great odds to attain a worthwhile goal.' That's pretty much the formula for all fiction, long or short."

"No kidding?"

"No kidding. Now there are three elements in that formula: the Appealing Character, the Great Odds, and the Worthwhile Goal, but if you have all those you ought to be O.K."

"I'll be damned," she said.

"Of course there are exceptions to that formula—the main character might not be appealing, or his goal might not be worthwhile in the traditional sense. Like in *The Day of the Jackal*, the main character was a professional killer and not a very likable fellow. And his goal, the assassination of de Gaulle, wasn't what you might call worthwhile. But still there were great odds, and the author had researched and paced his story so well that it didn't really matter—you still wanted the assassin, in some horrible way, to succeed and kill de Gaulle, even though you knew that he couldn't."

"Mmmmm," she said. "So who do *you* write for?"

"Me? Oh, lots of people. I'm freelance."

"Uh huh."

"I write books and magazine articles and screenplays and lots of unproduced TV pilots," he said.

"Yeah," she said, "I'll bet."

"I *do*," he said. "I swear to God."

"Mmmmhmmm," she said. "And what do you do for a *living*?"

"That's what I do for a living," he said.

"You mean to tell me you earn enough from writing to *live* on?" she said incredulously.

"Absolutely," he said.

"How much do you make a week?"

"I don't know how much it is a week, but I can tell you what I earn a year. About a hundred thousand."

She burst out laughing.

"A hundred thousand *dollars?*" she shrieked. "Get out of here!" She laughed some more.

"It's the truth," he said.

"Yeah? Tell me some of the things you've written, then."

"OK. Let's see. Have you heard of a book called *Knuckle Sandwich?*"

"Yeah . . ."

"I wrote that."

"Get out of here," she said.

"Have you heard of a book called *Fresh When Available?* Or one called *Modern Lit?* Or one called *Cut to the Chase?* Or another called *You Can't Get There from Here?*"

"Yeah . . ."

"I wrote all of those."

"Get out of here. I *read* some of those. The guy that wrote them is named . . . let me think now . . ."

"Lance Lerner?" he said.

"Yeah, that's it," she said, "Lance Lerner."

"That's me," he said, "Lance Lerner."

"Get out of here," she said a little less certainly, because now that he mentioned it he *did* look the slightest bit familiar to her. The face, that is.

"You don't believe me?" he said. "Check the ID in my wallet. It's in my inside jacket pocket, it's hanging in the closet."

"OK," she said, "I might just do that."

She went out of the bedroom and reached into the closet and found a man's sportcoat. She reached into the inside jacket pocket and took out a wallet and looked inside that and then she got the shock of her life—it really *was* Lance Lerner!

Lance Lerner, a famous author that she had personally herself seen on the *Tonight Show* with Johnny *Carson* on her very own *television* set was lying naked and stretched out and handcuffed to the bed in the very next *room!*

All at once she felt horribly embarrassed. To have been talking to a famous naked person and not even *known* it! What must he *think* of her?

The question now was, what should she do? Well, perhaps she ought to unchain him, for one thing. Although, come to think of it, had he *asked* her to do that? He had not. He was probably trying to worm his way into her confidence before doing that, but never mind. Why do it if he hadn't even asked?

Wait till she told Thelma about this! Thelma wouldn't believe her, of course. Maybe she should go and get her Polaroid Swinger and take some snaps of him so she'd have the proof, just like when you caught a big fish. Would the pictures be proof enough?

"Hey," he called from the next room, "did you find the wallet yet?"

"Uh, yeah," she said, "I found it all right."

What was she going to do? Here was one of the best-known authors in the whole country, and he was naked and completely helpless, and she could do anything she wanted with him. Anything. *Even have sexual intercourse.* Not that she *wanted* to have sexual intercourse with him. Not that she wanted to have sexual intercourse with *anybody*. Not that she particularly *disliked* the idea of having sexual intercourse. Not that she at *all* disliked the idea of having sexual intercourse with a famous author. How many women did she know who had had sexual intercourse with a famous author? None, that's how many. Would she be too embarrassed to even suggest it to him? Hell's bells, why suggest it to him? He was hardly in a position to say anything about it, one way or the other.

She walked slowly back into the bedroom. Her breathing had become shallow and rapid. Her face felt hot.

"Well," he said. "Are you satisfied now?"

"So you're Lance Lerner," she said.

"Yes," he said. "And what's *your* name?"

"Gladys," she said. "Gladys Oliphant."

"Glad to meet you, Gladys," he said. "I wonder, now that we've been properly introduced, if I might ask you a favor?"

"What's that?" she said, but she was barely listening to him now, so excited was she becoming at the prospect of having sexual intercourse with a famous author.

"Could you unlock me?"

"Hmmmmmm?" she said, and idly began unzipping her pastel pink nylon gown.

"I said would you mind unlocking me? I think Stevie left the key on the living-room coffee table."

"Mmmmm," she said.

She took the pastel pink dressing gown off her shoulders and dropped it on the floor. Blushing furiously, she walked slowly toward the bed. He had apparently guessed what she was up to, because his eyes got very big and he stopped talking.

She stepped out of her fuzzy pink slippers and faced him in her pastel pink panties and her pink lace brassiere. She was starting to sweat heavily. It stood out in large beads all over her body.

"I hope," she said shyly, "that you don't mind too much what I'm about to do, Mr. Lerner. It's a real opportunity, you see, and I'd really kick myself later if I passed it up."

He didn't reply, but when she took off her brassiere and stepped out of her panties and sat down on the bed, caving in the mattress, she noticed that his sexual organ had become hard again, so he couldn't have been as disgusted as she feared he might be.

Carefully, carefully, carefully, she stepped across his famous skinny body. She squatted over him, grasped his rigid penis and then slowly, slowly, slowly, she settled herself on top of him, keeping most of her crushing weight on her hands and knees.

If Thelma didn't believe her, it almost didn't matter anymore. She, for one, knew it was true, and that would have to be enough.

31

Stevie chased the two black guys west on 57th Street, shouting at them to stop or she'd shoot, but they didn't even slow their pace.

She started to fire a warning shot over their heads, but that was dangerous because the bullet could ricochet and kill an innocent bystander. Instead she stopped, held her breath, made sure the coast was clear, took careful aim with both hands at the one she was closest to, and fired.

The shorter guy screamed and dropped immediately to the pavement. The taller one looked back briefly and kept on running. She took careful aim at him, but now there were pedestrians in her line of fire and, as expert a marksman as she was, she didn't want to risk it. She raced after the fleeing robber, passing the one on the ground, who she quickly noted was still alive but not in danger of escaping. She scooped up his automatic, and continued running.

The taller guy reached Seventh Avenue and turned north. She figured he was trying for the park. They raced up Seventh Avenue, across 58th Street. One more block and she would lose him. She was damned if she was going to lose him—Stevie Petrocelli always got her man!

The light turned red as he reached 59th Street. He plunged into the busy thoroughfare, narrowly missing a taxicab, which swerved and hit a gray stretch limousine. Stevie followed, running hard, her hands out in front of her on her snub-nosed .38, trying for one more shot in the clear, which was all she needed to bring him down. Brakes screamed and tires screeched and more cars collided in an effort to avoid hitting the tall black man and the short white woman who was chasing him with a gun.

The tall guy had made it across 59th Street and had sprung for the high brick retaining wall which separated him from the park. It was a bad leap, she realized immediately. She was amazed that any black man that tall and that young and with legs that long had missed clearing the top of that wall, but that is exactly what happened. The robber slammed hard into the wall and toppled back onto the ground.

He howled in pain, but as she dove at him, he suddenly turned and thrust what he was carrying right into her gut. The *Random House Dictionary* knocked the wind out of her and she collapsed on top of him.

They lay there together for several seconds, gasping for breath, like sated lovers. Her snub-nosed .38 was pointed directly at his face. Neither of them could speak for fully a minute. A small crowd was cautiously pressing forward as they heard her barely audible whisper:

"You have . . . the right . . . to remain . . . silent. . . ."

32

At numerous points during his rape, Lance thought he would either suffocate or be crushed to death.

The woman on top of him was the fattest woman he had ever seen undressed. True, she did have a pretty face, but if anyone had told him that he would ever end up having sex with anybody as gross as this, much less have her be his first woman other than his wife in almost eight years, he would have told them they were out of their minds.

Still.

Still, there was something decidedly exciting about having, for once in his life, nothing whatsoever to say about a sexual experience, no way at all to feel responsibility or guilt, no need ever to worry about technique or foreplay or have to answer for the consequences. It was oddly liberating.

He was grateful that she had had the decency to help support her weight on her elbows and knees and not rest it all on top of him, and it was amazing but true that his hardened phallus was able to penetrate all those folds of flesh and actually make contact with something slippery that felt like a vagina. The pressure inside his groin kept building up and building up and finally he heard himself cry out in release. She felt it too, and it seemed to push her over the brink because she too cried out, then shouted, then screamed and shuddered and then, forgetting all about her knees and elbows and human decency, she began sinking slowly onto him, like a ship slipping below the waves.

"I love you," she sobbed, "I love you."

"Then . . . please . . . ," he gasped, "don't . . . crush me . . ."

"Oh my God," she said, redistributing her massive weight, "I'm sorry, I'm *sorry!*"

"That's . . . all right," he gasped. "I think I'm . . . OK now."

They were both silent for several moments, bathed in sweat and breathing hard.

"It was wonderful for me," she said. "Was it wonderful for you too, Mr. Lerner?"

"Wonderful," he said. "Absolutely wonderful."

At that precise moment they heard a shriek behind them. Lance couldn't see past the mountain of flesh on top of him, but Gladys turned and gave a little cry of surprise, and then Lance could see her too.

Standing in the bedroom doorway, her face bruised and her clothing torn and filthy, was Stevie.

33

"Hi there, Miss Petrocelli," said Gladys with a fishy smile.

"What in the name of Christ are you *doing!*" shouted Stevie.

"I, uh, came up here to fix your shower," said Gladys, carefully getting off Lance and standing up. "I discovered Mr. Lerner here, and, uh, we got to talking and everything, and we, uh, kind of got, uh, carried away, I guess."

"Carried away? You got carried *away?*"

"Yeah," said Gladys, swiftly scooping her bra, panties and dressing gown off the floor, "one thing kind of led to another and—"

"Get out of my house, you fat whale!" shrieked Stevie. *"Get out of my house this instant or I will shoot you for trespassing!"*

"Just going, just going," mumbled Gladys apologetically, trying to get into her dressing gown as Stevie began shoving her toward the door with both hands. Gladys turned back toward Lance and gave him a little wave. "So long, Mr. Lerner, nice meeting you. Hope to see you again."

"Out!" screamed Stevie. *"Out!"*

Doors opened in the hallway to see fat Gladys, still half naked, being shoved violently out of Stevie's apartment.

Stevie slammed the front door so hard it almost came off its hinges. She turned on Lance.

"What the hell have you been *doing!*" she yelled at him.

"What have *I* been doing?" He was incredulous. "What do you *mean* what have I been doing? I've been being *raped,* that's what I have been doing!"

"You're my *date!*" she screamed. "The minute I leave the house I come back and find you fucking my super behind my *back?*"

"Hang on there now, Stevie, for Christ's sake," said Lance. "Calm down a minute, will you?"

"Calm *down?* You screw my superintendent and then you tell me to calm *down?* Get out of here! I never want to see you again! Get out of my house!"

"How the hell can I get out of your house—you've chained me to your goddamned bed!"

She came for him and he was sure she was going to break his jaw, but then she stopped herself and merely stood there, breathing hard.

"You can order me out of here if you like," said Lance. "All you have to do is unlock these cuffs and I'll be out of here like a flash. But I'd really like to point out that I had nothing to do with this. I was chained to the fucking bed. I had absolutely nothing to say about it. I had absolutely no responsibility in this matter whatsoever, I can guarantee that."

"Oh, you had absolutely nothing to do with it, is that right?"

"That's right, absolutely none. For the first time in my life I am absolutely blameless."

"Tell me you didn't enjoy it," she said.

"I didn't enjoy it," he said.

"Did you have a stiff prick?"

He thought for a moment, and went for honesty.

"I admit that it was stiff. I did not tell it what to be. It has a mind of its own."

"Did you have an orgasm?" she said.

"Did I have an orgasm?" he said.

"Yes. An orgasm. What's the matter, don't you know?"

He swallowed hard.

"I, uh, believe that I might have had one, yes."

113

"You aren't sure?"

"No no, I did, I know I did. I'm sure."

"But what—you didn't enjoy it?"

"Not . . . all that much, no."

"Not all that much," she muttered.

She wheeled into the living room, tore back into the bedroom with a key and began furiously unlocking the handcuffs. In her rage she was not able to manipulate the tiny locks, and as she missed each one she cursed. Finally they were all opened and Lance withdrew his somewhat battered wrists and ankles and rubbed them hard to get the blood flowing again.

"I'd like to talk this over calmly with you," he said, "but you seem very upset."

"You're goddamned *right* I'm upset!" she yelled.

"*I* should be the one who's upset," he said, "not *you*—do you know how long you were gone?"

"I was gone just long enough to shoot one perpetrator and tackle the other and collar them both and turn them over to another cop to be booked so I could rush home and find you fucking another *woman*, that's how long!"

She began sobbing uncontrollably and pushing him out of the bedroom.

"I can see why you're so upset," he said. "Perhaps we can talk this over when you're not so upset."

She yanked open the front door and started pushing him, naked, out into the hallway.

"Hey, just a minute!" he cried. "At least give me my clothes!"

With a hysterical cry of anguish, Stevie shoved him into the hall and slammed the door. Other doors on the landing opened briefly, then closed. Lance stood there, dazed, then pounded on Stevie's door.

"Hey, open up!" he shouted. "Give me my clothes!"

"Go to hell!" she cried.

He pounded again on her door.

"Stevie, please! Open up! I need my clothes!"

He pounded some more, but it was hopeless. He looked around wildly for help. Two other doors on the landing were opened just a crack. He advanced toward them, and they closed like clams. He stood outside one and then the other and beseeched the inhabitants for articles of clothing or at least a sheet, but he was shouting at deaf ears.

It wasn't fair. In rape cases involving women victims, even

the most male-chauvinist cops no longer accused the victim of enticing the rapist, or at least the situation was a lot better than it used to be. But now, when the rape victim was a man, here was a *woman* cop behaving even worse.

He started walking cautiously down the stairs, trying to figure out how he was going to get home without his clothing. It was just possible that if he waited long enough Stevie would calm down and he'd be able to go back up there and get his clothes. It was also possible that he might find Gladys's apartment and persuade *her* to lend him something to cover up with.

He crept slowly down the stairs. Several doors opened a crack as he passed by them. At least three of the elderly tenants telephoned the police. On the first floor he knocked on all the doors, figuring that Gladys had to be behind one of them, but nobody answered his knocking or his calling. It was possible that he could find something in the basement he could wear home.

Lance reached the basement door, opened it, turned on the overhead bulb and made his way down the filthy wooden steps. He wandered around the basement, past the furnace, and into the laundry room. There was a clothesline with a lot of somethings on it, but in the dim light it was hard to see what.

He crept closer. His eyes became accustomed to the gloom. What they were were nine pairs of panties, five brassieres, seven pairs of transparent pantyhose, and a pale blue half-slip. There was absolutely nothing else, either hanging up on the clothesline nor in the washers or driers, not even an old drop cloth or a laundry bag.

Was it preferable to go out on 57th Street naked or in ladies' lingerie? He didn't know. He thought it over. People would feel more threatened on 57th Street by a naked him than a transvestite him, he decided. He pulled the pastel blue half-slip off the clothesline and put it on. Then he carefully made his way back to the filthy wooden steps and climbed back up to the lobby. It was lucky it was warm out.

Just as he reached the lobby door, a patrol car pulled up in front of the apartment building and two cops got out and came into the vestibule. When they saw him standing there in the pale blue half-slip, they drew their guns.

34

As a matter of fact, the cops were damned decent about the whole thing after the first few minutes.

All right, so they had a little fun frisking him and asking him what he was doing in the slip and trying to figure out where he kept his ID. All right, so they carried on a little longer than they absolutely needed to when he explained that he had been raped by a fat lady and then thrown into the hallway without his clothes by a policewoman. But he finally piqued the cops' curiosity enough that they actually knocked on Stevie's door to check out his story, rather than taking him right back to the precinct in his slip for booking, and then it all got better.

Stevie finally let the cops into her apartment, she grudgingly corroborated Lance's story, and ultimately Lance got his clothes back. And, after he had assured the cops he wasn't going to press charges against the hefty super, they slapped him on the back and left the building. Stevie still refused to speak to him, so he went home.

The following day was to be his first session of group therapy. The prospect filled him with dread. He wondered how much he would have to tell these people. He realized that withholding anything at all, no matter how painful, would hurt nobody but him. He would have to tell them everything, then. Except, of course, about being raped by Gladys and being captured by the cops while wearing a slip. And maybe one or two other tiny, insignificant things like that.

35

He felt like the new kid in class. That particular one had not been among his top ten feelings when he was a lad. There were four people in the smallish conference room, seated around a low, circular, white Formica-topped table—four, that is, besides himself and Helen Olden.

"This is Lance," said Helen. "He was in private therapy with me several years ago. His marriage just broke up, so he's come back. I've suggested that he join our group."

He was truthfully surprised that he had come at all. He and Helen had discussed it at great length during their last private session. Helen had called the group a safe place to experiment with dangerous feelings like anger and fear and—the most dangerous feeling of them all—love.

She had explained that relationships in the group were a model for all your relationships in the outside world, that however you related to people Out There is how you were going to relate to people in the group. And people in the group, unlike your friends, would tell you when you were full of shit. Friends, she said, made an unspoken bargain with you: "I'll tolerate *your* shit if you tolerate *mine*." People in the group, she said, were forbidden to do that.

Lance thought it sounded interesting, but he didn't think it would help him get Cathy back. He agreed to come, partly to humor Helen, and partly because he thought he might be able to write about it sometime.

The members of the group sat on their canvas-and-wood director's chairs and waited anxiously to see what the new member was like and which of the hoary numbers in their respective bags of tricks it might be necessary to run on him in order to neutralize the threat of his unfamiliarity.

"Lance," said Helen, "is a successful freelance writer, and he can tell you more about himself a little later on. Right

117

now, though, I'd like each one of you to tell him your name—first name only, of course—and a little bit about yourself and what you hope to get out of the group. OK, who wants to be first? Jackie?"

Jackie, a short, stocky man with thin hair and a face that resembled the nose-glasses sold in novelty stores—thick horn-rimmed spectacles, large hooked nose, bushy moustache and furry eyebrows—raised his hand.

"OK, teacher, I'll go first," said Jackie. "My name is Jackie, I'm fifty-three years old, and I work in toilets."

"You're a plumber?" said Lance innocently.

Everybody chuckled. It had been a joke. Lance felt stupid and even more the outsider, a feeling he had worn throughout his boyhood like his older cousin's hand-me-down clothes.

"I'm what they call a stand-up comedian," said Jackie, "but I work mostly in toilets. God forbid I should get a decent room to work in, I'd probably have a heart attack altogether. That's another thing, heart attacks. I've had three mild ones so far, and the next one will probably do me in." Everybody groaned. "I'm the group's hypochondriac," said Jackie.

Arnold, a timid-looking man in a three-piece suit and round wire-rimmed glasses, turned to Lance. "The one thing we don't tolerate in here is anybody who comes on like a victim," he explained.

"Yeah?" said Jackie. "Look who's talking—Arnold, the biggest victim on the eastern seaboard."

"All right," said Helen, "you can save that for later, Jackie. Arnold, why don't you go next?"

"My name is Arnold," said Arnold. "I'm thirty-three years old, I'm a Certified Public Accountant, I'm married to a wonderful wife, I have two little daughters, I have just begun to write my first novel, and I manipulate people by pretending to be weak."

"Thank you, Arnold," said Helen. "Laura?"

Laura, an attractive but pale woman of about twenty-eight or twenty-nine with long straight hair, smiled nervously at Lance. It was reassuring to find that *they* were nervous too.

"My name is Laura," she said. "I'm thirty years old and . . . Well, actually, I'm only twenty-nine, but I look thirty, and I'll *be* thirty in just two months, so I just . . . Well, let's see. I have also started writing my first novel, but basically I'm an Avon Lady. That is, I sell Avon home-care products to suburban women in the greater metropolitan

118

area . . . I'm not married. Recently I discovered that I'm a . . ." Laura's voice trailed off.

"Yes, Laura?" said Helen. "Go on."

Laura blushed. Lance felt himself willing to fall in love with her. Group members, as Helen had emphasized, were forbidden to see one another outside of the group. It was not inconceivable that he might wait till either he or she had achieved total mental health and left the group before claiming her. Not inconceivable, and also not likely.

"Recently," said Laura, "I discovered I'm a lesbian. That is, recently, while demonstrating some Avon products to a client, a suburban housewife in Great Neck, I allowed myself to be seduced, and—"

"Seduced, Laura?" said Helen. "I thought we agreed that—"

"All right, I set it up," said Laura. "I mean, I *was* seduced, but I *did* set it up. Or anyway, that's how it seems to the group."

"You've decided you're a lesbian just because you allowed one housewife to seduce you?" said Lance. The notion of Laura being seduced by another woman was beginning to turn him on. He suspected that this was inappropriate behavior on his part.

Laura blushed even harder.

"Well," she said, "it was, uh, more than one housewife, actually."

"How many?" said Lance, trying to make his voice as clinical as possible.

"Uh, well, actually it was seven separate occasions," said Laura.

"I see," said Lance. "Well, I'm sorry but I just don't think being seduced by even *seven* housewives makes you a lesbian."

"Thank you," said Laura. "You know, Lance, I knew I was going to like you the minute you walked into the room today."

"Thank you," said Lance.

"I think you're very kind and very sensitive, and I find you enormously attractive physically."

"*Thank* you," said Lance.

"I should also warn you that I try to buy people's love with compliments," said Laura.

"All right," said Helen. "Roger, you go next."

119

Roger, a handsome, thickly muscled man in his late twenties, faced Lance, smiling artificially.

"My name is Roger," said Roger. "I'm twenty-eight years old, I'm a *cum laude* graduate of the University of Illinois, where I played first-string varsity football for all four years. Today I sell insurance, chiefly health and major-medical, and I . . . Well, I'm writing a novel too, but it's not going very well, and . . . Oh yes, about two years ago I had an absurd household accident which left me crippled and . . . Well, I still have to walk with a cane, and I can't make love to my wife except to . . . I'm impotent, and it seems to be a medical problem, so there's nothing that can be done about it."

"Bullshit," said Arnold. "Four doctors so far have told you there's no medical reason why you can't get an erection."

"OK," said Roger sheepishly, "maybe I exaggerated."

Lance felt vaguely cheated. Helen was famous for having a preponderance of celebrity patients, yet none of the people here was remotely glamorous or recognizable. Of course, he'd been given only their first names—it was possible that, had they told him their surnames as well, he would discover them to be celebrity comics, celebrity CPAs, celebrity insurance men and celebrity Avon Ladies.

"Lance," said Helen, "it's your turn."

"All right," said Lance, having the distinct sensation that he was on a TV panel show. "Well, as Helen said, I'm a freelance writer. I just turned forty. My wife left me about six weeks ago, and I'm pretty broken up about that. What else? Let's see, I have a book being published September 15th, and . . ."

"Why did your wife leave you, Lance?" said Arnold.

"Well," said Lance, "I guess she felt that she had needs that I couldn't satisfy or something. She's, uh, gotten somewhat involved with the women's movement of late and . . ."

"Aren't you leaving something out, Lance?" said Helen.

"Leaving something out?" said Lance. "Oh. Yeah. That. Well, about three weeks before my fortieth birthday, y'see, I sort of decided that Cathy—my wife—was having an affair with my best friend, Les. So, uh, I—"

"What made you think that?" said Jackie. "Was she coming home with Vitalis on her collar?"

The group members chuckled tolerantly.

"How did it make you feel?" said Laura.

"Horrible," said Lance. "But I decided that all I wanted

was to even the score. So I took her best friend, Margaret, to lunch, and I suggested that we go to bed, and that was pretty much my undoing."

"You went to bed with your wife's best friend and she found you out?"

"Sort of," said Lance. Then he saw Helen raise an eyebrow at him and elected to amplify. "OK, well, it was worse than that. See, I thought she invited me over to her place to make love, but what I didn't know was that she and my wife and my best friend were planning this big surprise party for me. So I, uh, took off my clothes, and when I opened the bedroom door, the lights came on and there was everybody yelling 'Surprise.'"

"I don't mean to make light of your suffering," said Laura, suppressing a smile, "but that *is* a fairly amusing picture you just painted."

Lance nodded.

"I guess so. Maybe it's still a little too recent for me to see the humor in it, I don't know. Anyway, all I really want to do is get Cathy back."

"Have you been dating other women since Cathy left you?" said Arnold.

"Not exactly dating," said Lance.

"Have you been getting *shtupped?*" said Jackie.

"I suppose you could call it that," said Lance.

"Tell us about it," said Roger. "If you think it will help, I mean."

"Well," said Lance, "first of all, I was . . . raped by the super in the building where this policewoman I know is living."

"The super was a man or a woman?" said Laura.

"A woman, a woman," said Lance.

"How could a woman overpower you to rape you?" said Laura.

"First of all, this woman happens to weigh around two hundred and fifty pounds," said Lance. "And, second of all, I happened to have been, uh, handcuffed to the policewoman's bed."

"You know something, boychick?" said Jackie. "I think I'm going to look forward to hearing your stories more than episodes on *As the World Turns.*"

36

On the third day following the publishing party where he met her, Claire Firestone phoned and invited Lance to dinner. It was to be in just eight days, on a Wednesday night at seven p.m., at her apartment on Park Avenue. Lance was tempted to ask what he should wear, but decided that was just a bit too naive a question.

"Should I bring a date?" he said.

"Oh no, I don't think so," she replied. "I'll find you a suitable dinner companion."

The night of the Firestone dinner party he began dressing an hour earlier than usual. He put on a dark blue suit, took it off, put on a pair of slacks and a sportcoat, took that off, and finally settled on a black velvet suit with a soft blue shirt and a solid black tie. He was tempted to put on his tux, but decided against it. He didn't know what you wore to impress a publisher who held novelists in low esteem, but a tux seemed to be trying just a wee bit hard.

Lance arrived at the elegant Park Avenue apartment shortly before seven p.m. He toyed with the notion of walking around the block a few times to be not quite so punctual, then said the hell with it. He gave his name to the doorman and was led into the lobby. The elevator man took him right up in an oak-paneled car with a richly upholstered leather bench in the back.

The elevator doors opened directly into the foyer of the Firestone's apartment. A maid in a black uniform ushered him into a living room that was at least fifty feet long, took his order of a glass of white wine, and left. He sat down on a long couch upholstered in gray suede.

No other guests were there yet. The Firestones were

probably still dressing. He knew he should have taken a few turns around the block.

Everything in the living room was done in various shades of gray. The carpet, the couches, the chairs, even the smoked mirrors which lined the walls and ceiling and made the room look like it was big enough to house a 747. Several low gray marble coffee tables attended the couches. On the coffee tables were dozens of tiny crystal vases filled with single white flowers and tiny glass cups filled with lit gray candles.

The maid reappeared and handed him his drink, then withdrew. He was in the midst of rehearsing his first non-business remarks to Firestone when Claire entered the room.

She looked fabulous. A gray silk blouse revealed the shape of her nipples, and gray silk slacks clung to her pelvis and thighs.

"Lance," she said. "How nice to see you."

"Nice to see you, too," he said, standing to greet her.

"I see you already have your drink," she said.

"Yes," he said.

The maid reappeared and looked at Claire questioningly.

"A kir royale, please, Elizabeth," she said.

"What's a kir royale?" said Lance.

"Champagne and cassis," she said.

"Ah," he said. "Sounds good."

The maid withdrew.

There was a moment of silence while Lance tried to think of something to talk about. He was distinctly ill at ease. His hostess seemed quite calm.

"Lovely evening out," he said at last.

"Is it?" she said.

"Yes," he said. "Warm, I mean, but perfect weather for this time of year."

"Mmmmm."

Christ, he thought, the woman is going to think I'm a fucking idiot.

"Have you been out?" he said after another pause. "Today, I mean?"

"No," she said. "Not today."

"Ah," he said, cursing himself for not having any small talk, for never in his life having had any small talk, drifting into a fast rehearsal of what he was going to say to Firestone about his book.

"Yesterday," she said.

"What?" he said, alarmed, having no idea what she was talking about.

"Yesterday," she said. "I went out yesterday. To the office."

"Oh. Yes. To the office. You, uh, work in an office, do you?"

"Yes," she said. "I have an office at the publishing house. I go in two or three days a week."

"Is that so?" he said. "How about that."

"Yes," she said. "I look at manuscripts that come in over the transom, so to speak. I'm sort of a glorified reader. It's not much of a job, really—Austin just gave it to me to keep me off the streets."

"Ah," said Lance.

The maid returned with a pinkish drink on a silver tray. Claire took it and nodded. The maid withdrew.

"So that's a kir royale," said Lance.

"Yes," she said. "Would you like to taste it?"

"Oh. Sure."

She held it out. He sipped it.

"Mmmmmm. Good," he said, handing it back, again at a loss for something to talk about.

She took a sip of her drink herself. The silence began to be oppressive, although Claire seemed to be bothered by it not at all.

Lance glanced at his watch.

"So," he said. "Who all is coming tonight?"

"Well," she said, "it's turned out smaller than planned."

"Oh?"

"Yes. One couple canceled because of illness, the other had a family emergency. It'll be just us, I'm afraid."

"Just us?" said Lance. "Just . . . you and me and . . . Mr. Firestone?"

"Just you and me," she said. "Austin was abruptly called to London this afternoon. There wasn't time to call you."

He was silent for about a minute. He stood up.

"I'm sorry," he said. "I'll come back another time."

"Not at all," she said. "Please stay."

"I do think I ought to go," he said.

"I'll be very offended if you go," she said.

Lance stood slightly off balance, torn between the momentum of continuing toward the door and coming back into the room. He didn't know what she wanted from him.

"Are you serious that nobody else is coming?" he said.

"Absolutely serious," she said.

He walked uncertainly back into the room.

"Tell me again what happened. One couple canceled because of illness, and the other had a what? A family emergency?"

"That's right."

"What kind of family emergency?" he said.

She smiled.

"What kind would you like?" she said.

"What?" he said.

"What kind would you like them to have had?" she said.

"I'm . . . not really following this," he said.

"I'm sorry," she said.

"What, uh, excuse did the couple actually give you?" he said after a short pause.

"Who?" she said. "The Benedicts?"

"Yes," he said. "The Benedicts."

"They didn't give any," she said.

"They didn't give *any?*" he said. "Then why aren't they coming?"

"I'm afraid I forgot to invite them," she said.

He looked rapidly around the room for he knew not what—a hidden TV camera or Allen Funt or something like that. Nothing and no one came to his rescue. He began perspiring freely.

"What about the other couple?" he said. "The ones who canceled because of illness. Did you forget to invite them too?"

She frowned, as though blaming her faulty memory.

"I'm afraid I did," she said.

"I see," he said.

"Good," she said. "What do you see?"

"I see that I'm in a little bit of trouble here, and I see that it could get a whole lot worse," he said. "Let me ask you something." ·

"Shoot."

"Was it never your intention to have anyone else to dinner tonight?"

"Never," she said.

"I see," he said. "Well, if you wanted to have dinner with me alone . . ." he looked about uncomfortably and lowered his voice, "then why didn't you simply tell me so?"

"Oh, I don't know. You might not have agreed to come. You might have been afraid that I'd make sexual advances to you and that you'd be placed in a compromising situation with the wife of the man who's publishing your book."

"Well," he said, continuing to perspire, "that possibility might have crossed my mind. Would that fear have been justified?"

"Mmmmmhmmmm," she said. She was obviously relishing his discomfort.

"Great," he said, retreating again toward the door. "Listen, Claire, it's been lovely, but I really have to leave now."

"Why?"

"Well, if I stayed I'd probably drink a whole lot of kir royales and then I might just decide that hopping into the sack with you was something other than professional suicide."

"Lance?" she called softly.

"Yes?"

"Are you rejecting me?"

"Well, that seems to be the idea, yes."

"Rejection is very aphrodisiac to me, Lance."

"Swell. Listen," he said *sotto voce*, "you mean to tell me you would actually hump another man in the apartment you share with your husband?"

"I haven't yet," she said, "but there's a first time for everything."

"What about the servants?" he whispered. "Aren't you afraid they'd notice?"

"I don't see how they could *help* but notice," she said.

"Aren't you afraid they'd talk?"

"Not at all," she said. "I'm the one who hires them, I'm the one who pays them, and I'm the one who fires them. Besides, I've got a lot more on *them* than they've got on *me.*"

"Jesus," he said, "I'll just bet you have. Well, look, don't think it hasn't been stimulating."

He managed to reach the door before she spoke again.

"Lance," she said, "please don't go. I promise to be good."

He turned around. She looked contrite—chin lowered, lips pursed. Like a little girl.

"I promise I won't tease you anymore," she said.

"Was that what it was, teasing?"

"Yes."

"Why do you do that?" he said.

She shrugged.

"I don't know. Out of insecurity, I guess. I only do it with men I don't know."

"Insecurity?" he said. "Are you insecure with me?"

"A little."

"How come?"

"I don't know. Overly impressed by authors, maybe. Are you staying for dinner, then?"

"Can I really trust you?"

"Nope."

They both laughed. He went back inside.

Dinner was surprisingly nice. They ate facing each other across a glass table with the same small crystal vases with single flowers in them and with the same candles in little cups. The maid brought them an endless array of perfectly seasoned, wonderfully tasty things, most of which he didn't recognize. They drank a lot of wine.

She told him about being gawky and too tall and growing up with rich parents and horses in Virginia and then she confessed it was a lie. She had never been gawky, her parents weren't rich, there weren't any horses, and she had never been to Virginia. She had been beautiful always, with perfect bones since the age of ten, had modeled from twelve to twenty-two and fought off the boys since before the onset of puberty.

Austin had seen her picture in *Vogue* and married her within six months of meeting her when she was twenty-two. He at the time was forty-four and had already made his first few millions in the mail-order business before he switched to books—first textbooks, then trade books. He was now sixty-two, she said. He swam a mile a day wherever he was, had had three face lifts and looked sensational. She supposed he fooled around with other women, but she didn't care. He was an excellent provider, a strong protector when she needed strength, a considerate lover, and in the eighteen years they had lived together, she said, he had never bored her.

Had she had affairs while married to this seemingly model husband? She admitted that she had. Not many, but a few. But why? She didn't know. Possibly because she came in contact with a great many stimulating men and had a strong curiosity about them sexually and a strong need to control them through sex. Possibly she only did it for the excitement.

She needed excitement in her life, she said, and it was getting increasingly hard to come by. She already owned everything she'd ever dreamed of owning: a huge Park Avenue apartment, a good-size summer home in East Hampton, an apartment in London, a winter home in Acapulco, a chauffeured limousine, two sports cars, a yacht, a private plane, a staff of servants. There hadn't been any children, perhaps because both of them had been self-centered, ambitious, and vain. There wasn't much to look forward to now, except old age and losing what she already had. If she took an occasional lover, she said, it was her own affair, so to speak. What she and Austin did with their own bodies on their own time was their own business.

She asked him about his separation and he told her. She didn't laugh as he thought she might. And she didn't flirt with him again. Except when he was leaving.

When he was leaving she impulsively slid her arms around his neck, kissing him sweetly on the mouth, and swiftly ran her tongue over his lips.

"I thought you promised to be good," he said, beginning to get excited in spite of himself.

"The promise only applied to dinner," she said. "Dinner's over. All bets are off."

She kissed him again and undulated her body against his. He pulled away, but not before she'd noticed his hardness.

"Tsk, tsk," she said, frowning with mock disapproval.

"I think we should just be friends," he said.

"I have enough friends already," she said. "I think we should be lovers."

She grabbed him and kissed him again.

"What would your husband do if he walked in and found us like this?" he whispered.

She thought about this for a moment.

"He would probably tear your head right off your shoulders," she said.

It took him two minutes flat to make it out the door, down the elevator, and out onto the street.

37

"Yeah?" said Lance, picking up the phone.

"May I speak to Lance Lerner, please?" said a male voice with a coarse Bronx accent.

"This is he," said Lance.

"Mr. Lerner," said the voice, "this is Julius Blatt? I'm a public defender down at the Supreme Court in Manhattan?"

The caller sounded as if he wasn't sure of these facts and was checking them out with Lance.

"What can I do for you, Mr. Blatt?" said Lance.

"I have these two clients," said Blatt. "Ernest H. Roosevelt and Irving 'Goose' Washington? Their names ring a bell with you at all?"

"Roosevelt and Washington," said Lance. "Nope. Afraid not."

"They say they know you," said Blatt.

"They black kids?" said Lance.

"Yeah. They're being held for armed robbery—of the B. Dalton bookstore on Fifth Avenue. They're both writers, and one of them, Roosevelt, says he's a student of yours or something."

"A student?" said Lance. "I haven't had any students in years, Mr. Blatt."

"Well, he claims he's had some correspondence with you? Says he asked you for advice on writing, and you were generous with him and gave him lots of pointers? You sure that doesn't ring any bells?"

"I'm afraid not," said Lance. "I mean it's very likely I answered a letter he wrote me and gave him some advice. I do that quite a lot. But I can't truthfully say I remember him."

"Yeah," said Blatt. "Well, what we were hoping was that maybe you'd come down and be a character witness for him.

129

Tell the court something about his writing, that kind of thing, you know?"

"You want me to be a character witness for a guy who robbed a B. Dalton bookstore who I never even met and can't recall exchanging letters with?" said Lance.

"You willing to do it or not?" said Blatt.

"Not," said Lance. "I'm sorry, Blatt, but it's a ridiculous request."

"OK, OK," said Blatt. "No problem. I was just asking. You have to hit all the angles on this kind of a thing. Tell me this. If we go to trial soon, would you be willing to do a human interest piece on them for the *Daily News?*"

Lance sighed.

"I don't do that kind of thing, Blatt," he said. "I mostly write novels, you know? Why don't you get somebody like a reporter at the *Daily News* to do that for you?"

"OK, OK," said Blatt. "No problem. I was just asking. As I say, you got to hit all the angles on a thing like this. Tell me this. If we could manage to start up a grass roots movement to get these boys some national publicity, would you be willing to help us out?"

"What do you mean, help you out?" said Lance.

"I don't know yet," said Blatt. "I mean if I could make them a kind of cause célèbre, you know? Like the broad that killed the guard who raped her in the slammer, you know? Or like the Chicago Seven, you know?"

"What do you mean," said Lance, "something like 'Free the Dalton Two'? That kind of thing?"

"'Free the Dalton Two' . . ." said Blatt. "Hey, that's not too bad, you know?"

"I was kidding," said Lance. "That was not a serious suggestion."

"Why not?" said Blatt. "I kinda like it, you know? 'Free the Dalton Two.' It's kinda catchy, you know?"

"Do me a favor, Blatt."

"Sure."

"Don't use it, OK?"

"Why not? It's a great slogan."

"Just do me a favor and don't use it, OK?"

"OK, OK," said Blatt. "No problem, Mr. Lerner, no problem. But thanks."

38

The telephone rang, jarring him out of a complex and exhausting dream about moving and misplacing things, and large empty houses with windows thrown open to an impending storm and dry leaves scudding across bare living-room floors. He picked up his watch and tried to focus on the dial as the phone continued to ring. It was ten-thirty a.m., a not unreasonable hour for people to call. He picked up the phone.

"Yeah?" he said.

"Good morning, darling," she said.

"Who is this?" he said.

"Claire. How many people do you know that call you darling?"

"My mother and many gay gentlemen I know. How are you, Claire?"

"I'm wonderful. What are you doing right now?"

"Right now?" he said. "Right now I'm talking to you on the phone. I'm still in bed."

"Mmmmmmmmmmm," she said. "Why don't you put on your clothes, hop in a cab, and come over here to play?"

"No thanks," he said. "I'd rather not."

"Do you know what I'm wearing?" she said.

"How could I possibly know what you're wearing?" he said.

"I am wearing nothing," she said. "I'm all alone in a big scary bed and I want you to come over and play with me."

"I don't think so, Claire," he said. "But thanks for the offer."

"Maybe some other time?" she said.

"Yeah," he said. "Maybe so."

He hung up and had an intense fantasy about going over to the Firestone apartment and climbing into bed with Claire, as

131

the maid served them endless kir royales. Then he got up, showered, shaved, dressed, and went through the morning mail.

There were three letters addressed to neighbors a few doors east of him, two letters addressed to somebody three blocks down, and one addressed to him correctly that had been stamped ADDRESSEE UNKNOWN, RETURN TO SENDER, which had apparently been sent back and remailed and managed to get to him despite Postal Service perversity. There was also the front half of a huge envelope which had been savagely separated from the rest of itself and from whatever it might have contained and then been crumpled up and stamped on repeatedly. He wondered if such things happened to other people as well, or if the Postal Service just had a personal vendetta against *him*.

Of the nineteen letters correctly addressed to him, five were charitable solicitations bearing photographs of grotesquely disfigured adults, children and animals; three were offerings to buy mutant grapefruit, stunted Japanese miniature trees, and foot-long penis extenders; three were entreaties to write his congressmen on behalf of whales, baby seals, rabbits being used to test cosmetics, and refugees from a country he had never even heard the name of before; two were utility bills with elaborate instructions on how to decipher the new computerized format and no explanation of why the previous three computerized formats had fallen into disfavor; one was a cheery letter from Con Edison explaining that its campaign to persuade customers to save energy had been too successful and that Con Ed had therefore applied for and won another huge rate hike to make up for lost revenues; and four were aggressive personal entreaties to claim three million dollars' worth of prizes he had already won which were waiting for him in a warehouse somewhere, feeling rejected. Lance marveled at how computers had managed to type into every other line of all five lengthy letters either his name or his address or his shirt size.

The single personal letter truly meant for him was addressed in a vaguely familiar handwriting. He tore open the envelope and took out a message scrawled hastily on lined notepaper:

Dear Mr. Lerner:

I'm sorry about the photographs. If we hadn't been high we never would have sent them. It hurt me that you hung up on me but I guess I deserved it. I really respect your writing and would someday like to discuss with you the various career opportunities open to young women in the area of journalism. I promise not to act like some dumb sex-crazed groupie.

If you could spare a few minutes to see me, please call.

Sincerely yours,
Dorothy Chu

Dorothy Chu, the Chinese girl in the Polaroids! He searched the newest note for a phone number, but, like the last one, there wasn't any. He wondered if it was worth going down to Chinatown and trying to find her.

The doorbell rang. He supposed it was a messenger. He buzzed, heard the door open downstairs, then close, and footsteps come slowly upstairs. He went to the stairwell and peered down, and was totally unprepared to see Claire, in a light tan raincoat.

"Claire. I thought you were in bed."

"There didn't seem to be any point remaining there all alone," she said. "I hope I'm not interrupting anything."

"Well, frankly," he said, "I have a hell of a lot of desk work, and then I have to go out and do some errands."

She pushed him back into the apartment.

"I can't stay long," she said. "But I wanted to see you and tell you I'm sorry for last night."

"Sorry?" he said. "You didn't do anything to be sorry for."

"That's the problem," she said. "May I take off my coat?"

"Well, sure, but . . ."

She unbuttoned her coat and took it off. Except for a pair of T-strap heels, she was totally naked.

He felt suddenly dizzy and had to steady himself against the doorjamb. Her body was sensational. Small firm breasts of a twenty-five-year-old, flat stomach, small blond pubic thatch, legs that went from floor to ceiling.

"So," she said, "what do you think? Not too bad for an old lady of forty, eh?"

"Not . . . too bad, no," he said. "Look, Claire, I really don't think you should stay, I really don't."

"Now listen, Lance," she said evenly. "I am getting tired of being rejected. And so I am giving you a choice."

"Yes?"

"Either we go to bed right now, and I guarantee that Austin will never find out, or else I will go right home and call him up and tell him that you attacked me."

She was not smiling. He had no reason to believe she might be kidding.

"Well," she said, "which is it going to be?"

He sighed.

"All right, Claire," he said, "you win."

39

Lance led Claire into the bedroom. She immediately lay down on the bed, propped her head up with two pillows, and watched him with great interest as he took off his clothes.

"I love bodies like yours," she said. "Long muscles, and not an ounce of fat. That's one of the reasons I've been so persistent."

"Good," he said. He took off his jockey shorts and climbed wearily into bed.

"I've seen more enthusiasm from people going in to have root canal," she said.

"It's just that I'm used to picking my bed partners and the circumstances of bedding them myself," he said, aware that this was not an accurate description of recent experience.

"Well," she said, "then this will be a nice change for you."

He lay down beside her and began to stroke her face and neck and shoulders.

"Are you adept at cunnilingus?" she said. "I usually like to start with that."

"Veddy good, madam," he said, mimicking an obsequious waiter. "And are there any special instructions for the entrée?"

She chuckled and gently pushed his face toward her mons veneris.

He was furious with her, so furious he felt his erection wither. He feared his anger would make him impotent. His fears were well-founded, as are all fears of impotence, stage

134

fright, and other self-fulfilling prophecies. He went to work on her pudenda with tongue and lips and teeth and fingers and a vengeance that appeared to startle her.

"Don't be upset if I don't make it," she said after a while. "I hardly ever do."

He stopped what he was doing and regarded her coolly across a smooth landscape of belly and chest.

"I don't give a good goddamn if you make it or not," he said. "I happen to like eating pussy, and whether you achieve an orgasm or not doesn't affect my pleasure one bit."

Nobody had ever reacted that way to this statement, he sensed. She had doubtlessly used her difficulty in achieving orgasm as a punitive and emasculating weapon against her husband and lovers, even at the expense of her own pleasure. Being told that it was of no concern to Lance whether she came or not removed the point of her controlling edict and must have freed her to consider whether or not she was willing to go on denying herself pleasure, because, shortly after he'd made his statement, she began to moan with pleasure.

Skillfully escalating her excitement onto higher and higher plateaus, Lance was eventually able to push her over the threshold into a deep and powerful release that left her sobbing with ambivalent gratitude. He regained his potency and injected himself into her. She dug her nails and her teeth into his flesh, but it was she, not he, who shouted. Lance hung on for dear life, trying to contain his orgasm. The pressure in his groin built up and up until he feared he would explode, and then he did, and they finished together, with her clasping his body to hers so hard he thought he'd shatter.

He lay on top of her as both of them gasped for breath. He felt spent and drained and sucked dry of every drop of fluid in his body—sperm, sweat, blood and spit. He felt he'd probably never have the strength to move again.

"How was it?" he said when he could find the strength to speak.

"Why, weren't you there?"

"I mean," he said, "How was it for *you?*"

"Nice," she said.

"Just nice?"

"Very nice," she said.

"Nicer than with Austin?"

She made a cry and slapped her forehead.

"Why do men always have to know if they were the best lay you ever had?" she asked. "Why can't you just be satisfied that it was very nice?"

That night he dreamed he was standing in a large hotel room that bore some resemblance to Claire's apartment and some to his own, although it wasn't an apartment and it wasn't in New York. There was no furniture in the room, not even a bed, but there was a phone and it rang. He answered it and was told by the operator that an unidentified person had called to say he would make an attempt on Lance's life sometime within the next hour.

A policeman happened to be in the room and told Lance not to worry, that he'd see to it that all exits would be covered and that no harm could befall him. Then, somehow, Claire—or was it Cathy?—was in his arms. She was frightened and he was reassuring her. They were on what appeared to be a little balcony adjoining the hotel room, and as he hugged her and reassured her he noticed that the door to the next room had slowly opened and the shadow of a large man had fallen diagonally across the floor. He knew it was the policeman and wasn't alarmed, but when he looked up he saw to his horror that it wasn't the policeman at all, it was a gorilla about eight feet tall.

The gorilla appeared to be in something of a drug-induced stupor, and it also appeared to be in flames. Lance knew, in the way that we know things in dreams, that the gorilla was wealthy, as gorillas went. Terrified, but figuring that a good offense is the best defense, and recalling from childhood that you must never show an animal your fear, Lance took a step toward the gorilla and began a low, bestial growl in his throat.

He awoke from the dream, thrashing wildly about in his bed, and growling so loudly that he was hoarse for several hours after he got up. He didn't know what the dream could have meant. He suspected he was in more trouble than he had thought. He felt that Helen would be able to explain the dream to him and, perhaps, help prevent its recurrence.

40

"Well, I talked to Lerner," said the short man in the modishly cut three-piece suit to the two depressed-looking black youths in the filthy green visiting room.

"What he say?" said Ernest H. Roosevelt.

"Well," said Julius Blatt, "he may not be able to see his way clear to testify for you in court as a character witness, but he did suggest something that I think is a hell of an idea. He suggested—"

"He ain't going to testify for me?" said Ernest. "Why not?"

"Well, I don't know exactly," said Blatt, "but he did offer to start a grass roots movement to get you some publicity and raise money to get you guys out of here."

"*Publicity?*" said Goose. "What the fuck we need with *publicity?*"

"Just a minute, bro'," said Ernest. "Tell me what the man suggest."

"Well," said Blatt, "he tried to sell me on the idea of starting this huge publicity campaign to get into the media with. He wants the slogan to be 'Free the Dalton Two.' I said I didn't know, I'd try it out on you before I let him go ahead with anything."

"'Free the Dalton *Two*'?" said Goose. "What we need with *that?*"

"'Free the Dalton Two,'" said Ernest slowly and carefully. It sounded OK. It sounded classy. It sounded like he and Goose could become some kind of something in the media with that. It sounded like maybe it could help him sell his novel.

"Tell the man yes," said Ernest. "Tell him he got my permission to put it in the works."

"You got it, my man," said Blatt, and slapped Ernest's surprised palm.

41

"Who is the gorilla in your dream?" she asked.

"I don't know," he said. "I didn't get too close to him, but from the little I saw I don't think it was a well-known one."

Helen gave him a perfunctory smile.

"Whom do you think the gorilla *represents?*" she said.

"I really don't know," he said. "I was hoping that perhaps *you* might."

She gave him one of her long-suffering looks.

"OK," he said, "maybe this is something. In the dream I had the impression that the gorilla was sort of well-to-do. A wealthy gorilla. Also he was kind of on drugs, I think. And he was in flames, although he didn't seem to be in any pain that I could see."

"A wealthy gorilla," she said. "On drugs and in flames."

"Yeah," he said.

"What does that image bring to mind?" she said.

"I don't know," he said.

"Come on, Lance. A wealthy gorilla—*stoned* and on *fire?*"

"I don't know," he said. "I sense that it must mean something very obvious, but I just can't see it. I mean I know that the subconscious mind is into a lot of symbolism and puns, but I just can't see it."

"Lance, listen to me. The gorilla is on *fire* and *stoned*. What do these two words mean to you, Lance—*fire* and *stone?*"

"I'm sorry," he said, "I'm sure it's really obvious to you, but I just can't see it."

"Are you deliberately trying to torture me?" she said.

42

As a reward for bringing her to orgasm, Claire Firestone staged a huge weekend dinner party in her East Hampton house, at which Lance was, if not the guest of honor, at least the guest she invited first.

A minor theater critic named Shipley and his wife unfortunately had been planning their own dinner party in East Hampton on that very evening for the past three weeks. The moment the Firestone party was announced, Shipley guests began phoning in cancelations due to illness at a rate that caused Ada Shipley to wonder whether Legionnaire's Disease hadn't suddenly flared up on eastern Long Island.

Truman Capote had already accepted the Firestones' invitation, as had Woody Allen, George Plimpton, Alan King, and, as a special treat, Firestone was flying Marlon Brando in by private plane.

A middle-aged literary agent named Arthur Black had a case of social frenzy so great that the very notion of attending a "B" party while in the same community an "A" party was going on without him was enough to send him into cardiac arrest. Although he had managed to wangle an invitation to the Firestones', he was nevertheless unable to come up with an acceptable excuse for canceling his invitation to the Shipleys'. On the night of the parties, Black was reduced to making his *au pair* girl telephone Ada Shipley to say that the Blacks would not be able to attend because they had a flat tire. Ada Shipley, who already knew that the Blacks had got themselves invited to the Firestones', offered the use of the Shipleys' Honda to transport the Blacks to the Firestones'.

A homosexual movie critic from the *New York Daily News* named Ralph Raitt, whose elderly mother lay dying of cirrhosis, had already canceled his invitation to the Shipleys' to be in the intensive-care ward with Mom. But when he received his invitation to the Firestones' he noted, to his mortification, that he was actually beginning to root for the old lady either to get dramatically better immediately or else die in time for him to hot-foot it out to the Firestones'. After all, he reasoned, the old gal was already in a coma and was dying anyway—what did it matter to *her* when she went?

As luck would have it, Raitt's Mom's EEG went flat only six hours before dinner time on the appointed day. Raitt did about twenty minutes of heavy soul-searching, arranged with a funeral home for a speedy cremation, and stood up for the entire three-and-a-half-hour ride out to the Hamptons on the Long Island Railroad.

Raitt's social frenzy was in a league with Black's, but it was nothing new. For twelve years a rich publisher named Corman had held an annual Memorial Day party in his East Hampton house. It was one of the most prestigious parties of the year, but Corman had tired of it, and this year he'd simply decided not to have it. Most of the guests who'd been yearly invitees feared that the party was still going on, and that they had simply been dropped from the "A" list due to lack of recent professional achievement or the unwitting commission of some small social awkwardness. Ralph Raitt was the only one of these who, when asked if he'd been invited to the Corman party this year, actually went out on a limb and said yes.

Lance had not been anxious to face his little house in the East Hampton woods in the weeks since the separation. He called Cathy and asked if she was up for going out there with him now that the weather had turned hot—they never went out between November and June, and he'd had no desire to stay there without her.

Cathy declined his invitation. He said they could even have separate bedrooms if that would put less pressure on her, but the answer was still no. He was momentarily despondent, but determined not to let it throw him. He decided he could hazard a short weekend in the Cathyless cottage so long as he wouldn't have to do it alone.

He telephoned Stevie to invite her out for the weekend of the Firestone party, and although she hung up on him the first three times he called, he was finally able to keep her on the line long enough to tender the weekend invitation through the stratagem of screaming out: "MARLON BRANDO WILL BE THERE!"

When she heard why Lance was calling her, Stevie speedily forgave him for being raped by her hefty super. She got another cop to trade her two night tours, and she accepted Lance's invitation.

The Firestones' East Hampton house was a cavernous old three-story affair on the Atlantic Ocean. It featured a half-timbered front, a double-height, exposed-beam ceiling, a profusion of little leaded-glass windows, and a swimming pool with a cement bar and bar stools imbedded in the bottom at the shallow end.

Lance drove up to the Firestones' with Stevie in his rotting old Porsche convertible and allowed an off-duty East Hampton cop to direct them to a parking space. Lance took a deep breath of sea air as they got out of the car and wondered why he had allowed his dread of being without Cathy in their little house to keep him in New York.

They entered the Firestone house, which was already half-filled with people, and Stevie began recognizing celebrities and throwing their names at Lance so swiftly it reminded him of the old Lucky Strike tobacco auction commercial.

"There's Gay Talese," said Stevie, "and his wife, Nan. There's Frank Perry and his wife, Barbara Goldsmith. Oh my God, there's Hal and Judy Prince, Steve Sondheim, Jimmy Kirkwood, Sidney Lumet, David and Leslie Newman, and George Plimpton and his wife, Freddie."

"C'mon," said Lance, "I want to get a drink."

"Oh, Jesus," said Stevie as they passed the piano, "it's Woody Allen, Marshall Brickman, Buck Henry, and Paul Simon."

Lance noted that several of the guests were sporting painful sunburns. Interesting, he mused, how we emulate the skin pigment of the least successful ethnic groups in the society.

Claire spotted Lance and drifted over. She looked as sensational as ever, in a simple white jersey dress that clung to her body as though it had a self-adhesive lining. He could see not only her nipples but her areolas in sharp relief against the material.

"Claire Firestone," said Lance, "I'd like you to meet Stevie Petrocelli. Stevie, Claire."

Stevie tore her eyes away from Woody, Marshall, Buck and

141

Paul just long enough to size up her hostess, who was doing the same to her.

"Pleased to meet you, sweetheart," said Stevie to Claire, who raised one eyebrow.

"Lance tells me you're a policewoman," said Claire, trying to home in on her target. "That must be exciting work."

Stevie shrugged.

"It's a living," she said, her eyes professionally working the room. "Did Marlon arrive yet?"

"Oh, then you *know* him?" said Claire with a slightly bemused smile.

"I had occasion to spend a little time with Bud, as we call him, a couple of years ago," said Stevie. "Lucy Saroyan introduced us—that's Bill's daughter, you know."

"I know," said Claire sweetly. "I think we must have had to meet *all* of Marlon's friends by now."

"Didn't you just love little Wally Cox?" said Stevie. "He was the cutest thing. Bud was really destroyed by his death."

Claire glanced swiftly at Lance and rolled her eyes ceiling-ward.

"I'll bring *Bud* by as soon as he arrives," said Claire to Stevie, moving on. "I know you two will have a lot of catching up to do."

"Seems friendly enough," said Stevie, watching Claire greet guests. "Although she's going to need paramedical assistance getting out of that dress."

They pushed their way to the bar, as Stevie continued her recitation of recognized faces.

"There's Gilda Radner," she said, "Danny Aykroyd, John Belushi, Lorne Michaels, Jean Doumanian, Mike Nichols, Patrick and Cynthia O'Neal, and there's Jack Rollins, Woody's manager."

The bartender, a black with a missing thumb and an air of snobbism that endeared him to a number of employers guilty about their wealth and looking for punitive proxies, icily informed Lance that kir royales were too much *trouble* in a party of this size. Lance accepted white wine as a substitute. But Stevie, who hadn't even wanted a kir royale, took the bartender's remark as a personal insult and speculated aloud how far she thought she might be able to navigate the bottle of kir up the bartender's rectum.

Stevie's observation caused somebody behind them to explode with laughter. They turned around to see a man about six foot five, with close-cropped white hair fading to black at the sideburns. The man's face looked as though it had been born with a perfect tan that had never peeled nor faded in sixty-two years. He had bushy black eyebrows and cold blue eyes, and although Lance had never met him nor even seen his picture he knew the man was Austin Firestone.

"Don't you know you're speaking to a member of a disenfranchised ethnic group?" said Firestone to Stevie with a gigantic twinkle in his eye.

"What, you mean they stopped giving out franchises to thumbless bartenders?" said Stevie.

Firestone chuckled and introduced himself. Lance, balancing resentment about the canceled tour and guilt about Claire, nonetheless found himself instinctively drawn to the tall tycoon.

"Say," said Firestone, focusing in on Lance, "aren't you the author of a book we're publishing next month?"

"That's me," said Lance, flattered that Firestone had recognized his name, but irritated that he obviously didn't remember the title of his book.

"Uh . . . *Carousing*, isn't it?" said Firestone.

"Close," said Lance, "but no cigar. It's *Gallivanting*."

Firestone snapped his fingers.

"*Gallivanting*," he said. "Damned fine book, as I recall."

"Really?" said Lance. "Then why the hell aren't you going to promote or advertise it?"

Stevie gave Lance an interested look.

"What do you mean?" said Firestone. "I thought we were."

"You call interviews on FM radio and in the Moonie newspaper a promotion campaign?" said Lance, aware that he was coming on too strong, but not knowing how to stop.

"Is that all we're doing?" asked Firestone. "What's the budget?"

"Five thousand," said Lance.

Firestone was momentarily puzzled, then he snapped his fingers again.

"*Moola*," he said.

"Pardon me?" said Lance.

"Our lead title next month—*Moola*. It's by Andrew Goodbody, the Wall Street Gnome. It's going to sell about two million copies in hardcover."

"That's a self-fulfilling prophecy if I ever heard one," said Lance. "But what does it have to do with me?"

"Look, Lerner," said Firestone, "I'm a good businessman.

My people tell me *Moola's* going to go through the roof, so we're really doing a media blitz on it. If they thought *Carousing* was going to go through the roof, we'd be blitzing that too."

"*Gallivanting*," said Lance, "not *Carousing*. Look, you promote *Moola* like a bestseller, it'll *be* a bestseller. You don't promote *Gallivanting*, it'll go straight into the toilet all right, just like your people think—not because it's a dog, but because nobody will have even heard it was on sale. You call yourself a good businessman? Why publish *Gallivanting* at all? You're just throwing away the cost of printing and binding."

Firestone took a long reflective swallow of his drink. His eyes never left Lance's face.

"What would you consider a fair test of whether or not your book had legs?" he said at last.

"Send me out on tour as they promised me when I signed the contract," said Lance. "I'm a great promoter. See whether sales improve enough in the cities I do interviews in to warrant putting more money into the promotion budget."

"How many cities would you consider a fair test?" said Firestone.

"Ten," said Lance, then wondered if that was too high or too low.

Firestone took another long pull on his drink.

"Let me think about it," he said. "I'll tell you before the end of the evening."

Just then there was a commotion and it looked as if everyone was suddenly being sucked out of the room by a giant vacuum cleaner.

"Well," said Firestone, "it looks to me like Brando's arrived."

43

There he stood, Marlon Brando. The Marlon Brando of *On the Waterfront* and *The Wild One* and *The Men* and *Viva Zapata!* and *Julius Caesar* and *The Young Lions* and *A Streetcar Named Desire,* but mostly the Marlon Brando of *On the Waterfront.* The Marlon Brando of "Oh, Chollie, I coulda been *somebody,* I coulda been uh con*ten*duh."

Lance had seen Brando over a dozen times in *On the Waterfront* alone, and now here he was, a quarter of a century later, standing in the living room of a woman whom Lance had fornicated with, standing not six feet away. Never mind that so many years had passed and that Marlon had swallowed the Goodyear blimp. He was still Marlon, and the fifty or so people who pressed in on him, some to introduce themselves, some merely to shake his hand or stand there looking at him and just smile foolishly—even those who were celebrities themselves—were quite aware of it.

Through the folds of fatness, the old Marlon smiled back at them over the years, that same wonderful crooked little smile that had made them all fall in love with him when he was beautiful, and the smile had not changed.

To Lance's chagrin, Stevie pressed forward, caught Brando's eye and called out, "Howya doin', Bud?"

To Lance's utter astonishment, Brando said softly, "Howya doin', Stevie?" You could have knocked Lance over with a goddamn feather . . .

Celebrities and noncelebrities alike swirled around Brando like schools of fish around a whale. Brando nodded, smiled, and every now and then murmured something in the famous voice. After a while Lance got tired of the spectacle. Also he had to pee. He made his way to the bathroom.

Others had the same idea. There were two people ahead of him in line, a middle-aged man and a woman of forty. A

145

beautiful young woman strolled up and joined the line. The woman and Lance smiled briefly at each other, acknowledging their mutual need to eliminate. He toyed with the notion of giving her his place in line and decided not to—gallantry seemed extraneous in the crapper.

When it was finally his turn to go into the bathroom he was surprised and repelled to find turds in the toilet bowl. He flushed, but they did not go down. He urinated, gave the mechanism a while to rest itself, then flushed again. They spun merrily in the whirlpool, they teased the opening of the drain, but they didn't enter.

Lance was certain that if he left now, the beautiful young woman in back of him would think the turds were his. Although he would probably never see her again, he didn't want her to remember him as somebody who left turds in toilet bowls. He waited a couple more minutes, then flushed again. Again the turds tickled the drain opening, even poking a timid snoot inside it, but then withdrew.

There was a knock at the door.

"Be right out," called Lance.

The hell with it, he thought. He put the lid down on the toilet and was about to open the door. He went back to the sink, turned on the water, then turned it off again. Bad enough to have her think he was a person who left toilets unflushed, he didn't wish to also leave the impression he didn't wash up afterwards.

Lance opened up the bathroom door. The beautiful young woman seemed irritated at how long he had taken. He flashed her a tentative smile. She pushed past him into the bathroom, began to close the door.

"Uh, listen . . ." he began.

She turned back toward him.

"Yes?" she said, her irritation now quite apparent.

"They aren't mine," he blurted.

"What?" she said.

His face broke out in prickly sweat.

"Never mind," he said, and scurried away in confusion.

He had half a dozen brief conversations with people he knew, and resented the fact that he frequently found their eyes not on him but elsewhere, working the room. He would have resented it even more if his own eyes hadn't been doing the same thing.

Austin Firestone passed him in the hallway.

"All right, Lerner," said Firestone, "I've thought it out."

"Yes?" said Lance.

"I'll give you a five-city tour. You increase sales in those cities by a substantial enough margin, maybe I'll give you a few more."

Lance nodded.

"Fair enough," he said. "How's about raising the print order?"

"How many copies in the first printing?" said Firestone.

"Fifteen thousand," said Lance.

"We'll keep it at fifteen for now," he said. "If sales start to go up after the first couple of cities, we'll order a second printing."

Firestone started to move away.

"Wait," said Lance. "Print orders are self-fulfilling prophecies too, you know. Any book with a print order as small as fifteen thousand is never going to be taken seriously by anyone—not by your salesmen, not by the jobbers, and not by the retailers either. A print order of a *hundred* thousand, though, automatically causes everyone to—"

"I *said* fifteen is enough for now," said Firestone in a voice that turned Lance's blood to permafrost, "don't push your luck, Lerner."

Firestone strode away. Lance's heart was pumping double-time. Don't push my luck, is that it? he thought. Don't push my luck? Well, I'll damn well push whatever I *want* to push, big guy, including your horny wife.

He went back to the thumbless black behind the bar and demanded a kir royale.

"I regret," said the bartender in a patronizing tone, "that owing to the size of the present crowd—"

"Don't give me that crap," said Lance quietly. "You pour some champagne and some cassis into a glass *pronto,* pal, or you're going to be missing more than thumbs."

Eyes the size of golf balls, the bartender reached for the champagne bottle.

147

44

There was something oddly familiar about her, but he doubted that he knew her. She wore bleached jeans and a T-shirt with printed lettering on it that was so faded and cracked it was almost illegible. She had the slim figure of a girl of about seventeen or eighteen and long straight black hair and the stunningly beautiful face of an Oriental model he had once seen in *Vogue*.

"I guess I shouldn't have come," she said in a wounded tone. "I don't know why I did, except maybe I wanted to see if I had the balls."

"I'm sorry," said Lance, "but I don't believe that we—"

"Dorothy Chu," she said somewhat petulantly. "We already have a relationship: I call you on the phone and you hang up on me."

"Dorothy!" he said. "My God, come in."

She entered the apartment shyly and looked around.

"Nice place," she said. "How come you don't have any furniture?"

"My wife took it," he said.

"She leave you or what?" said Dorothy, checking out the layout.

"Well, sort of," said Lance.

"I don't blame her," said Dorothy. "You probably hung up on her once too often."

"Dorothy, listen," said Lance, "I didn't hang up on you."

"You didn't?" she said. Her petulance, no longer sure of itself, faltered.

"No," he said. "I tripped on the phone and it disconnected. I tried to get you back, but you didn't leave me your phone number."

"No kidding?" she said. Her face was breaking out in the most beautiful smile.

"I swear to God," he said. "I would have called you back if I could have. I even looked you up in the Manhattan directory, and you weren't listed.

She squealed and impulsively threw her arms around him and kissed him. It was over before he had a chance to enjoy it.

"I'm sorry," she said. "I tend to be overly impulsive at times."

"Hey, don't apologize for hugging and kissing someone," said Lance. "It was a lovely gesture."

She looked at him and smiled self-consciously, color coming into her cheeks.

"I feel kind of stupid," she said.

"How come?" said Lance.

"Because I don't know what to *do* now. I came over here because I was hurt and wanted to give you a piece of my mind, and now that that isn't appropriate anymore, I don't know what else to do. Except maybe leave."

"Oh, don't leave," said Lance. He loved how she looked and how direct and vulnerable she was. He was also trying to figure out how old she was and whether it was possible to somehow get her to hug and kiss him again without appearing to be a dirty old man.

"OK," said Dorothy.

"Sit down," said Lance.

Dorothy looked around, saw no chairs, and sat down cross-legged on the floor, in a modified lotus position. He loved the way she did that. An adult probably would have made some snide remark about the lack of furniture and made him feel bad. He sat down across from her and tried to get his legs into the same position, but it was a little painful so he didn't push it.

"I still don't know what to say," said Dorothy, blushing. "You'll have to start."

"Oh, OK. Well, let's see. What shall we talk about? Why don't you tell me about you?"

"OK, like what?"

"Well, like, what does it say on your T-shirt?"

"Oh, this?" she said. She squinted down at her chest. "It says, 'If God had not intended man to eat pussy, then why did he make it look so much like a taco?'"

They both blushed and giggled.

"Glad I asked," he said. "Well. Tell me. What made you write to me in the first place? What did you want?"

149

She shrugged.

"I don't know. Like I said, my friend Janie and I are sort of writer-groupies. We're both big fans of yours, and we're both writers, and, well, we just wanted to sort of meet you and get some advice from you and stuff."

"Advice? What kind of advice?"

"You know. About writing and everything. About how to crash into print. I'm really quite serious about my writing."

"I see," said Lance.

"I'm writing something now, in fact, which I sort of hoped you might take a look at and tell me if it was any good and whether it was, you know, commercial."

"What kind of thing is it?" said Lance. "A novel?"

She shook her head.

"Huh-huh. A poem."

"A poem?" said Lance.

"Not a *poem*, really, more like a trilogy."

"A trilogy?" said Lance. "About how long is it?"

She shrugged.

"I don't know exactly, I mean I haven't numbered the pages. There must be over a thousand, though."

"Ah."

"What's wrong?" said Dorothy.

"Well, I'd love to read something you wrote, but if it's a poem over a thousand pages long, I don't know if I—"

"It reads very quickly," she said.

"I'm sure it does," he said, "but I'm a little strapped for time right now. I'm about to have a novel of mine published and I have to go out on the road for several weeks and promote it. I don't really even have time to do my *own* things now—my errands and things—much less read a—"

"Hey, that's OK," she said. "I understand. I guess it was a little presumptuous of me to ask you anyway."

"Not at all," he said. "It's just that I don't really have the time right now."

"What errands do you have to do?"

"Pardon me?" he said.

"What errands and things do you have to do?"

"Why do you ask?" he said.

"I don't know. I was just thinking. I'm on vacation from school right now, and I'm kind of looking for a summer job. Maybe I could work for *you*—run your errands and straighten up your place and stuff."

Lance considered it. Many of the things he had to do were

things you couldn't delegate—like going to the dentist, getting a haircut, and so on. But there *were* a great many things that could be done by someone else, provided they were intelligent. Dorothy did seem to be intelligent.

"I'm very intelligent for my age," said Dorothy, seemingly reading his thoughts.

"What is your age?" said Lance.

"Sweet seventeen," said Dorothy.

"And never been kissed?"

"Oh," said Dorothy, "I've been kissed, don't worry. About everywhere you could think of."

"I see," said Lance, beginning to have a lustful fantasy about her and then quickly cutting it short. Please, God, he prayed silently, don't let me ever believe it would be a good idea to have sex with this child.

"I guess maybe I shouldn't have said that," said Dorothy. "When I'm nervous I tend to babble a little."

"Oh, that's all right," said Lance. "I do the same thing myself. Why are you nervous, though?"

"I told you. You're one of my heroes. I'm really impressed with you. I think you're one of our finest writers."

"Well, that's very flattering," said Lance. "Thank you."

"You're welcome. Of course, I'm only a kid, so what do I know?"

Lance smiled wanly.

"A word of advice, Dorothy," he said. "Once you've given a compliment, leave it alone. Don't try to take it back again."

"I'm sorry," said Dorothy. "I wasn't disparaging you, I was disparaging myself."

"Why do you have to disparage either one of us?" said Lance.

"I don't know," said Dorothy. "Maybe because it makes me feel like I'm at home with my folks."

"Your folks give you a hard time at home?" said Lance. She nodded.

"They're very traditional. Very Chinese. Do you know anything about the Chinese?"

"I'm afraid not."

"They're very conservative. Next to them Ronald Reagan is a radical. You should hear their views on sex."

"What are their views on sex?"

"I don't know. They won't discuss it with me. They've tried to prevent me from seeing men altogether."

"Have they been successful?" said Lance.

Dorothy shrugged.

"Yes and no. I mean I've been to bed with a couple of boys, but I didn't enjoy it too much. Maybe that's because of their lack of skill—do you think so?"

"Maybe," said Lance.

"I hope to God that's it," said Dorothy.

"How do you mean?" said Lance.

She looked at him carefully, as if trying to decide how much to say.

"I mean I hope it's not that I like girls better," said Dorothy.

Lance nodded, beginning to feel like a psychiatrist. He wasn't sure why she was telling him this, but he didn't think he wanted her to stop talking just now.

"What makes you think you might like girls better?" said Lance.

Dorothy shrugged again, looking down at her hands, and absentmindedly tried to form a hangnail on her left thumb.

"I don't know," said Dorothy. "It's just that sometimes when I'm with a girl I really like, like my friend Janie, and especially if we're doing drugs, well . . . I get these feelings."

"What kind of feelings?" said Lance.

"Mixed," said Dorothy. "Sort of loving and platonic, and also sort of horny. I'm not sure I want to have horny feelings about other girls."

"It's quite normal, you know, for girls to have sexual feelings about other girls," said Lance.

"Yeah?"

"Yeah."

"It doesn't make you a lesbian?"

"Not at all."

"What does?"

"I don't know. I suppose if you have sex only with women for a long period of time, then people might say you were a lesbian."

"What if you have sex mostly with men, and then just a *little* with women? Does that make you a lesbian?"

"I don't think so. I think that makes you a bisexual."

"I don't think I'd ever really want to do it with a woman," she said. "I've had fantasies about it, I mean, but actually doing it would be really gross."

"OK," said Lance.

"Anyway, I didn't mean to talk so much about sex and lesbians. I really just wanted to come over here and meet you.

152

And if you think you'd have enough work to keep me busy, maybe I could work for you for a while until you go out on tour."

"Do you type?" said Lance. "I'm not saying that I have all kinds of typing to do, but there might be some every so often."

"I'm a fantastic typist," said Dorothy. "I'm not bragging, I really *am*. Saying you're a fantastic typist is just stating a fact. Also I take pretty good shorthand, would you believe that?"

"That's pretty impressive," said Lance.

"Yeah. My folks insisted I learn all that stuff so when my writing career went down the tubes I could always be a secretary."

"What would I have to pay you?" said Lance.

"I don't know," said Dorothy. "Whatever you like."

"How about three dollars an hour?" said Lance.

"How about six?" said Dorothy.

"I, uh, don't really think I can afford six," said Lance.

"OK, why don't we split the difference, then, and say five?"

"Uh, Dorothy, splitting the difference between three dollars and six is not five," said Lance. "It's four and a half."

"OK, four and a half," said Dorothy. "Tell me something." "Yes?"

"Once I start working for you and being in your apartment a lot and stuff, do you think you'll ever make a pass at me?"

"I hope to God I'm never that stupid," said Lance.

"Good," said Dorothy. "Not that I'd hate it or anything, I mean, because you really are attractive and everything, but I guess we ought to keep our relationship professional. Plus which you *are* a little old for me. Hey, what do I call you, Lance or Mr. Lerner?"

"How about Gramps?" said Lance.

45

Lance telephoned Claire to thank her for the party. It had
been, he declared, a complete success. It had indeed, she
said. Lance told her he felt that the five-city tour that
Firestone had granted him was at least a start. Not as many
cities as he had hoped for, but at least a start.

"You now have five cities," said Claire in the cadences of a
game-show host. "How would you like to turn five into ten?"

"Pardon me?" said Lance.

"I said, how would you like to double the number of cities
on your promotional tour?"

"Uh, I'm not sure I get your meaning," said Lance. "Are
you suggesting that there is something I could do that I
haven't already done which might accomplish such a thing?"

"There might," said Claire coyly.

"And would that favor be of a sexual nature?" said Lance.

"It might," said Claire.

"Let me understand something," said Lance. "Are you
telling me you have the power to influence Firestone to make
strictly business decisions?"

"Oh, nothing is strictly business with me, Lance," said
Claire.

"In other words," said Lance, getting hot under the collar,
"you have had the power all along to get me such a thing, but
instead you're using it to force me to exchange sexual favors
for it?"

"Whoa, boy," said Claire. "That is not what's so at *all*."

"Then what is?" said Lance.

"Here is what's so," said Claire. "I happen to be a
somewhat bored woman who happens to be able to exert
certain types of influences on certain people, including my
husband, for certain specific things at certain specific times.

Not in all areas and not at all times, but enough to be effective. *How* I do this is my business. *When* I do this is my business. It is not always easy work, I might add. It is most definitely work. And when I do work for somebody, I like to get repaid in some form, or else I feel taken advantage of. Now then, the form of repayment in your case—and in very few others, I might add—happens to be sexual. If it pleases you to do me sexual favors, Lance, I will be delighted. If not, so be it. I imagine I'll get over it somehow. But be very clear about one thing: nobody is *forcing* you to do anything at all. *You* are the one who will decide if you want to do it. Not me. *You.* You are a completely free man, lover. That's what makes you such a challenge."

Lance thought it over. What she had said was certainly straightforward. And it was not as if she were Gladys Oliphant.

"What do you want me to do?" he said.

"Have you ever made love in a moving limousine?" she asked.

A uniformed chauffeur rang his doorbell later that afternoon, and escorted Lance to the limousine. Lance thought he could detect a faint smile at the corners of the chauffeur's mouth but he couldn't be certain.

Inside the limousine Claire was waiting for him. She was wearing a long ivory-colored dressing gown. Lance got in and sat down beside her. The chauffeur closed the door behind Lance and then got into the front seat, put the car in gear and drove.

Claire smiled at Lance, then reached forward and closed the sliding glass panel that separated the front and back seats. She drew a gray curtain across the glass as well, then sank back in her seat.

"What are you drinking?" she said, indicating the bar which stood between the two richly upholstered jump seats on the floor in front of them.

"What do you have?" said Lance.

"Everything," said Claire.

"All right," said Lance smugly. "I'll have a White Russian."

Claire nodded. She opened a panel on the bar and withdrew a bottle of Kahlua and a bottle of vodka. Then she opened another panel and took out a container of cream. She took a glass from the top of the bar and mixed the drink so swiftly he was sure she must have spent time as a professional bartender.

He took the drink from her and thanked her. It tasted surprisingly good.

"Aren't you having anything?" said Lance.

"Already have," she said, indicating an empty champagne glass on the bar. "May I offer you anything else before we begin—an hors d'oeuvre? A phone call? A little TV?"

He looked at the TV over the bar and the phone to its left and tried not to act overly impressed.

"Not just now, thanks," he said.

"Maybe later?"

"Yes. Maybe later."

He drank some more of his drink. Claire reached over and began unbuttoning his shirt. He looked out the window. They were turning onto Park Avenue. Claire removed his boots and his trousers and underpants. He wondered if people outside the limousine could see in. The car was moving fairly swiftly so perhaps they couldn't.

Claire began to play with his penis. As it grew stiff, the car slowed down and stopped at a stoplight. A very proper-looking couple in their sixties stood just back from the window. Claire met their gaze, smiled sweetly at them and removed her dressing gown. Now quite naked and still smiling sweetly at the astounded couple, Claire raised herself slightly off her seat, grabbed Lance's penis and settled herself slowly down on top of it.

Lance was so embarrassed he hid behind her back. The couple, frozen in their tracks, did not move as the light turned green and the limousine surged forward.

After the first embarrassment with the couple on Park Avenue, Lance began to enjoy the outrageousness of it all. They drank, they made love, they watched *Star Trek* reruns on TV. Claire called her office and made a few other short phone calls. Lance asked her if one could make long distance calls from the limousine, and by way of response she made a longish call to a friend in Paris. While she talked, she busied her hand in his crotch.

That evening a dozen incredulous people would report to friends or family what they had witnessed that afternoon when a sleek gray stretch limousine had pulled up at a stoplight. Not one of them would be believed.

When the chauffeur finally opened the door to let Lance out at his apartment, Lance and Claire were both dressed again and it was dusk.

"Thank you for a wonderful afternoon," he said.

"Oh no," she said, "thank *you*. And congratulations."

"Congratulations?" he said.

"On your five additional cities," she said.

The following morning the telephone rang at nine-thirty, awakening him from a fitful sleep.

"Lance? Howard. Hope I didn't *wake* you?"

"You did," said Lance.

"Well, it serves you *right*. For not having to be up when I do. Guess what I pulled *off* for you—you're not going to *believe* it!"

"What did you pull off for me, Howard?"

"I put a *hell*uva lot of pressure on Firestone, and I *got it*."

"Got what, Howard?"

"Five additional *cities* on your *tour!*"

46

Hiring Dorothy had proven to be a brilliant decision. She managed to shop for groceries, take his boots to the shoe-maker to be resoled, go to the health-food store to stock up on vitamins, go to the post office with parcels, and replenish his liquor cabinet in about a third the time he would have used himself.

Today he planned to have her go to the library and do some research for him, but when she arrived at his door she looked as though she'd been crying and might start again at any moment.

"Hi, Dorothy," he said. "Is anything wrong?"

She shook her head.

"I'm sorry," said Lance. "I didn't mean to pry. It's just that you looked very sad and I thought you needed to talk."

She nodded.

"I do need to talk," she said.

"What's wrong?" said Lance.

Dorothy started to cry, took out a crumpled piece of Kleenex and dabbed at her eyes.

"I'm in big trouble," she said at last.

"What kind of trouble?" said Lance.

"You remember that discussion we had? About lesbianism? Well, last night I told Janie what you said. She thought you were very wise. She's a big fan of yours, too—did I mention that?"

"Yes."

"Well anyway, we were over at my house, and we were doing some grass, and we were talking over what you and I discussed, you know? And Janie said that she was very relieved, because *she* was worried about stuff like that too. About whether she had lesbian tendencies and everything. And she said that she was relieved to hear that sometimes I felt horny towards her—like an asshole, I had told her that—because sometimes she felt horny towards *me*."

"Yeah . . . ?"

"Yeah. So I said that was nice. So she said the grass was making her feel horny towards me *now*. So I said that was nice. I mean what was I going to say? So she said she wondered what it would be like to kiss me. On the lips and everything. So I said I didn't know. So she kissed me."

"Yeah . . . ?"

"I don't mean a peck on the cheek, I mean a real kiss. On the mouth. With tongues and everything. Yecchh!"

"You didn't like it, huh?"

"Not really. Well, maybe a little bit. But it just felt so *gross,* you know? To have another girl's tongue inside your mouth? So I kind of pulled away from her and she could tell I was grossed out, and she got really hurt. She probably gets paranoid on grass like *you* do. Anyway, she starts crying and saying I'll probably never want to be her friend again and everything . . . So I went and hugged her. I mean I really *love* that girl—we've been through some real shit together and I really *love* her. As a friend, you know?"

"Yeah."

"So anyway, there I am, hugging her and consoling her, and she keeps on crying. Crying and saying how I probably find her repulsive and everything, and how she probably ruined this wonderful friendship we had. I got so sad that *I* started crying. There we were, two assholes, hugging and crying. I told her nothing could ever ruin our friendship and that I loved her. I kissed her a whole lot of times, to sort of show her how much I loved her, but definitely keeping clear of the old mouth-a-rooney, you know? But in a way that was worse than if I hadn't kissed her at all."

"Why's that?"

"Because. She saw how I was avoiding kissing her on the mouth and she ended up feeling even more repulsive than before. So, just to show her I didn't find her repulsive, I kissed her on the mouth."

"Yeah . . ."

"I stuck my tongue in there too, just to sort of make my point, you know? And . . ."

She began to cry again.

"And what?" said Lance.

"And," said Dorothy, dabbing at her eyes and nose, "I started *liking* it. I started getting really turned *on*. Janie did too. So we just stood there, kissing and getting turned on, and before I knew it we were taking our clothes off, and then there we were in bed together, *naked*, for God's sake!"

Lance could visualize the scene very clearly. It was getting him excited, which he didn't think was an appropriate reaction for him to have. He thought he ought to say something helpful or understanding, but he couldn't think of anything.

"Uh, did you each take your *own* clothes off, or did you undress each other?" he said, immediately sensing it was the wrong question.

"Each other," she said. "God, it was weird, lying in bed naked with your best friend, having sex."

"You did, uh, have sex together then, did you?" said Lance.

Dorothy nodded, then cried some more.

"Yeah," she said. "Well, sort of."

"Sort of?" said Lance.

"I mean, *she* did," said Dorothy.

"You mean she . . . ?"

"She went down on me. I felt *really* weird then, you know? To have my best friend down there licking away at my thing? I mean what kind of *people* must we be if we would have sex with our best friend? The worst part was I even *enjoyed* it! God! Now I'm a dyke for life."

159

Lance was having trouble speaking. The image was too powerful. He wanted to comfort her, but he didn't dare touch her for fear of giving her the wrong idea. Or the right one. Why is it, he thought, that the notion of two women together is stirring to both women and men, but the notion of two men together in unappealing to women and to heterosexual men?

"Listen, Dorothy," said Lance. "You haven't done anything wrong. You'd be surprised how many people have experimented like you and Janie and done that kind of thing."

"Have *you?*" said Dorothy through her tears.

"Sort of," said Lance.

"You went to bed with your best *friend?*" said Dorothy.

"That's right," said Lance.

"Far *out,*" said Dorothy. "I would never have thought *you'd* go to bed with another man."

"It . . . wasn't a man, exactly," said Lance. "It was my best *female* friend, but it was certainly a weird experience."

Dorothy was incensed.

"How can you even *compare* that with what I did?" she said. "How can you even speak of them in the same *breath?* I thought you were going to tell me something weird, and you tell me how you fucked a *female friend?*"

"OK," said Lance, "you want to hear *weird, I'll* tell you weird. How about this: All my adult life I've had fantasies about *nurses*—about nurses wearing translucent white *uniforms,* and being seduced by two of them while I'm a patient in the hospital and having a *threesome* with them."

"Are you *kidding* me?" said Dorothy. "You call that *weird?* That's the most boring fantasy in the world. There's not a guy in the *world* that doesn't have that fantasy."

"OK," said Lance, beginning to feel challenged, "then how's about this: I let a policewoman I know handcuff me to her bed naked while she went out to the liquor store, and while she was gone a fat woman who weighed about three hundred pounds came up to her apartment to fix her shower head and raped me."

Dorothy studied him carefully.

"Is that a fantasy or it really happened?" she said.

"It really happened."

Dorothy nodded her head.

"That's weird," she said.

"You're damn right it is," said Lance triumphantly.

"You let a policewoman handcuff you naked to her bed?"

"Damn right," said Lance.

"I think you may be a lot weirder than I am," said Dorothy.

"What?" said Lance. "Hey, c'mon now, Dorothy, what *is* this?"

"Letting a policewoman handcuff you naked to her bed?" said Dorothy. "Are you *kidding* me? That's *gross.*"

Lance felt extravagantly stupid. What in God's name had made him confess that?

"Dorothy, I was merely trying to make you feel less weird by telling you one of my own experiences," said Lance. "I was just trying to help you, and I end up feeling like a real asshole."

"I'm sorry," said Dorothy. "I know you were just trying to make me feel better. But getting handcuffed naked to a bed and being raped by a four-hundred-pound woman —*yecchh!*"

"I didn't say *four* hundred pounds, I said *three* hundred pounds, and besides—"

"OK, OK," said Dorothy. "I'm sorry I said you were gross. And I really do appreciate what you were trying to do."

"Good," said Lance. "Now then, do you feel better?"

Dorothy thought a moment, as if she were checking her mood thermometer, and then shook her head and began to cry again.

"What's wrong *now?*" said Lance, annoyed that he hadn't totally cleared up the problem.

"I haven't told you the worst part yet," said Dorothy.

"Yes you did," said Lance. "You said the worst part was that you even enjoyed it."

"That's not the worst part," said Dorothy. "That's only the *second* worst part. The worst part is that my mother walked in on us."

Dorothy began sobbing uncontrollably.

"Oh, boy," said Lance softly. He tentatively reached out to hold her and comfort her, then withdrew his hand. "What did she do?"

"She said I had dishonored the family. She kicked me out of the house!" said Dorothy, and completely fell apart.

Lance went over to her and took her in his arms. They hugged for several minutes and she continued to cry. As he feared, the close proximity of her body against his was making it difficult to concentrate on his vows to himself.

"What are you going to do?" said Lance, once Dorothy had quieted down.

"I don't know," she said. "I really don't. I guess I could go and stay at the YWCA, but that really sounds grim."

"It does," said Lance.

"Can I ask you something?" said Dorothy.

"What?" said Lance, although there was no doubt in his mind what the question was going to be, only how he would answer it.

"Can I bring my sleeping bag over here for a while and sleep on your floor until I find something more permanent?"

He thought about her question for several moments, but he finally said aloud what he had thought he would:

"Of course you can."

47

Dorothy Chu moved into Lance's apartment that very evening. She brought with her a sleeping bag, a knapsack filled with clothes, a backpack filled with various books of poetry she especially prized, the manuscript of her epic-length poetic trilogy, and a large if somewhat moth-eaten stuffed panda.

Lance decided she should spread her bedroll on the living-room floor, right where the sectional sofa had stood before the Motherloaders had removed it under Cathy's direction. It was agreed she would use the small upstairs bathroom for everything except baths or showers, when it was permissible for her to use the master bathroom off Lance's bedroom, but by appointment only. It was agreed she would roll up her sleeping bag every morning and keep her things very neat and out of sight. It was agreed that she would respect Lance's privacy and that he would respect hers and that both of them, when not in the bath or shower or their respective beds, would appear fully clothed at all times.

At first Dorothy quite scrupulously followed the ground rules that Lance had laid down. She kept her bedroll neat and out of sight during the day. She made appointments for the bath or shower hours in advance.

Then she began to get a trifle lax. One evening he walked into his bathroom to take a pee and found her in the tub. She had forgotten to make an appointment and was deeply apologetic. He asked why she hadn't at least closed the door, and she said that she couldn't stand closed doors because she was claustrophobic. She swore it would never happen again, and he forgave her, but some small damage had been done that could not be undone: he had seen her, for however short a time, naked. The sight of her lovely girlish body, nude in his tub, was one he could not eradicate from his memory, try as he might.

On another occasion he stepped into the shower, only to find that she had hung up several pairs of her bikini panties to dry there. He was irritated and noticed, to his extreme discomfort, that when he handled the still-moist garments to remove them from the shower, he found his fingers tingling.

On yet another occasion he walked into his bathroom to see her sitting on the john, her pants down at her ankles, reading. She apologized like crazy, explained that her john upstairs was stopped up and didn't flush properly, but once more the damage had been done.

The weather was extremely hot. Several times he caught her walking around the apartment in her underwear. On one particularly hot day he caught her typing in his study wearing only panties. What did she want—to drive him insane? He lectured her like a beleaguered father. She answered him like a resentful teenaged daughter. She said he was uptight about the human body, like all older men. The words stung. He searched within himself and was forced to admit that he was at least somewhat ambivalent about the human body, if not precisely uptight. To try to escape the most-ancient category in her catalogue of older men, he resolved to alter his attitudes. He tried not to scold her when she broke the rules and appeared before him less than fully clothed. He tried not to even appear upset when he got out of the shower once and found her standing at his sink, brushing her teeth. He began to get used to seeing her walk around the house with little on, if anything at all. His hands began, ever so slightly, to shake.

His friend Les came over once and saw Dorothy walk through the hall in her underwear. Les raised an eyebrow. Lance explained that Dorothy was living with him temporarily, but that nothing sexual was going on between them. Les waited for the put-on to end and the truth to come out, but Lance swore it was the truth. Les finally believed him, and inquired whether he might perhaps take Dorothy to a movie one night. Lance said absolutely not. Dorothy was much too young for Les, he said. Both Lance and Les were surprised at the ferocity of Lance's edict.

Something was happening to him. It did not appear to be anything good.

One night Lance passed by the living room and heard the sound of sobbing. He peeked in and found Dorothy face down on her bedroll, crying into her pillow, clutching her panda. Lance entered the room and softly called her name. She didn't appear to hear him. He bent down and softly touched her shoulder.

"Dorothy?"

"Yeah?"

She didn't turn around. He thought she might be crying because of something he had done to her, although he couldn't imagine what. He felt horrible.

"Dorothy, what is it?" he said.

She turned over. Her eyes were very red and very wet.

"It's Janie."

"What *about* Janie?" he said.

"They got Janie," she said and began to sob again. It was like a line in a World War II movie—*They got Janie.* He imagined Janie climbing out of a foxhole and being suddenly riddled by Kraut machine-gun bullets.

"Who got Janie?" he said.

"My parents. They told her father what she and I were doing. They threw her out of the house."

More sobbing.

Well, he thought, at least Janie's alive. At least she wasn't going to show up in the movie's next scene in a shallow grave with her rifle plunged into it, bayonet first, her helmet dangling from the stock.

"Where will Janie live now?" asked Lance, and immediately regretted the question.

Janie Wang moved in late that night.

Janie was taller than Dorothy, larger boned, flatter faced, wider hipped, smaller breasted, more Oriental looking. She wasn't quite as beautiful as Dorothy, but she was beautiful.

164

She, like Dorothy, had long straight black hair and wondrous cheekbones. Like Dorothy, she still slept with a stuffed animal—an incongruously blue teddy bear that looked like it had been around as long as Lance himself.

Lance made an attempt with Janie to re-establish the ground rules, but he knew it was hopeless. Their cosmetics and clothes were everywhere. Long black hairs clogged his drains. Janie appeared to have claustrophobia as severe as Dorothy's where bathrooms were concerned, so Lance was continually walking in on her on the john as well. Before long, both Janie and Dorothy passed in and out of his bathroom when he was using it as freely as when he wasn't, as freely as if it were their own. And he never saw either of them fully clothed again.

He found he didn't really mind it. It was like one happy family. Better yet, it was like the fantasies of his youth—to be invisible in the girls' dormitory. He liked the idea that they felt relaxed enough to go about the most intimate of activities in his presence without being self-conscious. They frequently hugged and kissed and caressed each other when he was in the room, though nothing more. He felt strangely honored that they were willing to share their displays of affection for each other with him.

They discussed their daily activities together at dinner and always asked his advice. The three of them went places together at night. They began to have private jokes together. They decided they were a family. Every night, at their request, Lance tucked Dorothy and Janie into their sleeping bags and told them bedtime stories of his own devising. They began to have their favorites, and made him repeat these incessantly, like small children.

They told him that they loved him and he didn't doubt it. He loved them too. His friend Les came over and saw the two of them living there with Lance and rolled his eyes. Lance swore that they were not a ménage-à-trois, but Les couldn't be convinced.

"You sonofabitch," Les chuckled enviously, shaking his head, "you crafty old sonofabitch. How the hell do you do it?"

Lance decided that Les was too obtuse to be a close friend anymore.

Often at night he would lie in his bed downstairs and listen to them up in the darkened living room, whispering and giggling. He wondered if they were having sex. He wondered if they wanted only each other. He wondered what they really thought of him. He wondered if he were jealous of the intimacy they shared with each other which excluded him. He wondered how long their present relationship would endure. He sensed that it was about to change, but he didn't know in what direction. The possibilities filled him with inexplicable anxiety.

48

Julius Blatt simply didn't understand it.

The idea was a natural. A hundred-dollar-a-plate benefit dinner organized around Lerner's slogan, "Free the Dalton Two," was only a fucking brainstorm. He already had half a dozen celebrities committed as either sponsors or speakers— celebrities a whole lot bigger than Lance Lerner, as a matter of fact—by the time he called Lerner and asked him to be a speaker at the dinner.

Blatt hadn't even been sure that Lerner was big enough to ask in the first place. The fact that he had called him at all was only a courtesy to the man who had thought up their slogan. So it was especially puzzling, *and* hurtful, to have Lerner react the way he had and to have him say the things he had. Blatt had actually thought he was doing the man a favor, and here he goes and says all these mean and hurtful things.

If, as Lerner maintained, he really hadn't wanted Blatt to use the line "Free the Dalton Two," then why had he given it to Blatt in the first place? And why would he object to their using the line anyway? Probably because Lerner was now sorry he'd given it to him for free. Money-grabbing bastard—that's all those writer bastards cared about anyway.

Well, fuck him. Blatt didn't need Lerner, and neither did

Goose or Ernest. As a matter of fact, now that he thought about it, Blatt wasn't even altogether sure it hadn't been he himself who had come up with the slogan during their conversation.

49

The members of Lance's therapy group were unexpectedly tough on him. They distrusted the familial feelings which he swore he felt for Dorothy and Janie. They said he wasn't being honest with the group or with himself. They said he wanted to have a ménage-à-trois.

He told them they were full of shit. He said that maybe—maybe—that had been true in the beginning, but that now those feelings had evolved into something higher. He said he felt paternal feelings for the two girls, that he wanted to be their father and their older brother and their friend. He said he didn't want to be their lover.

They told him he was full of shit. He appealed to Helen, told of how he tucked Dorothy and Janie into bed every night with their stuffed animals and improvised bedtime stories. He said he'd even had a notion he would look into the legal possibilities of adopting them. Helen, too, said that he was full of shit.

The group asked Lance what he was doing for sex these days. He told them about the session in the limousine with Claire. He said that he had still not given up on Cathy. Cathy's birthday was coming up soon, he told them. He was trying to figure out whether he should buy her a present.

"Why don't you take her out to dinner on her birthday?" asked Helen.

"Oh, I don't think so," said Lance.

"Why not?" said Laura.

"Because. She'd never agree to go," said Lance.

"How do you know?" said Arnold.

"I just know," said Lance. "She's my wife. I know her."

"You know her so well that you thought she was having an affair with your best friend, but she wasn't, and you thought she would never leave you, but she did," said Arnold. "You sure know her well."

"Hear, hear," said Roger.

"Very nice, Arnold," said Helen.

"Thank you," said Arnold.

"Touché," said Lance. "Look, maybe I *don't* know her as well as I think I do. Maybe I'm just afraid to call her and ask her."

"Are you afraid she'll say no," said Helen, "or are you afraid she'll say yes?"

Lance thought it over.

"Both, I guess."

"Give it a try, Lance," said Helen gently. "You might just find that whatever her response is, it's the one you want."

"And if she says no," said Jackie, "you can always go out for chinks with the teenaged dykes."

50

Lance's call caught Cathy off guard. She was almost pleasant. He asked her to dinner for her birthday and she declined, as he'd expected. But when he asked her what she planned to do instead, she couldn't come up with any alternatives that didn't sound depressing.

Lance realized her first refusal hadn't shattered him and that he was truly willing for her to do what she wanted. This realization afforded him the freedom to be looser and lighter. As their conversation continued he found himself getting back to the old him. He was peppy, confident and funny, and Cathy seemed surprised and charmed in spite of herself.

When he repeated his invitation to dinner, she accepted. He suggested the Four Seasons, the elegant East Side restaurant that had been one of their favorites. She seemed pleased by the suggestion. He asked what time she wanted him to pick her up. She said she preferred to meet him at the restaurant.

They arrived at about the same time. He saw her get out of her cab, caught a glimpse of her upper thighs as she emerged from the cramped space, and remembered what she looked like naked.

They kissed lightly and went in. He had asked that they be seated in the main room next to the marble reflecting pool and they were. She looked fabulous—even better than the terrible time he had seen her last at the Russian Tea Room. Her hair was pulled back in a way that he had never particularly liked while they were together but which he had to admit was very flattering. She wore a sleek black dress and silver jewelry that he had not given her. Where, he wondered, had it come from?

"So," he said, smiling.

"So," she said, smiling.

"You look lovely."

"Thank you."

There was a pause. They both continued to stare at each other, slightly forced smiles on their faces.

"It's good to see you again," he said.

"It's good to see you, too," she said.

"I mean that," he said.

"So do I," she said.

It was not going to go well, he thought suddenly, and cursed Helen and the group for encouraging him to bring her here. Try as he might, he could think of absolutely nothing to say to her. Their captain took drink orders and withdrew.

"It's warm," he said suddenly.

"In here?" she said, surprised, because in fact the interior of the restaurant was quite comfortably cool.

"No, outside," he said.

"Ah," she said.

"For this time of year," he said.

"You think so?" she said.

"Well, no," he said, "but I couldn't think of anything else to say."

His admission released some of the pressure and they both laughed.

"Christ, this is hard," she said. "Why should it be so hard?"

169

"I don't know," he said. "It's ridiculous. I mean here we are, people who know each other more intimately than anyone in the world, and we're reduced to speculation about the weather."

"I know," she said. "Well, I feel better now. How have you been, Lance? You look very well."

"I've had my ups and downs," he said. "As you know, I'm about to leave for a ten-city promotional tour for my book."

"Yes, how did you manage that?" said Cathy. "The last time we talked I think you said they'd changed their minds and weren't going to send you anywhere. Did Howard change Firestone's mind or what?"

"Well, no, not exactly. I pretty much did it myself. I talked to Firestone himself—as a businessman, not as an author— and I think it did some good."

"How did you manage to see him?" said Cathy. "I didn't think he ever talked to authors."

"Well, that's not untrue," said Lance. "But I happened to meet *Mrs.* Firestone at a party, and I told her what a hard time I was having getting to see her husband, and she set it up for me."

"Ah," said Cathy.

Talk of Claire was beginning to make him nervous. He decided to redirect the conversation elsewhere.

"So," he said, "what have you been up to?"

"Oh, lots of things," she said. "There are tons of new fall books to get through and assign, and I've been doing some of my own writing. I've started a novel."

Lance didn't know how to react at first. He thought she might be mocking him.

"Why are you looking at me that way?" she said.

"I don't know, I just thought you hated the whole process of novel writing so much."

"In *you*," she said. "Not in me."

"I see. But you want to write novels?"

"Yes."

"What made you choose the novel form?"

She shrugged.

"I want to make something of myself," she said. "I want to be acknowledged as a person in my own right, not as somebody's wife, or as somebody's editor, either. I want to be noticed. Writing is not a bad way to be noticed, I've noticed, and I seem to have some ability in that area."

Lance nodded.

"So what am I going to write?" she said. "A poem? A short story? The market for short stories died with the *Saturday Evening Post*. The market for poems never existed. I'm not interested in learning to be a journalist, I sense that writing for movies and TV is a closed shop, and writing for the theater is a worse gamble than three-card monte—you've told me that for years. So, that's why I'm writing a novel."

"What's it about?"

She smiled self-consciously.

"A woman who leaves her husband and tries to find out who she is," she said, "what else?"

"Maybe I can help you," he said.

"I don't *need* your help," she said with surprising rancor, and immediately softened. "I'm sorry, I didn't mean it to come out like that. It's just that this is something I have to do myself. To find out if I can do it by myself. To find out if I can do *anything* by myself. How can I find that out if I let you help me?"

"I see your point," he said.

"Do you?" she said.

"Yes."

"Thank you."

"How far have you gotten on the novel so far?" he said.

"Oh, not far," she said. "A chapter or so, that's about all. There's too much to do at the *Times,* and also I've been going out a lot."

He got a sudden sinking sensation in his stomach, and she must have picked up something because she quickly tried to make it sound as though she hadn't been speaking of dates.

"I've been going to lots of dinner parties, I mean," she said. "I guess people feel sorry for me or something, so they keep inviting me."

"Oh, really?" he said. "Who's invited you?"

"Oh, let's see," she said. "The Bernsteins, the Newmans, the Ramsays, the . . ."

"You know something?" he said. "Since we've been separated I don't think one of our friends has called me—for dinner or anything else."

"You aren't hurt, are you?" she said.

"Oh, no, of course not," he said. "Well, maybe a little. It's as if they felt they had to choose between us. And all of them seem to have chosen *you.*"

"Oh, come on, Lance," she said. "You don't really think that's true, do you?"

"I actually do," he said.

"Well," she said, "if it is, it's only because they probably feel that the woman of the couple needs them more than the man. That's all it is."

"I don't know," he said. "I think it's more than that. I think they're avoiding me."

"*Avoiding* you? Why?"

"I think they think that separation and divorce are a disease, and that I'm the carrier. If they're exposed to me, they could catch it and their own shaky marriages would sicken and die."

"Oh, Lance, that's ridiculous," she said. "Our friends' marriages aren't shaky. You're just projecting. Misery loves company."

"Is that so?" he said, beginning to get irritated. "You really think that we're the only ones who have troubles?"

"I *think*," she said, her voice taking on a harder edge, "that most of the couples we know do have *some* troubles, but I *don't* think that they have let them progress to the point that they are going off to have affairs with their wives' best friends in order to . . ."

The waiter returned with their drinks. They sat glaring at each other till he left. Then Cathy dropped her eyes.

"I'm sorry, Lance," she said. "I didn't mean to get so argumentative. I really wanted tonight to be nice."

"So did I," said Lance. "And it *will* be. And thank you for apologizing. It was actually my fault for bringing up the—"

"No, no," she said, "it was *my* fault."

"Oh no you don't," he said, picking up the mock fight. "It was *my* fault, you bitch."

They both laughed, clinked glasses and drank off their drinks. It had gotten off to a bad start, but it would go better now. Maybe.

They ordered dinner. Conversation at dinner went better than conversation at drinks. They had dessert and after-dinner drinks and Cathy, in a burst of warm feeling for her estranged husband, asked if he would like her to come back to their apartment for a nightcap.

Lance, envisioning her running into his two half-clothed Chinese nymphets, replied that he would much rather see *her* apartment. Besides, he said, it would give him an opportunity to visit their furniture.

* * *

Cathy's new apartment was in a squalid building on the far West Side. He tried not to notice or comment upon the frayed carpeting or the heavy smell of cat urine in the hallways or the peeling paint on the hall walls. It was impossible to tell what color the paint had been when new.

Cathy unlocked her door and they stepped inside. It was a tiny three-room apartment. She had had it painted white and it looked a lot better inside than out, but their furniture looked like it had been crammed into the tiny living room with a shoehorn.

"Well, well," he said, trying to sound jolly, "very nice. Hello, couch. Hello, chair. Hello, other chair."

Cathy giggled. Lance walked around the cramped room, addressing every piece of furniture in turn.

"Hello, coffee table. Hello, lamp. Hello, wastebasket."

Cathy giggled a bit less enthusiastically. Lance got down on all fours.

"Hello, rug. Hello, little round rubber trays to keep the sofa legs from sinking through the carpet."

Cathy jammed a cocktail napkin in his mouth to shut him up and fixed him a drink. He drank it. They sat down on their couch and each of them had another drink. Lance put his arms around Cathy's shoulders. He was starting to feel very mellow. He leaned over and kissed her. She did not pull away. She did not melt, but she did not pull away. Did she want to make love? He couldn't tell.

They kissed some more, and she began to respond. He stroked her face and hair. They kissed some more. He lay her gently back on the couch and began kissing her face and neck and ears. He thought he heard her moan. They kissed some more. He began to unbutton her dress. They slid to the floor.

Before long, to his extreme surprise, they were making love. It had never felt so exciting while they were living together as man and wife. He felt no resentment or anger. He didn't know why and he didn't care. He was dizzy with pleasure and, apparently, so was she. She had never been so responsive since they'd first met. Just before she was ready to climax she cried out: "Go for it, lover!"

He had never heard her say such a thing. Where had she learned it? Surely not from *him*. He was shaken but decided not to spoil what was happening by bringing it up. Cathy was more loving than she had been in a very long time. They lay in each others' arms for a long while without speaking.

"Cathy?" he said at last.

"Yes, baby?"

"I love you."

"I love you too," she said.

"I'm glad I had the guts to invite you to dinner tonight," he said.

"So am I," she said. "If you promise not to say hello to every article of furniture in the bedroom, I would love you to sleep here with me tonight."

"I promise," he said.

She led him into her teeny weeny white bedroom. They fell asleep in each other's arms, in her teeny weeny bed.

The following morning they awoke and made love again. They had not made love the night before and the morning after in years.

"Cathy?" he whispered.

"Yes, darling?"

"Come back. Come back and live with me and let's continue the marriage."

She cupped his face in her hands. She stroked his cheek. She kissed him on the lips.

"Lance," she said.

"Yes, Cathy?"

"I need to live alone for a while. I really do."

"Why?"

"I just do. It's been an incredible growth experience for me. I'm going through some wonderful changes. I need to do this now. I want you to have it be all right with you."

He nodded, noting that the expression "have it be all right with you" sounded unfamiliar.

"Would you at least consent to a dating relationship with me while you're living here?" he said.

She looked at him and smiled.

"Perhaps," she said.

He smiled. She kissed him.

"This is very lovely," he said. "Being with you like this."

"It is," she said. "But I'm so hungry my stomach thinks my throat's cut. How about some eggs?"

"Perfect," he said.

Cathy got out of bed nude and pranced into the teeny weeny white kitchen.

Lance lay in bed awhile, thinking. It had gone surprisingly

well, he thought. Helen and the group were right, God bless them. He felt very close to Cathy now. He was disappointed that she didn't want to come back to him yet, but he was glad she had agreed to a dating relationship. A few more dates like this and she couldn't resist returning to their home.

Which brought up an interesting question: Did he still *want* her to return to their home? He did, he decided, and he was puzzled that the question had come up at all.

He got out of bed, stretched, and looked around. On the tiny bedside table was a small lamp, a box of Kleenex, and a pile of snapshots. He idly picked up the snapshots and started leafing through them.

The first one was a close-up of Cathy in a white tennis shirt, holding a tennis racket over her shoulder. The second one was a long shot of Cathy serving. The third one was a long shot of a man in a white tennis shirt and shorts, with a floppy white tennis hat obscuring the upper part of his face. Who was this man—one of her dates?

The next one was a close-up of Cathy and the man, kissing. Lance began to get slightly dizzy and slightly nauseous, because he recognized the man that Cathy was kissing—it was *Howard!* Howard-fucking-Leventhal, his editor!

Lance couldn't believe it. Howard must have telephoned Cathy the instant he heard that they were separated, right after Lance visited Howard in his office and told him. The bastard! The opportunistic, hypocritical bastard! Lance wanted revenge. What kind of revenge could he exact on Howard? Living well is the best revenge, someone had said. A good swift chop in the Adam's apple is pretty good revenge too, he thought.

Lance walked weakly into the kitchen.

"Well, *there* you are," said Cathy brightly. "Your order is almost ready, sir—Adam and Eve on a raft with a side of down, right?"

In reply Lance merely looked at her.

"I'm afraid I found something I'm not glad I found," he said, holding out the snapshots for her to see.

She saw what he was holding and burst into tears.

"I just happened to see this pile of snapshots on the night table," he said. "So I did what anybody would do if they passed a pile of snapshots on a night table—I picked them up and looked at them."

Cathy continued to cry.

175

"The snapshots seem to feature my wife Cathy Lerner and a gentleman who happens to be my editor, name of Howard Leventhal."

Cathy stopped crying and blotted her eyes with a tissue.

"Oh, Lance," she said, "I feel terrible."

"*You* feel terrible?" he said. "It isn't *your* wife who's going out with Howard Leventhal."

"Lance, promise me something," said Cathy.

"What?"

"Promise me you won't tell Howard," she said.

"You mean Howard doesn't *know* he's going out with you?" said Lance.

"I mean," said Cathy, "promise me you won't tell Howard you found out we're dating. It would just *kill* him if he knew that you knew. He'd never be able to face you again."

"Oh, well, we can't have that, can we?" said Lance. "We certainly can't have old Howard not being able to face me. Tell me. What are we going to do to enable *me* to face *him?*"

"Oh, Lance, I'm so sorry," said Cathy, beginning to cry again. "Is it really going to be hard for you?"

"Cathy, what kind of a man would go out with his friend's wife?" said Lance.

Cathy looked at him closely.

"Is that a serious question?" she said. "Coming from a man who—"

"What *I* did was different," he said. "What *I* did had to do with balancing the scales, with revenge, with an-eye-for-an-eye. But what kind of an editor would go out with his author's wife?"

"What's wrong with going out with your author's wife if they're separated?"

Lance thought that one over.

"You mean outside of the fact that Howard is an opportunistic, hypocritical bastard, and that your going out with him has got to make him even more ambivalent towards me and my novel than he was already, which could seriously jeopardize the success of my book, if not my entire career? You mean outside of *that?*"

"Yes," she said. "Outside of that."

"Outside of that," he said, "there's nothing wrong with it at all."

He remembered how solicitous Howard had been about the separation. How eager he was to learn the particulars. And all the time the main thing he had on his mind was how

176

quickly he could move in on Cathy himself. The bastard! The scummy bastard!

He tried to visualize Howard and Cathy together. Howard and Cathy *naked* together, making love. He felt sick to his stomach. So *that's* where she got her "Go for it, lover!" How *dare* Howard teach his wife such flip and intimate expressions! As if sex with Cathy were some kind of sport in a beer commercial!

He felt faint. It was an instant replay of his apparent cuckolding by Les. It was both better and worse than that, actually. Worse because this one was really true, better because . . . because why? Because he had been through all this before when he thought that Cathy was sleeping with Les. In a way he would have *preferred* it be Cathy and Les. For some strange reason, though, one of the many powerful feelings he was feeling was relief. He wondered about that.

"Cathy? Tell me something," he said.

"What?"

"Do you love him?"

"I don't think so," she said. "I don't really know."

"I see," he said. It hadn't been the answer he was expecting. "Tell me, when you're with him, do you ever talk about me?"

"Talk about you? No. Why would we talk about you?"

"I guess I just don't like the idea of the two of you talking about me, that's all. You don't ever . . . make fun of me, do you?"

"Of course not. Why would we make fun of you?"

"I don't know. Howard must have really been tickled at the thought that I was pining away for you and he was shacking up with you. He *is* shacking up with you, I assume?"

"I think that's between me and Howard," she said evenly. "But Howard has tremendous respect for you, Lance, he really does."

"Yeah, he's proven that."

"He *does*. He's really very fond of you. He's said so a number of times."

"I can just imagine."

"Well, he does. We both do. And we're not making fun of you behind your back."

"Good. Because you and I did live together for a long time, and you do know a lot of stuff about me that I'm not dying to have you tell the world."

"You're being silly, Lance."

177

"Maybe so. But if I growl in my sleep when I'm having a bad dream, I don't want to read about it in Liz Smith's column."

"Liz Smith wouldn't be the slightest bit interested in the fact that you growl in your sleep."

"You haven't told *Howard* that I growl in my sleep, have you?"

"Of course not," she said.

"Have you told him any of the stuff we did together, like talking in bunny voices?"

"Of course not," she said.

Her cheeks flushed and she turned away.

"Good," he said. "I'd hate it if you told him about that. Cathy?"

"Yes?" she said.

"Why Howard Leventhal of all people?"

"What do you mean?" she said.

"I mean what do you see in him?"

Her eyes glazed hard, as though they had been fired in a kiln.

"He's very nice," she said defensively.

"Yeah? Well, I just think you deserve something better than Howard Leventhal," he said, starting to put on his clothes.

"What's wrong with him?" she said.

"Well, nothing, really, I guess. I mean I guess it's not *his* fault if he's balding, paunchy and speaks in an effeminate manner . . ."

"Lance!"

"I'm sorry. I didn't mean that. I don't know why I said that. I mean Howard is really very nice, as you say. Plus which he's literate, he has a steady job with regular hours, and he's always free evenings and weekends. And after you've been with him long enough you'll hardly even *notice* he's balding, paunchy and speaks in an effeminate manner."

"I really don't think I can continue this discussion, Lance. I really don't think it's fair to Howard."

"No, I know it isn't. You're right. I promise I won't even *mention* Howard's baldness or paunchiness or his effeminate way of speaking again."

"I *mean* it Lance. I am not continuing this dis—"

"OK, OK, OK. Look, I guess I should be going, but just tell me one more thing, all right?"

"What?"

"Why did you leave that pile of snapshots on the night table for me to find?"

"Who knew you were going to go poking around through my private things?"

"Yeah, right."

"I didn't do it intentionally. I didn't know you were going to come over here and we were going to make love and you were going to spend the night."

"No, you didn't. But once I got here and we made love and you asked me to sleep over, you could have thought of it *then*."

She shrugged.

"Cathy?" he said softly.

"Yeah?"

"I think you *wanted* me to find those snapshots. Maybe not consciously, maybe subconsciously. I think you wanted me to know that you were going out with someone as good as Howard, even if he *is* balding and paunchy and speaks in an effeminate manner. I think you wanted me to know that a man I work with and respect takes you seriously as a woman."

"I . . . don't really know how to answer that," she said.

"That's OK," he said. "You don't have to."

He finished putting on his clothes.

"Well, I guess I'll be going," he said sadly.

She nodded.

"I'd just like you to know," he said, "that you didn't have to prove that to me—that men I respect take you seriously as a woman. I mean I already knew that."

"That's very sweet of you," she said.

She followed him to the door.

"I'm sorry," she said. "About the snapshots, I mean."

"So am I," he said.

"It was a wonderful birthday," she said.

"For the most part," he said.

"Do you still want to have a dating relationship?"

"I don't think it would be too hot of an idea under the circumstances," he said.

"I guess you're right."

"So long, Cathy."

"So long, Lance."

When he got downstairs to the lobby, he opened the door and, although it had done him no harm, he punched it.

51

It was necessary during the first week of September to go in and confer with Howard about the imminent promotional tour. Lance did not know how he was going to be able to do it. If he didn't do it the book would suffer. He did it.

Lance was amazed at how easy it was. He acted polite, if a bit stiff, towards Howard, and it wasn't until Howard lowered his voice and put on his sympatico frown to ask how things were between Lance and Cathy that Lance looked at the letter opener on Howard's desk and was tempted to drive it into Howard's right eyeball.

The moment passed, and Howard's right eyeball remained intact, innocent of how close it had come to being punctured.

Howard once more expressed his delight at the doubling of the number of cities on Lance's tour and once more took full credit for the improvement. Howard admitted, when Lance raised the issue, that the size of the first printing and the budget for advertising were still too small. Howard regretted that only Firestone himself, however, could change that. Lance suggested that Howard go to work on Firestone again—perhaps he would be as successful with him as he was with the tour cities.

On his way out of Howard's office, Lance passed what he now realized was the office that Claire used on those days she deigned to come to work at all. He asked the secretary at the desk outside Claire's office if Claire was in. The secretary, a blond girl with high cheekbones who could have been Claire at twenty-one, asked who she should say was calling.

"Studs Lerner," said Lance, and watched the girl pick up the intercom and announce that a Mr. Studs Lerner was outside without an appointment. The girl nodded and hung up the intercom and ushered Lance into Claire's office.

It was an extremely large office for a part-time employee. It had an industrial gray carpet, a long gray suede couch, a low marble coffee table and two large corner windows. Claire's desk was a huge antique partners desk half a football field away from the couch. She greeted him with a warm smile and a proffered hand. He took her hand and kissed it in a mock gallant gesture.

He told her of his meeting with Howard and then, because he had to tell *someone* and he wasn't due to see either Helen or the group for several more days, he told her of his date with Cathy, and of Howard's duplicity. Claire seemed both sympathetic and amused. It wasn't quite the reaction he had had in mind, but he should have known how she would react, given what he knew of her own perversity.

When he again mentioned that Howard was claiming credit for the increase in the number of tour cities, Claire laughed out loud. But she did agree with Lance that the 15,000-copy print order on his book was way too small and that the $5,000 advertising budget was absurdly tiny too.

"How would you like to double your print order and triple your ad budget?" she said.

He looked at her warily.

"What would you want in exchange for that?" he said.

"First, close the door," she said.

He went and closed the door.

"Second, climb under my desk."

"Are you serious?"

"Absolutely," she said.

"What if your secretary comes in?"

"I love to live my life on the brink, in case you hadn't noticed," she said.

"I've noticed, I've noticed," he said. "Boy, you'd sure make one dandy secretary of state."

Lance crawled under Claire's desk. He knelt between her spread thighs and raised her skirt. She wasn't wearing panties. He went to work on her. She began to squirm on her chair. And then she hit the intercom button on her desk. Lance couldn't believe it.

"Fiddle?" said Claire, her voice practically normal.

"Yes, Mrs. Firestone?" replied the tinny voice of the girl outside the door.

"Could you come in a second? And bring your steno pad."

"Yes, Mrs. Firestone."

"Are you insane?" Lance hissed up at her.

"Yes," she said. "Thank you for asking."

"I'm not going on with this," he said.

"Oh, yes you are," she said.

52

Fiddle Coleridge brushed the straight blond hair out of her eyes, picked up her steno pad and got up from her desk.

Fiddle didn't think most employers dictated letters while they were in conference, but perhaps the letters she wanted to dictate had to do with this man, Studs Lerner, whom she was in conference with. And then again, perhaps they didn't. Mrs. Firestone was a quirky and irrational employer. Not that Fiddle didn't like her. On the contrary, she was mad for her. Mrs. Firestone had told her on more than one occasion that she herself had been very much like Fiddle when she was in her twenties. Then too, Mrs. Firestone had hinted that, were Fiddle to work out at a secretarial level, perhaps one day she might be made a junior editor.

Fiddle opened the door to Mrs. Firestone's office and was surprised not to see Mr. Lerner. She looked around the room, but he was nowhere to be seen. Was there another exit from Mrs. Firestone's office? A secret panel perhaps?

"Sit down, Fiddle," said Mrs. Firestone. Her voice seemed strained, as if she were containing angry feelings. Fiddle prayed it wasn't she that Mrs. Firestone was angry at.

"Yes, ma'am," said Fiddle. She pulled up a chair, snapped open her steno pad, and waited, pencil poised, for Mrs. Firestone to begin.

"This is to Mike Fieldston, head of Promotion and Advertising," said Mrs. Firestone. "Dear Mike . . ."

Mrs. Firestone drew in her breath sharply and winced as though she were in pain.

"Mrs. Firestone . . ." said Fiddle anxiously. When she had

been a girl of six, a favorite aunt had had a heart attack while reading her a bedtime story and had expired on the spot.

Mrs. Firestone appeared to recover and acted as though nothing had happened. Perhaps it had merely been gas. Fiddle decided not to mention it.

"Dear Mike," said Mrs. Firestone, "Pursuant to discussions with buyers at B. Dalton in Minneapolis, Kroch's & Brentano's in Chicago, Doubleday in New York, and the Walden chain in . . ."

Once more Mrs. Firestone caught her breath and squeezed her eyes tightly shut.

"Mrs. Firestone?" said Fiddle, now starting to become genuinely alarmed.

Mrs. Firestone, eyes still closed, continued to dictate, her phrases punctuated by little gasps. Fiddle, fearing that a beloved mentor and a junior editorship were teetering on the brink of extinction, felt her own heart begin to pound. She stared at Mrs. Firestone in mute horror, too well-bred to acknowledge the older woman's symptoms until she herself acknowledged them first, but no longer able to scribble shorthand squiggles on the lined green pad.

"Fiddle," Mrs. Firestone gasped, "are you getting this or aren't you?"

"I'm trying to, ma'am," said Fiddle, her pulse racing.

"I don't hear your . . . pencil moving," said Mrs. Firestone with difficulty.

As Fiddle stared in horror, Mrs. Firestone, eyes still squeezed shut, sank down a couple of inches in her chair. The fingers of both her mentor's hands extended, then clenched into fists. A sheet of onion-skin under Mrs. Firestone's left hand crumpled into a tiny ball.

"Mrs. Firestone," said Fiddle, "may I ask you a question of a personal nature?"

"You may . . . not," said Mrs. Firestone. "You may take . . . dictaaaaaaaaaaaaaaaaaaaaaaaaation!"

The last syllable seemed as if it would go on forever, although it probably lasted no longer than six or seven seconds, and when it was concluded Mrs. Firestone sank back in her chair and smiled the biggest smile that Fiddle had ever seen her smile. She was so still that Fiddle was certain she was dead. Her only consolation was that Mrs. Firestone had apparently died happy.

Fiddle didn't know what to do. When she was six and it had been her aunt, she had merely screamed for her Mommy.

Screaming for her Mommy now would not be appropriate. She was terribly frightened. She supposed she should get up and go to her desk and call the police. She wondered, since she had been the only one present when Mrs. Firestone passed away, whether the police would want to question her. She didn't think she would be able to take it. She would crack for sure under the third degree. Perhaps they would send her to prison. Daddy's lawyers would try to get her a reduced sentence, but they were corporate tax lawyers, not criminal defense lawyers, so what could they do with a murder rap?

Fiddle got unsteadily to her feet. Her steno pad slid to the floor. Miraculously, Mrs. Firestone's eyes snapped open at the noise.

"Well, Fiddle," she said cheerily, "now then, would you read that back?"

53

Howard telephoned Lance late that night. He seemed very excited. At first Lance thought it had something to do with Cathy.

"You'll never *guess* what I pulled off for you, bubbeleh," Howard exulted, "you'll never *guess*. You want to guess?"

"You doubled my print order and tripled my ad budget," said Lance wearily.

There was a stunned silence at the other end of the line.

"How did you *guess*?" said Howard.

"I wouldn't want you to spread it around," said Lance, "but I'm psychic."

54

By September 10th the first of the reviews of *Gallivanting* began to trickle in. They were, for the most part, quite good. There was really only one reviewer who took Lance to task, a novelist named Ferdfleisch whose review, unfortunately, ran in the prestigious *New York Times Book Review*.

Ferdfleisch accused Lance of writing below his level, of descending to superficial humor, of trivializing his own seriousness for fear of being judged by harsher standards. It was probably coincidental and irrelevant that three years earlier Ferdfleisch had approached Lance for a quote for the dust jacket of Ferdfleisch's current novel and that Lance, after reading the manuscript and finding himself in philosophical disagreement with it, had to tell Ferdfleisch that he couldn't give him the quote. Only a cynic would have felt there had been any connection between Lance's failure to give the man a quote and Ferdfleisch's harsh review.

Had Cathy been aware that Lance's novel was going to be assigned to a fellow to whom Lance had declined to give a quote? In all fairness, she'd probably known no more about it than Lance himself.

In point of fact, Ferdfleisch's criticism was not wholly unfounded, for Lance preferred to put even his more serious themes in humorous form, believing that humorous material was both more valuable and more difficult to write than serious, that the only reason authors wrote serious books was that they lacked the skill or patience to write humorously, that *War and Peace* would have been a better book had it been written humorously, and that Tolstoy would have done so had he had the craft.

It was also true that Lance placed rather more credence on others' opinions of him and his work than he ought to have, and usually stood ready to re-evaluate everything in his life on the basis of the last thing screamed at him by a street-corner degenerate. Although no street-corner degenerate had succeeded in publishing a critique of Lance's novel, a reviewer in an obscure rural newspaper in South Carolina had written a review which criticized Lance for a number of things that, in fact, were not even *in* Lance's book. There was very good reason to suppose that this reviewer had not even read the book he was reviewing, but his criticism stung Lance nonetheless.

Why is it, Lance wondered, that the unfavorable reviews are generally easier to remember than the favorable ones? Possibly for the same reason that beautiful women admire men who don't value them. Was that also the reason, he wondered, that he had had such a motley string of literary agents over the years?

Lance's current agent, a man named Kronk, was currently going through a mid-life crisis which had caused him to decide that the literary life and the world of commerce were intrinsically less valuable and durable than the rural life. Kronk had bought a ranch and was breeding beefalos, although his tendency to form deep emotional relationships with the animals conflicted with his ability to send them off to market and had already cost him, by his own estimate, close to half a million dollars on the one herd.

Kronk had thus far not had much success trying to sell *Gallivanting* as a movie. The problem, he'd told Lance, was that these days studio people in Hollywood were somewhat prejudiced against novels as a basis for a motion picture, especially those that were close to being published. They reasoned that if the novel were still available for purchase it must not be a very hot property. Studio people, Kronk said, preferred to buy options on nonfiction articles in magazines like *New York* and *Esquire* and *Texas Monthly* and develop them into plotted pictures. The fact that this technique hadn't worked since *Saturday Night Fever,* said Kronk, was no evidence to them that the process wasn't valid.

One of Kronk's chief values as an agent was his ability to collect money for work that Lance had written. Lance had grown weary of the excuses that had been given him routinely over the years in lieu of payments from book publishers, magazines, movie studios, television networks, theatrical producers and independent contractors: that although the book had sold half a million copies he had still not earned back his advance royalties; that there had been more returns than copies printed; that the publisher had a full year to render statements and another six months to pay royalties; that a check was due him but would be late because it had to be signed by the head of the accounting department who was on vacation in Tibet; that the girl who normally issued the checks had been stricken with ulcerative colitis and wouldn't be back in the office for eighteen weeks; that his check had been erroneously made out to the Philadelphia Society for the Jewish Blind and would now have to be canceled and reissued; that the check had been mailed twelve weeks ago to an address that Lance hadn't lived at since college, and so on.

The real reason that it took so long to get paid—and the *only* reason, said Kronk—was that companies made enormous interest on late payments, and that freelance writers as a group had somewhat less clout than shepherds. Since Kronk had been representing him, Lance had been able to collect most monies due him an average of three months earlier than before.

Lance telephoned Kronk to commiserate with him about the feisty review in the *Times* and to confer about the promotional tour, but Kronk's secretary said that her employer had been called away on an emergency—the breech birth of a baby beefalo.

Publication day was almost at hand. Mike Fieldston sent over by messenger an itinerary of travel details and scheduled interviews for Lance's ten-city tour.

The tour would begin on September 15th in Pittsburgh, then go on to Cleveland, Cincinnati, Chicago, Detroit, Minneapolis, Los Angeles, San Francisco, Dallas and Houston. The trip would take two weeks. Except for a layover on the weekend in Detroit, he would be in a different city every day. He looked over the schedule and shook his head. Most days began with interviews on TV news shows at about six-thirty a.m. He was what they referred to on these programs as "color."

55

Gladys Oliphant was ecstatic.

At first, of course, she hadn't been sure. The morning nausea she'd attributed to some week-old lasagna she had eaten. The warm, flushed feeling she attributed to the weather. The sleepiness she attributed to the long hours she was now putting in every night on her novel. The increased need to urinate she attributed to her increased consumption of beer during her writing sessions.

But when her period kept failing to materialize, she finally suspected what the matter was and went to the doctor for the test. The doctor confirmed her suspicions: Gladys was pregnant!

There was not the slightest doubt in her mind who the father was: Lance Lerner was the only man who had made love to her in several years. There was not the slightest doubt in her mind what to do about the pregnancy: she had always wanted a baby, and now she was going to have one fathered by one of the most successful writers in the country. With a writer father and a writer mother, there was little doubt that the child would become a writer as well.

Gladys knew that Mr. Lerner would be as tickled by the news of his impending fatherhood as she was herself. She could hardly wait to tell him.

56

The evening of publication day, September 15th, Lance shared a bottle of Korbel champagne with Dorothy and Janie in his apartment in modest celebration. Then he packed his garment bag and his shoulder bag, gave the girls some final instructions about the apartment, the mail, and so on, kissed them both goodbye and went to the door. They followed him to the door and kissed him again, then went down the stairs with him and followed him into the street.

A cab came towards them and Lance flagged it down. It screeched to a stop and he began to get into it. Dorothy clung to him, kissed him repeatedly and whispered "I love you" in his ear. She was crying.

He was terribly moved, and embraced her.

"Please," she said, "don't die in a plane crash."

It was a somewhat unsettling request. He hadn't been planning to die in a plane crash, and yet, since the crash of the DC-10 in Chicago on May 25, 1979, with a planeload of publishing people on their way to the American Booksellers Association convention in Los Angeles, some of his old fears of flying had returned to him. Fears of the commonplace—defective aircraft, dangerous flying conditions, pilots with the level of competence of your average department-store clerk. But also fears of the unusual—midair collisions with meteor showers or returning spacecraft or flocks of wild geese.

He distrusted every announcement made to him over the public address system, correctly assuming that the true state of affairs was being, at worst, wholly lied about or, at best, euphemized in the same manner as the routine safety announcements. When they said, "Your seat cushion may be used as a flotation device," what they really meant was, "If we crash in the ocean, your seat cushion may stay afloat for a few minutes after the plane sinks."

189

Lance sensed that there were things he could do to increase his chances of survival on the flights he took, but the only precaution he'd adopted thus far was to avoid DC-10s.

He got out of the cab at the American Airlines terminal and checked in for his 9:00 p.m. flight. It was just 8:30. He found, as usual, that his gate was on the other side of the airport.

He stood in line at security and wondered whether he would make the metal detector beep. Lance's peculiar problem with metal detectors was that he carried around such a heavy load of nonspecific guilt that every time he heard the metal detector beep when he walked through it he had an insane fear that this was the one trip when he had absent-mindedly packed a Luger in his luggage. Didn't it occur to them that one could hijack a plane with weapons that wouldn't make a metal detector beep?

The woman ahead of him in line at the metal detector seemed exceedingly edgy. Around her neck was a Pentax in a black leather case. She turned to Lance.

"Excuse me," she said, "but will the X-rays fog my film?"

"No," said Lance, "but they *will* cause cancer and birth defects."

"Oh, no problem," said the woman, facing forward again, "just so they don't fog my film."

Lance went through the metal detector without a beep and boarded the plane to Pittsburgh. With his sixth sense he was beginning to detect the first unmistakable warnings of disaster lying somewhere ahead, but he didn't know how far ahead and he couldn't guess just what form the disaster would take when it appeared.

57

Upon boarding the plane to Pittsburgh, he was not at all surprised to find that the temperature in the cabin was approximately ninety-eight degrees Fahrenheit. Shortly after takeoff it usually dropped to a degree or two above freezing. He generally brought with him a long underwear T-shirt and a sweater to ward off frostbite, and changed clothes in one of the plane's tiny lavatories. Any time it took him more than sixty seconds, some shmuck was banging on the door, asking if he was all right in there—if you were in the john any longer than the time necessary to urinate they figured you were having a stroke or engaging in unnatural sex acts.

When the drink cart came down the aisle after takeoff, Lance obtained two Bloody Mary mixes without vodka. As soon as the stewardesses were three rows past him, Lance reached into his shoulder bag and withdrew a flask of vodka and surreptitiously poured a couple of fingers into each drink. He resented paying two-fifty apiece for vodka miniatures that cost the airline a couple of cents, but sneaking his own vodka into their Mr. and Mrs. T or Snap-E-Tom made him feel like an axe murderer.

By the time he reached Pittsburgh, he was slightly juiced. His schedule of interviews indicated that his first one was tonight, on a live radio program from midnight till two a.m. It was called *Middleman at Midnight*.

When he got out of the terminal at the Pittsburgh airport he was surprised to find it was about fifty degrees and raining. When he'd left New York it had been at least ninety. He flagged a cab, put his luggage inside, and gave the cabdriver the address of the radio station.

The cab let him off at a quarter to twelve in what looked like a deserted industrial park. As the rain slanted into his

face, Lance slowly circled a series of rakishly modern build-
ings, unable to find either a street number or an unlocked
entry door. From a public phone across the street, he dialed
the radio station. It was now midnight, and he was supposed
to be on the air.

After forty-five rings a grouchy male voice answered.

"Hi," said Lance, shivering in the cold, trying to speak
above the whine of the wind and the splatter of rain. "This is
Lance Lerner. I'm a guest on your show, *Middleman at
Midnight*, but I can't seem to find the entrance to your
building."

"Who'd you say this was?" said the voice.

"Lance Lerner," said Lance. "Author of *Gallivanting*? I'm
supposed to be on *Middleman at Midnight*."

"I doubt it," said the voice.

"What do you mean you doubt it?" said Lance.

"I mean," said the voice, "that *Middleman at Midnight* was
never *on* this station, plus which it went off the air about six
or seven months ago. I sure don't know what you're doing
here now."

"I sure don't either," said Lance with disgust and hung up
the phone. By the time he managed to get another cab to go
to his hotel he was soaked to the bone. And his first interview
the following morning was at six-fifteen a.m.

It was a great beginning.

58

When the wakeup call came it was still dark out. He knew
he'd had only four hours of sleep and that getting out of bed
in his condition was going to be a major accomplishment.
With four hours of sleep he had the capacity to fall asleep
instantly at any stage in the getting-up process. Fortunately,
he had a technique:

He reached for his battered Porsche watch and squeezed it so hard the pain in his hand kept him awake long enough to sit up and swing his legs over the side of the bed. As soon as his legs were over the side of the bed he dropped to the floor and did fifty pushups. By the time he had finished the pushups, he was breathing hard enough to keep him awake till he got to the bathroom.

Once he'd washed his face and brushed his teeth, he picked up the phone again and called room service. He ordered two eggs over easy, a large grapefruit juice and coffee, and asked how long it would take to be delivered. A half hour, said the Hispanic voice at the other end of the line.

He went back into the bathroom and got into the shower, mentally reviewing all the steps in his daily process of getting ready to face the world—exercising, showering, shampooing, shaving, brushing, blow-drying, dressing, eating. With all those things to do every morning and the difficulty he experienced in merely getting out of bed, he found it a complete waste of time to be up and around for only one day before beginning the whole process all over again—if you're going to *get* up, you might as well *stay* up for at least a week at a crack.

Within sixty seconds of entering the shower he heard a violent knocking on his hotel-room door. Cursing, he stuck his head out of the shower and yelled, "Who's there?"

"*Rune* sorbis!" said a heavy Hispanic accent.

It never failed. When you asked room service how long it would take for your food to arrive they always said thirty minutes. If you waited thirty minutes before getting into the shower, they came in thirty-one. If you waited forty-five they came in forty-seven. If you jumped in the shower immediately upon ordering, they came in a minute and a half. They had an uncanny ability to know when you were naked and soaking wet. Once he'd outwitted them—he had waited forty minutes and they still hadn't come, so he turned on the shower without getting into it. Sixty seconds after he'd started the water, room service knocked on the door. The waiter had been palpably disappointed to find he was still dry.

He arrived at the TV station at six-ten a.m. An attractive young man and woman were sitting at an ersatz breakfast nook beside a window through which could be glimpsed a lovely ersatz pastoral scene. They were alternately doing news, weather and spunky repartee. Spunky repartee at that hour of the morning, Lance felt, was unnatural. He suspected they were on speed.

A relentlessly energetic young person guided him over a maze of thick serpentine cables and had him crouch down just out of camera range, waiting for a commercial break to go up onto the set.

"Our next guest," said the suspiciously spunky woman after the break, "is a man who single-handedly sailed from New York City to the Isle of Skye using only a dinghy and a sail made out of a bed sheet."

Lance looked around the studio for the man she might be describing and found that the relentlessly energetic young person was motioning for *Lance* to go up to the ersatz breakfast nook.

"Uh, I think there's been some mistake," said Lance in confusion.

"Good morning, Mr. Lerner," said the spunky young man. He extended his hand for a shaking and pulled Lance on camera.

"Good morning," said Lance, "but I think there's been a mistake here."

"I want to hear all about Mr. Lerner's voyage across the Atlantic in that *dinghy*," said the spunky woman, "but first we have to pause for one more commercial message."

The red light on the camera went out.

"Listen," said Lance, "I think there's been a mistake here."

The spunky man frowned.

"What kind of a mistake?" he said.

"About who I am," said Lance.

"Aren't you the author of *Gallivanting?*" said the spunky woman, now also frowning.

"Yes," said Lance, "but the book is a novel about a young man dating and having romantic relationships with women, and it's not about sailing across the Atlantic in a dinghy with a bed sheet for a sail."

The man and woman looked at each other, no longer spunky.

"There must have been some mix-up," said the man, "but it's a little too late to do anything about it. We've got the stills set up on the easels and everything."

"Excuse me?" said Lance.

"We're a live show, Mr. Lerner," said the woman. "Our